# "Have lunch with me?" he asked.

"What?" Anne stared at him, her eyes wide and startled. "I...I can't."

"Why not? You have to eat. I have to eat. Why not eat together?"

Why not eat together? All the reasons why not tumbled through Anne's mind and finally came out as one simple protest. "I don't know your name."

"Neill Devlin," he said promptly.

"Anne Moore." The response was automatic, as was accepting the hand he held out, but she had to struggle not to jump at the electricity that arced from that casual touch.

"Now that we've been introduced, have lunch with me." Neill's tone was light, easy, making it seem ridiculous to have doubts, foolish to refuse.

"I...there's a diner down the street," Anne said slowly. She never did things like this. Agreeing to have lunch with a total stranger was completely out of character. Then again, just lately she'd started thinking that her character was pretty damn dull.

**Dallas Schulze is "...a powerhouse of mainstream women's fiction."**
**—The Paperback Forum**

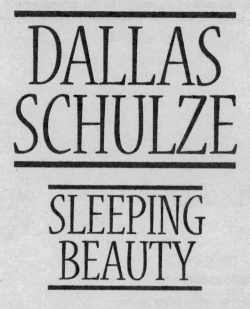

# DALLAS SCHULZE

## SLEEPING BEAUTY

MIRA

ISBN 1-55166-553-0

SLEEPING BEAUTY

Visit us at www.mirabooks.com

Printed in U.S.A.

# SLEEPING
# BEAUTY

# Once Upon a Time...

There was a woman who lived in a rose-covered cottage. She was a woman soft of heart and warm in spirit, with hair the color of new honey and twilight-colored eyes—eyes that, often as not, held a look that hinted at gentle secrets and close-held dreams.

She had spent her whole life in the small town where she was born, sheltered and protected by her family beyond what was usual, for evil had once set a shadowed hand among them, and they lived with the fear of its return.

Out of love, they bound her close with ties of fear and guilt.

Out of love, she accepted the soft bonds, though they grew tighter with each passing year.

She stayed safe within the walls of the rose-covered cottage, dreaming dreams of faraway places, exotic lands she would never see, adventures she'd never have. And if—just now and then—she dreamed of a man with a heart strong enough to break through the loving ties that bound her, well, that was a secret best kept between her and her heart.

This was real life, after all, and no one knew better than she that life was not a fairy tale.

# Chapter One

Neill Devlin had never believed in hell, at least not in the fire and brimstone, hot lava and damned souls sort of hell. It was a metaphor, the moral to a story, and he didn't believe in it any more than he believed in witches on broomsticks, fairies dancing on buttercups or happily-ever-after. He was holding firm on the last three, but it was obvious he'd been wrong about hell. It existed, all right, but it wasn't some dark netherworld, filled with molten lava and knife-edged rocks.

Hell was right here, in the middle of Indiana, in the middle of summer, in the middle of seemingly endless miles of cornfields, stranded on a dirt road halfway between nowhere-in-particular and somewhere-up-ahead, with the hot August sun beating down out of a cloudless, pale blue sky and only the lifeless hulk of a seventy-year-old motorcycle for company.

"Next time you get a bright idea for a vacation, Devlin," he muttered as he began pushing the bike down the road, "save yourself some trouble and just check into the nearest asylum for the terminally stupid."

Under the current circumstances, it was hard to remember why this trip had seemed like such a good idea when he'd started out. In the last eight years, he'd written three bestselling nonfiction crime books. A month ago, he'd finished book number four, and both his editor and his agent assured him that this was his best work yet, sure to shoot straight to the top of the *New York Times* list. He wished he could share their enthusiasm, but, after spending two years delving into the madness that had led a woman to kill her own children in the name of the Lord, he wasn't feeling particularly good about what he did for a living. He wasn't, in fact, feeling particularly good about the world in general.

The truth was, at thirty-five, after spending most of the last decade staring into the darkest corners of humanity's heart, he was burned out, wrung dry and in desperate need of a break.

He was also sick to death of Seattle's rain and its organic-food-eating, latte-drinking, grunge-music-playing inhabitants. He wanted to go somewhere where he could order a cup of coffee without someone asking him if he wanted a half caf, double-cream foamy with a twist of lemon. He wanted to order a steak, pan fried, rare enough to moo when he stuck his fork into it, no authentic mesquite grill, no béarnaise butter, no arugula and macadamia nut salad on the side—just a slab of unadorned meat without so much as a sprig of parsley to distract from the cholesterol-laden glory of it. And he didn't ever again want to hear anyone chirrup with joy over the wonders of the Pacific Northwest. As far as he was concerned, the whole damned place could sink into the ocean. It was so waterlogged already that he doubted anyone would notice the difference.

His parents had retired to Florida—Ft. Lauderdale, where nothing but an occasional hurricane got between the inhabitants and the sun. Just thinking about it made him feel warmer. He'd been staring out the window of his rented condo, watching a gray, misty rain fall, when the idea came to him, and his first impulse was to pick up the phone and arrange for a flight. In twenty-four hours or less, he could be lying next to the pool, letting the Florida sun bake the Seattle chill from his bones.

Then again, he'd been working nonstop for the last three months, running short on sleep and living on instant coffee and take-out food. Images from the book still filled his mind and haunted his thoughts. Past experience told him that he needed some time to decompress, time to step away from the dark corners he made a living exploring.

If he went home now, his mother would take one look at the shadows in his eyes and start worrying and baking—her response to most of the world's ills. His father would immediately drag him into the garage-turned-woodworking-shop, hand him a hammer and put him to work on whatever his latest project happened to be. Brandon Devlin was a great believer in the therapeutic effects of physical labor. A few days of their unspoken concern and he would have gained ten pounds, have blisters on every finger and be starting to envy his friends who never spoke to their parents.

That was when the idea had come to him. Sitting in the condo's basement garage was the 1930 Indian motorcycle he'd bought six months ago and had barely had time to look at since. A cross-country road trip. It was exactly what he needed—

a few weeks on the road with nothing to do but admire the scenery and nothing to worry about except where to stop for the night. No one was expecting him anywhere, so he could take all the time he wanted. Hell, he could spend the next year on the road if the mood struck him. Maybe there was even a book in this, something different, something that didn't require him to delve into the dark heart of madness.

It had taken him less than a week to tie up the loose ends of his life in Seattle—turn the condo back to the rental company, pack up and store the handful of things he'd gathered over the last two years, and call the few people who might notice he was gone. Then, feeling like a cross between *Easy Rider* and Alexis de Tocqueville, he left the gray, Seattle drizzle behind, heading south and east in search of sunshine and the legendary sense of freedom and adventure that came with life on the road.

After three weeks, he'd come to the conclusion that life on the road was highly overrated. He'd seen a lot of beautiful country, but, after a week or so, one spectacular sunset started to look pretty much like the ones that had come before. It was only sheer stubbornness that had kept him from chucking the whole idea and driving straight to the nearest airport a week ago.

But this was the final straw. He'd had enough of living like a nomad. Enough of staying in motels with paper-thin walls and a stingy supply of hot water. Enough of "home-cooking" that came straight from a can. His butt was numb, and his legs felt permanently bowed from straddling the bike. His shirt was sticking to the sweat on his back, and there was an ominous threat of a blister forming on his left heel. He was hungry, thirsty, and the damned bike was getting heavier with every passing minute. He wanted a cold drink, a hot shower, a meal that owed nothing to Chef Boyardee macaroni and a bed with a mattress younger than he was. The only way he was going to get a book out of this life experience was if he moved into the horror genre, he thought sourly.

A shallow breeze drifted past, a faint breath of air that drew a whispery rustle from the tall rows of corn that lined both sides of the road. Speaking of horror, he was starting to feel like he was trapped in an old *Twilight Zone* episode—the one where Billy Mumy kept sending people to the cornfields.

"No wonder they were terrified," Neill muttered. "It must have been summer in Indiana."

The hiccuping whine of an engine broke the stillness, and he stopped, bracing the bike against his leg as he turned to look back down the road. He allowed himself a brief fantasy of Cindy Crawford pulling up in a stretch limo. She just happened to be on her way to the nearest airport and was dying to give a lift to a slightly-the-worse-for-wear writer. Then again, the battered red pickup that appeared through the cloud of dust didn't look half bad, either, especially since the driver slowed as soon as he saw Neill, brakes scraping in complaint as the truck halted next to him.

"Need a ride, mister?" The face that peered at him across the tattered seat was lined by years and weathered by the sun. Faded blue eyes, a sharply hooked nose and a narrow mouth hidden beneath a scraggly band of salt-and-pepper whiskers with pretensions toward mustache-hood.

"I'd appreciate one. Is there room for my bike in the back?" Hell, who needed Cindy Crawford? She probably couldn't even drive a truck.

"You know, if you'd buy a real car, you wouldn't have to spend half your life at David Freeman's garage and the other half earning enough money to pay for repairs to that heap of junk." Lisa Remington slowed her car and flicked on the turn signal, waiting until a feed truck went past before turning left across Signal Avenue into the gas station.

"Lucy *is* a real car," Anne Moore protested.

"Depends on your definition of 'real,' I guess. Personally, I think a real car should hold more than one and a half people. And have the ability to go more than thirty miles an hour."

"Lucy holds two people quite comfortably."

"Only if they're contortionists," Lisa muttered.

"And she'll go more than thirty miles an hour."

"Only if you get out and push."

Anne laughed, reaching for the seat belt as Lisa pulled up next to the garage. It was an old argument, one neither of them expected to win. "You're just jealous because my car has a personality."

"Like a professional hypochondriac. If it isn't the brakes, it's the engine or the transmission. You only bought the stupid thing because no one else wanted it."

Anne shrugged, but couldn't deny the accusation. "They were going to send her to the junkyard."

"That's where it belongs," Lisa pointed out.

"Shh, she might hear you," Anne said, grinning as she nodded to the open garage door.

Lisa gave the ancient VW Bug that sat inside a

sour look. "Nothing that old can possibly have any hearing left. Do you know how old that thing is in dog years?"

"If she was a dog, I'd worry," Anne said dryly. She pulled the door handle. "Thanks for the lift."

"Hubba hubba." At Lisa's soft exclamation, Anne, one foot already on the ground, turned to look at her. Lisa was staring, mesmerized, toward the open garage, and when Anne followed her gaze, she could understand why.

*Hubba hubba, indeed,* Anne thought. The man leaning over the VW's engine compartment was a jeans manufacturer's dream come true. Faded denim clung lovingly to narrow hips and long legs.

"If I were a man, I'd say something sexist, like 'That's the most incredible butt I've ever seen,'" Lisa breathed reverently.

"It's not sexist when it's true."

"He must be from out of town. I'd know if a butt like that lived in Loving," Lisa said with conviction.

"Do you suppose the rest of him lives up to the rear view?" Anne's hand still gripped the door handle, but she'd forgotten all about getting out.

"It couldn't possibly."

As if in answer to the question, he straightened and half turned toward them. The dim light inside the garage made it impossible to see his features clearly, but what they could see was more than enough.

"Look at those shoulders," Lisa sighed.

Anne was already looking. The black T-shirt molded his torso, revealing broad shoulders that tapered into a narrow waist and flat stomach. He was tall—an inch or two over six feet—and every inch of that was lean muscle. Thick dark hair fell onto his forehead, and, even from a distance, the overall impression was one of rugged masculine beauty.

"I hate to use such a cliché, but there's a genuine hunk," Lisa said.

"Maybe he has buck teeth."

"Or crossed eyes."

"Or he's gay," Anne said with gloomy certainty. They were both silent a moment, contemplating the depressing likelihood of that.

He moved farther into the garage, out of their sight, and both women sighed. Anne shook herself a little and remembered to pull the door handle. "I wonder who he is."

"Maybe David finally hired someone to help in the garage," Lisa said. "He's been threatening to find part time help for the last couple of years."

"More likely he's just passing through town,"

Anne commented as she pushed open the door. More people moved *out* of Loving, Indiana, than moved into it, and, even from a distance, there was a coiled, restless look about the stranger that made it difficult to imagine him settling in a sleepy little farming town.

"Are you coming to dinner with Jack tonight?" Anne asked as she started to slide out of the car.

"Sure. Where else can I go to have my character called into question and my fashion sense insulted, all in one fun-filled evening?"

"It's not that bad."

"Sure it is. Your mom detests me. She detested me fifteen years ago when Brooke was alive and I was her best friend, and she detested me when I moved back to Loving two years ago. Hell, she probably even detested me the ten years I was in California." Lisa shrugged, one corner of her mouth angling down in a rueful smile. "One thing you've got to hand her is that she's consistent."

"She doesn't detest you," Anne protested weakly. "She just...worries that—"

"That your brother is going to ask me to marry him," Lisa said bluntly.

"It's not that. Exactly." Catching her friend's eye, she amended the statement. "Not *just* that, anyway. She just doesn't want to see Jack—"

"Make a mistake?" Lisa asked, dry as dust. She shook her head when Anne flushed. "Don't let it bother you. I don't. Your mother thinks that if Jack marries me, he'll stay in Loving and keep his job as sheriff." Exasperated, Lisa shoved her fingers through her hair, tousling the deep red curls into even greater disarray. "He's thirty-five, for God's sake, but, I swear, she still thinks he's going to go back to med school and become the world famous surgeon she planned on your father being. That ended when Brooke died. Why can't she just accept that?"

A lot of things had ended when her sister died, Anne thought, but all she said was, "Acceptance isn't a big part of my mother's vocabulary."

"A masterpiece of understatement."

Neither of them spoke for a moment, and then Anne broke the silence. "I think the politically correct phrase would be a *mistress*piece of understatement," she said solemnly.

Lisa considered for a moment and then shook her head. "No, I think it would have to be a *person*piece of understatement."

"A personpiece?" Anne wrinkled her nose. "Makes me think of Hannibal Lector."

Lisa waggled her eyebrows. "You bring the fava

beans and I'll bring the Chianti. We can tell your mom it's a hostess gift.''

Anne was smiling when she got out of the car, but the smile faded as the car pulled away. She'd known Lisa most of her life, though when she was a child, the six-year difference in their ages had been an unbridgeable gap and Anne had known her only as her older sister's friend. Their friendship had started two years ago, when Lisa moved back to Indiana.

On the surface, they didn't have much in common. Lisa was an artist. Anne worked as a secretary in a bank. Lisa had moved to California when she was twenty, had married a musician and traveled all over the country with him. When they divorced, she took her half of their community property and went to Europe for six months. Other than a trip to the Disney World amusement park when she was a child, Anne had never been more than a couple of hours' drive from Loving. She'd also never had a serious relationship with a member of the opposite sex, unless you counted Frank Miller, and she really hated the idea of counting him. After more than a year of casual dating, she could barely remember what he looked like between dates.

But despite their differences—or maybe because of them—she and Lisa had become close friends, and the fact that Lisa and Jack were dating would have made it a picture-perfect situation if it wasn't for her mother's politely implacable hostility, Anne thought, as she stepped out of the bright sunlight and into the dim garage.

Maybe there was a God after all, Neill thought, looking at the woman who'd just walked into the garage. She'd stopped just out of the sunlight, waiting for her eyes to adjust to the relative gloom. Maybe it was shallow to ascribe a ride into town, a cold Coke and half a dozen Oreos to divine intervention, but, when you threw in a pretty blonde in a blue-flowered sundress, there was no longer any room for doubt. God was in His heaven, and, if all wasn't completely right with the world, well, at least things were definitely looking up.

Her eyes still dazzled from the sun, she hadn't seen him yet, and he was in no hurry to make his presence known. Leaning against the cluttered workbench, Neill admired the view. She wasn't very big—not much over five feet—but she was very nicely packaged. The short, flippy skirt of the sundress revealed lightly tanned legs—delightfully long legs for such a small woman—and the rest of her was just as appealing. She had the kind of figure that had been fashionable back in the fifties—

a little too full in bust and hip for the current fashion, with a narrow waist that emphasized the curves. If she was like most women he knew, she probably thought she needed to lose ten pounds, but, as far as he was concerned, she looked just about right—soft and supple and very, very female.

*And it's obviously been way too long since you spent time in the real world, Devlin.* Neill shifted, uncomfortably aware that his jeans were suddenly tighter than they had been. He was a couple of decades past the age when just looking at a pretty woman was enough to get him hard. Then again, he'd spent most of the last year buried in research, and for the past six months the closest he'd come to a carnal relationship was biting into a hot pizza.

She walked over to the scruffy VW Bug, the hem of the flowered dress swinging gently against her legs. As she leaned over to peer uncertainly into the engine compartment, the thin cotton draped lovingly around the soft curves of her bottom and Neill choked on a mouthful of cola.

Startled, Anne jerked upright and spun toward the sound, one hand pressed to her suddenly thumping heart, her eyes searching the dimly lit garage. Someone was straightening away from the workbench, moving toward her—a man, a stranger.

The realization made her skin ice over and filled her throat with the acid taste of old fear.

"Sorry. I didn't mean to startle you." The rueful apology stopped her convulsive move toward the door and escape. She drew a shallow breath, struggling for control as he came closer. "I guess you didn't see me," he said, stopping a few feet away and smiling at her.

Black T-shirt, snug faded denims, worn black boots and thick, dark hair the color of midnight. It was the hunk, she realized, the man she and Lisa had been shamelessly ogling just a few minutes ago. Anne breathed more deeply, feeling irritation replace the momentary panic. She'd thought she was past reacting like that, years past it. Yet here she was, bolting like a silly little rabbit just because she happened to be momentarily alone with a strange man. And it wasn't even as if they were really alone, she thought, hating the fear that had her glancing toward the office.

"David got a call a few minutes ago," Neill said, seeing the direction of her glance. He kept a careful distance between them and made his voice low and soft. He didn't want to do anything to bring back the sharp look of fear that had turned her gray eyes almost black. Such pretty eyes, he thought. *She* was pretty, like the girl on an old-fashioned box of candy. Big gray eyes, the kind of skin that could only be called peaches and cream, hair the color of pale honey, a short straight little nose and a soft bow of a mouth, the lower lip just a little fuller than the upper, the kind of mouth that made a man want to taste that faint hint of a pout. As a general rule, his taste ran to tall, leggy brunettes, but he was willing to concede that his focus might have been a little too narrow in the past. There was definitely something to be said for short, curvy blondes.

"Your car?" he asked, nodding to the Bug.

"Yes. She's in for a tune-up."

"She?" Neill deliberately made his grin puppy-dog friendly. "What's her name?"

"Lucy," Anne said automatically and then flushed, bracing for laughter. Not everyone understood the impulse to name a car.

"Some cars just seem to require a name, don't they?" His smile widened in friendly amusement. "My older sister had a thousand-year-old Volvo sedan named Morris that someone had painted pink. I was in junior high, and my mother used to ask Darcy to pick me up after school. I was convinced my mother hated me. It was bad enough to have my big sister picking me up, but that car..."

He shuddered at the memory. "How macho can a guy be if he's forced to ride in a pink Volvo?"

"It must have been very traumatic." Anne smiled, the last trace of fear evaporating. It just wasn't possible to be afraid of a man whose sister had driven a pink Volvo named Morris. And there was that smile. And the way his eyes laughed even when he wasn't smiling.

No buck teeth, no crossed eyes and, since he was looking at her with unmistakable male appreciation, it seemed unlikely that he was gay. In fact, there wasn't a flaw in sight, she decided, catching back an appreciative sigh. Early to mid-thirties, with a lean, rangy body, blue, blue eyes, nearly black hair, strong, angular jaw and a mouth that looked as if it smiled more than it frowned. The man was practically a poster boy for tall, dark and handsome.

"I never have been able to figure out what it is about Bugs that makes people so crazy about them." Looking at Anne's car, he shook his head at the phenomenon. "A friend of mine got one for his sixteenth birthday. No air-conditioning, the heater was a joke, and when it came to hills, passengers were required to get out and push. But he loved that car. I wouldn't be surprised if he had it bronzed and keeps it on the mantel next to his kids' baby shoes.''

She chuckled but, at the same time, reached out to pat the car's fender reassuringly. "Lucy has heart," she told him.

He nodded, that smile flickering in his eyes again. "Seth used to get that same look when he talked about his car." He slid his hands into his pockets and let the smile reach his mouth. "Personally, I think it's the ugly puppy syndrome. You gotta love the car because you figure no one else will."

Anne's smile took on a sheepish edge. "They were going to strip her for parts."

He laughed. "So you bought her to save her from a wrecking yard?"

"More or less." She stroked her hand over the fender, and Neill tried not to think about having those slender fingers on his skin.

*You've definitely been spending too much time alone, Devlin.*

"Are you working for David?" Anne asked shyly. Later, she would be amazed at the easy way they were talking. She'd never been the kind of person who struck up casual conversations with strangers, yet here she was chatting with the best-looking stranger to cross her path in all her twenty-five years.

He shook his head. "My bike gave a death rattle a few miles out of town." He nodded toward the red and silver motorcycle sitting just inside the garage. "I lucked out and caught a ride into town. Otherwise, I'd still be lost somewhere in the cornfields. For a minute there, I was pretty sure Rod Serling was going to pop up and start intoning some moral lesson."

Her soft gurgle of laughter had Neill smiling. A cola, some cookies and a little conversation with a pretty woman—yeah, life was definitely on the upswing.

"I'm sure David will be able to fix your bike," she said.

"You should be careful about making promises I may not be able to keep." David Freeman's voice preceded him as he stepped into the garage. He was a short, stocky man with medium brown hair and ordinary features made memorable by unexpectedly pale blue eyes. Neill had liked him on sight and liked him even more when the mechanic had immediately recognized the Indian motorcycle for what it was. He'd pointed Neill in the direction of the soft drink machine and promised to take a look at the bike as soon as he finished the tune-up he was in the midst of.

"How's it going, Anne?"

"Good. Or it will be if you've got Lucy back in working order."

*Anne,* Neill thought. The name had an old-fashioned femininity that suited her. It didn't take much imagination to picture her in a long dress with a ruffled bonnet framing her face. Not that he didn't much prefer the modern version, he admitted, allowing his eye to drift to the smooth length of leg left bare by the flippy little skirt of her sundress.

"I've got your baby running again," David said, moving over to stand next to her. Neill caught the look the other man shot in his direction and wondered if it was his imagination that put a warning in it. And was there something proprietary in the way David touched her arm as he explained the work he'd done on her car?

Neill was surprised to feel a twinge of disappointment at the thought that she might be spoken for. He was just passing through. If he was incredibly lucky and the mechanic could resurrect the Indian in the next couple of hours, he would be on the road before nightfall. If not, then tomorrow or the next day. One way or another, he wasn't going to be around long enough for it to matter whether Anne of the pretty gray eyes and soft smile was seeing someone.

*Way too long without a social life,* he thought as he watched her pull a checkbook out of the small purse she carried. If they were lovers, would she be paying him for working on her car? Not that he cared, Neill reminded himself as he turned restlessly away. Just idle curiosity, an occupational hazard for a writer. He tilted his head back and downed the last of the now lukewarm cola. Turned back when he heard the trunk slam. She was just sliding into the car, giving him a last glimpse of long, slim legs.

She pulled the door shut, looked at him through the open window and smiled shyly. "Good luck with your motorcycle."

"Thanks." Just as well she was leaving, Neill thought. Another few minutes and he might have found himself asking her out. Too many nights spent alone, too much time staring at a monitor with nothing but his own words for company. Still, he found himself walking to the garage door, watching the silly-looking little black car turn onto the main road.

"Forget it." Behind him, David Freeman's voice was dry as dust.

"Why?" Neill turned, his eyes holding both question and a faint challenge. He didn't pretend not to know what the other man was talking about. "Is she spoken for?"

"Not that I know of."

"Then why should I forget it?"

David shrugged, his dark eyes unreadable. "Just take my word for it. Or not. Doesn't matter much one way or the other, does it, since you're just passing through? I'll take a look at your bike now. See what the problem is."

He walked away, but Neill stayed where he was a moment longer, his eyes shifting back out to the road. The little black car was long gone and Free-man was right—it didn't matter.

Damned if he knew why he found that so irritating.

# Chapter Two

The phrase "steel magnolia" could have been coined with Olivia Moore in mind. The only daughter of a wealthy Atlanta businessman, she'd been raised in a world of wealth and privilege. Her parents had expected her to make an appropriate marriage—a Southerner from her own social class—but she'd surprised herself no less than them by falling in love with John Moore, a country doctor of no particular social standing and a Yankee to boot.

When they couldn't talk her out of the marriage, Olivia's parents gave her a spectacular wedding, attended by the cream of Atlanta society. They also settled an equally spectacular sum of money on their daughter, to ensure that she could maintain the lifestyle to which she was accustomed, even in the northern hinterlands to which her new husband was taking her.

The money ensured that Olivia never had to worry about living on her husband's income, nor within the confines of the lifestyle she'd married into. She redecorated her new home—a rambling monstrosity with ridiculous Tudor pretensions—with fine antiques and made twice yearly trips to New York to refurbish her wardrobe. The local women, who had been perfectly willing to accept young Doc Moore's new wife into their social circle, soon found that Olivia wasn't interested.

In a town where nearly everyone knew everyone else, at least by sight, she made acquaintances but no real friends. The lack didn't bother her, since she had no particular interest in becoming intimately acquainted with farm wives and shop clerks. She would have been faintly surprised to know that the locals thought her a terrible snob. It was so obvious that Loving, Indiana, simply could not provide the sort of society to which she was accustomed that it never occurred to her that anyone could think otherwise. Fourth of July barbecues and Harvest Fairs were quite simply beneath her.

She had been, she felt, a good wife. She'd been disappointed when John refused to consider staying in Atlanta, where she had friends and family, a social life that mattered, but she hadn't insisted that he change his mind. Nor had she complained about the lack of amenities in the small farming community to which he'd brought her. If, with the clarity of a few months' hindsight, she'd seen the wisdom in her parents' arguments against the marriage, pride would not allow her to admit as much. Divorce was unthinkable—an admission of failure she refused to make. It never occurred to her that John might feel the same regrets. After all, she had given up a great deal, while he had gained... Well, he'd gained a wife who was not only beautiful but was from a much higher social strata than he could ordinarily have aspired to. The idea that he might have regrets would have astonished her.

Having made her bed, she determined to lie in it as graciously as possible. Had her husband shown the least trace of ambition, she could have used her considerable social skills to help advance his career, but, as long as he was content to practice medicine in this backwater community, there was no question of advancement, so Olivia had turned her attention to their three children.

She had, from the start, tried to instill in them a

sense of their own worth. It was important that they understand that the real world lay beyond the suffocating confines of Loving, Indiana. In this, she'd been hampered by John's sudden, unexpected refusal to allow her to send them to boarding school. Her arguments that they needed to start, early on, associating with the right sort of people and making the kind of connections that could benefit them later in life had fallen on deaf ears.

It was, as far as she was concerned, entirely as a result of his unreasonable attitude that their only son had dropped out of medical school to become the local sheriff, a position with few benefits and no opportunity for advancement. The fact that Jack didn't seem interested in advancement was also to be laid at his father's door. If John had only shown more ambition, set an example for their son… But he hadn't, and now, at thirty-five, Jack seemed content to remain in what his mother considered a dead-end job.

As if that wasn't distressing enough, he'd gotten involved with a woman whose fashion sense seemed to be derived from circus magazines. Olivia looked down the table to where Lisa sat across from Anne, barely suppressing a shudder of distaste. She was too…everything. Too tall, too quick to laugh. Her features were too sharp, her movements too quick, her hair too red. There was no refinement about her, no elegance, and not even ten years in California could explain the impulse that had led her to pair a turquoise pinafore with yellow daisies dancing around the hem with a purple T-shirt, matching tights and Mary Janes with hot pink buckles. In combination with her fiery red hair and multicolored earrings that looked like nothing so much as fishing lures, she provided a splash of eye-searing color amid the muted grays and blues of the tastefully decorated dining room.

The fact that Lisa had grown up with Olivia's oldest daughter did nothing to reconcile her to the possibility that Jack was serious about her. She'd considered Lisa a bad influence when Brooke was alive, and the nearly fifteen years since her daughter's death had done nothing to improve her opinion. It was a pity the woman hadn't stayed in California, far away from Jack, because it was perfectly obvious that she was completely unsuitable. Not that she was foolish enough to say as much to Jack. He was too much his father's son—his stubbornness increasing in direct proportion to the stupidity of his actions.

If his father said something, he might listen, but John, as usual, had refused to interfere. He liked Lisa, he'd said. She made him laugh. Olivia's acid rejoinder that that was an admirable quality in a stand-up comic but hardly a first priority for a daughter-in-law had received nothing more than a shrug in reply, and the abstracted look in his eyes had warned her that there was no point in continuing the discussion. More and more, John had developed an annoying tendency to divorce himself from whatever was going on around him.

Left on her own, she'd first tried to ignore the whole thing, hoping it was a phase Jack was going through—an early midlife aberration of some sort—but when they'd been dating a year and a half, it had become obvious that ignoring Lisa wasn't going to make her go away. It had been her suggestion that he bring the woman to Sunday supper. She'd hoped that seeing Lisa here, in the quiet elegance of his family home, would help to open his eyes to her complete lack of suitability, but it didn't seem to have had the desired effect. Perhaps the time had come to take more direct action.

"I had been wondering where you shop these days, Lisa?" Olivia blotted her lips with a corner of her linen napkin and sent a closed-mouth smile down the table. "You must find the local shops very limited after living in Los Angeles for so long. Particularly for someone with such a…unique sense of style."

Anne closed her eyes briefly, her fingers tightening on her fork. Just when you thought it was safe to eat dessert, she thought, nearly choking on a laugh that would have held more than a touch of hysteria. Actually, the only real surprise was that it had taken her mother this long to comment—albeit obliquely—on Lisa's outfit, an outfit Lisa must have put together with the sure knowledge that it would send her hostess's blood pressure through the roof.

"It is difficult, Mrs. M," Lisa said, taking the question at face value, as if the patently false concern had been real. "Luckily, I have a friend in L.A. who sends me things. She found this dress in a terrific thrift shop on Santa Monica Boulevard." Lisa smoothed her fingers happily over the shoulder of the turquoise pinafore. "Of course, it needed a little repair work, but you can't be too picky when it comes to used clothes."

Anne made a quick grab for her glass, drowning a laugh with iced tea. She knew all about the stores where Lisa's friend shopped. Thrift shop was a bit misleading, since vintage clothing was anything but thrifty. But Lisa's tone managed to convey the image of her friend scavenging garments from barrels full of castoffs.

"No, I don't suppose one can be too picky

about...used clothing,'' Olivia said, her patrician features frozen with distaste. "Of course, I suppose, if you must watch your pennies, thrift shops must be a godsend." Her smile was razor sharp. "I know how difficult it is for creative people to deal with the financial end of things. How is your little business doing these days, my dear?"

Lisa's smile tightened, her eyes glittering dangerously. Personal attacks rolled off her back, but she took her work seriously and expected the rest of the world to do the same. "Very well, thanks. I just shipped several designs to a boutique in San Francisco last week. And I have a special order ready to go to a client in Manhattan."

"Is that the one with all the fruit?" Jack asked suddenly, rousing himself from an abstracted silence. When Lisa nodded, he grinned. "Stupidest hat I've ever seen in my life," he told his mother cheerfully. "Looks like a can of neon fruit cocktail exploded over a safari helmet. I still say charging someone five hundred bucks for a hat they aren't even going to wear has got to be illegal."

"My biggest fan," Lisa said dryly, bumping his arm with her elbow.

The tightness around Olivia's mouth made it clear that she recognized his sudden contribution for what it was—her son was not only letting her know that Lisa's "little business" was doing very well indeed but that he was a firm supporter of it.

"That's wonderful," Olivia said insincerely. "I must admit, I had wondered about making collectible hats." Her light laugh hinted at the utter absurdity of the idea. "I didn't even know there was anyone who would want to collect something like that, but there's no telling what odd notions people will get, is there? You only have to look at pet rocks to know that they'll collect the oddest things."

"They will, won't they?" Lisa agreed, teeth only slightly gritted. "I guess I'm just lucky that there are people who consider my hats at least as interesting as a pet rock."

Just another evening spent in the warm bosom of her family, Anne thought. The only thing that could compare to it might be tap dancing barefoot through a minefield while someone lobbed bowling balls over her head. When she was younger, she could remember watching reruns of *The Brady Bunch* on TV and wondering if there really were families like that. If there were families who actually talked to each other; a place where you had only to turn to your family to find the solution for every problem, large or small.

It had always been a puzzle to her that they'd

known they could turn to each other. It couldn't be just a matter of birth or marriage because, if that was the case, she would have that same feeling about her own family. She couldn't remember a time when she'd felt as if she could take her problems to her family. It wasn't that they didn't love each other, she told herself, ignoring the niggling hint of question in the thought. Of course they loved each other, because that was what families did. She'd long ago grown out of the idea that real life was anything like a sitcom, but there was still that small, wistful part of her that wondered what it would be like to sit down to dinner and actually talk to each other, she thought as she pushed a piecrust crumb around the edge of her plate.

She didn't need to look at her father to know that, though he was sitting at the table, he was not really there. It was a knack he'd developed years ago—that ability to go away somewhere, to retreat from whatever was happening around him. She'd often envied him that ability, but tonight, when she glanced at him, it suddenly occurred to her that it was a lonely way to live.

And her brother... Jack had always been something of a mystery to her. When she was a child, the nearly ten-year difference in their ages had lent him an almost mystical aura in her eyes. Tall and lean, with hair the color of sunshine and deep blue eyes, she'd been dazzled by the physical perfection of him and by the fact that he'd been an adult while she was still a child. It was only when she became an adult herself that she'd begun to see the man behind the picture she'd created.

She frowned a little as Jack reached out to lift the wine bottle from the center of the table and tilt the remainder of it into his glass. On the surface, he seemed satisfied with his life, but there was a darkness in his eyes, a shadow lurking behind his smile, and she wondered at its source.

"Earth to Anne. Anybody home?" Jack's voice startled her. She looked up, suddenly aware that it wasn't the first time he'd spoken.

"Sorry." Her fork clinked against the edge of her plate as she set it down. "I guess I was somewhere else for a minute there."

"Thinking about the hunk?" Lisa asked with a teasing grin.

"No." But Lisa's question brought him instantly to mind. She'd thought of him several times during the afternoon, wondering where he'd come from, where he was going, half wishing she were the sort of woman who could have asked those questions. Or maybe even the sort of woman who would make a man like that change his plans and stay in town, just hoping for a chance to get to know her.

Seeing the faint hint of color come up in Anne's cheeks, Lisa leaned forward, her green eyes bright with interest. "Did you talk to him?"

"Why do I have the feeling that I've missed half the conversation?" Jack complained. "Who are we talking about?"

"There was a guy at David's garage when I took Anne to pick up that junk heap she drives. Greatest butt I've seen in years."

"Should I be jealous?" Jack asked.

"Maybe just a little," Lisa said, grinning. "It really was an exceptional butt." She looked back at Anne. "Did you talk to him?"

"A little." She lifted one hand to halt the questions she could see trembling on her friend's lips. "His motorcycle broke down, and he got a ride into town. David was going to look at it. That's all I know."

"Does he look as good up close as he did at a distance?" Lisa asked irrepressibly.

"Now I'm definitely jealous," Jack said dryly. "If this guy is still around, I'll have to run him out of town immediately."

"I can't believe you're joking about this." The harsh anger in her mother's voice cut through the light conversation like a dagger slashing through fine silk. Looking at her, Anne was startled by the emotion that tightened her face. In her experience, her mother made a point to avoid strong emotion. *Nothing ages a woman faster than strong emotion, Anne. It's not fashionable to say as much these days, but a lady is always restrained in her emotions.*

"Joking about what?" Anne asked, bewildered. She shot a questioning look at Jack, but, after one sharp glance at his mother, he was absorbed in watching the play of light through the parchment-colored wine in his glass.

"You actually spoke with this man?" Olivia demanded, pinning Anne to her chair with the sheer force of her anger.

"A little." Understanding glimmered and set a knot in her stomach. She lowered her hands to her lap, her fingers twisting together. She was suddenly sixteen again, home late from school, listening to her mother's hysterical sobs as she listed all the terrible things she'd thought might have happened to her only remaining daughter. "He was very pleasant," she offered quietly, knowing it wouldn't be enough.

"That doesn't mean anything," Olivia snapped. She shoved her plate back with a quick, impatient gesture that sent it clattering against her wine glass. The glass tipped and would have fallen if Jack's hand hadn't shot out, catching it and setting it upright again. His mother didn't even notice the small incident. "He was a stranger. He could have been anyone, done anything."

"I'm sure it was perfectly safe, Livvy." John Moore spoke for the first time since the meal began, his voice soothing. "It was broad daylight, after all."

"And we all know how safe that makes her, don't we?" The shrill question was followed by a thick silence.

Against her will, Anne's eyes went to the neat arrangement of framed photos on a low side table. There were several pictures, but the largest was of a pretty blonde with golden hair and deep blue eyes. The photo showed a girl on the brink of womanhood, her eyes sparkling with anticipation for the life that lay ahead of her. A life that had ended barely a month after the picture was taken.

"Well, nothing happened," John said after a moment.

"Not yet, but how do we know this man didn't follow her home? He could be waiting for her even now."

"I'm sure he's not." Anne kept her voice calm.

"He could hardly have followed me without a means of transportation, and since he didn't even know my name, it's not likely he could find out where I live, is it?"

The flat, disinterested tone had the desired effect. The hectic color that had tinted Olivia's cheeks began to recede, and she slowly relaxed the grip she'd taken on the edge of the table.

"I suppose not." She pressed her fingertips to the base of her throat, visibly gathering the threads of her usual control. "But I don't like the idea of you going back to that empty cottage," she said fretfully. "I've never understood why you insisted on moving out. It's not as if there isn't more than enough room in this house."

"I need a place of my own," Anne said, feeling the knot in her stomach tighten. They'd had this argument three years ago when she'd decided to move out. She wasn't going to have it again.

"I know, I know—you needed your privacy," Olivia said bitterly. "I never have understood why you felt you had to move out just for that. You could have stayed here and had all the privacy you wanted."

Anne swallowed an hysterical little bubble of laughter, aware that her mother actually believed what she was saying.

"It's not like I moved very far," she said, by-passing the issue of whether or not she should have moved at all. "The cottage is only a couple of hundred yards away."

"Far enough. You can't even see it from the house."

*Which was the only reason I agreed to move in there,* Anne thought. Despite her assurance about respecting her privacy, her mother wouldn't have thought twice about keeping tabs on any comings and goings at the cottage. *Not that there was anything to keep track of,* Anne admitted silently and with some regret.

When Anne didn't volunteer to pack her things and move back into the family home, Olivia's mouth compressed with irritation. She would have liked to pursue the issue but knew she wouldn't get anywhere with it, just as she hadn't gotten anywhere three years ago. It had been a shock to find her usually malleable daughter suddenly digging in her heels, insisting that it was time she had a place of her own. She'd had to content herself with the knowledge that at least she'd persuaded Anne to move into the ridiculous Victorian confection of a cottage at the bottom of the driveway, rather than getting a place somewhere in town. There was no point in rehashing the subject, particularly not with

Lisa sitting there, listening to every word. You didn't air family troubles in front of an outsider and, if she had her way, that was exactly what Lisa was going to stay.

"I still can't believe you talked to a stranger like that," she said fretfully. "As if you were just any-one."

*As if there had ever been a time, in the last fif-teen years, when I've been allowed to forget that Brooke Moore was my sister,* Anne thought bit-terly. As if she'd ever been able to be "just any-one."

"He was just someone passing through," was all she said. "I'm sure he's halfway to Chicago or New York or wherever he was originally headed by now."

"Not New York," Jack said suddenly. "Not un-less he had a rocket-powered motorcycle."

"Could have been nuclear," Lisa said, gamely picking up on his transparent bid to lighten the atmosphere. "I bet you can download plans for a nuclear-powered motorcycle off the Internet."

"And probably pick up everything you need to make it at the local hardware store."

"This is hardly a joking matter," Olivia said stiffly, but the moment of crisis had passed and they all knew it.

Just another warm evening spent in the bosom of her family, Anne thought wryly. She stood up and began gathering the dessert plates. All this because she'd exchanged a few words with a man she would never see again. And wasn't it ridiculous to feel regret at the thought? He would probably have turned out to be a dead bore. Any man who was that good-looking probably had an ego the size of Kansas. Still, she allowed herself a wistful moment to wonder where he was now.

At that particular moment, Neill was unpacking his duffle bag under the watchful eyes of Claudette Colbert and Bela Lugosi. They stared down at him from their respective posters—Colbert looking sultry and dangerous as Cleopatra, and Lugosi looking like an orthodontist's dream come true as Dracula. It was, he thought, an interesting combination with which to decorate a motel room. But then, even on short acquaintance, he could tell that his temporary landlady was an interesting woman.

When it became clear that nothing but an act of God was going to get the motorcycle back on the road that night, David Freeman had recommended The Blue Dahlia Motel.

"My great-aunt Dorothy owns it. It's nothing fancy, but it's clean, and the rates aren't bad." He pulled a grease-stained rag out of his back pocket, found a reasonably clean corner and began wiping the grease off his fingers. It was late, and he was getting ready to close the station for the day. "Truth is, there isn't a whole lot of choice in a town this size. Gert Billings rents out the second bedroom in her house from time to time, but she's looking for something a little more long-term than you're likely to be. 'Sides, you're a little on the young side."

"For what?" Neill asked, startled.

"For Gert. She's been on the lookout for a husband since Willie died a couple years back."

"Willie was her husband?"

"Actually, he was her brother." Neill's eyebrows rose, and David laughed. "Willie was a terrific handyman. He could fix damned near anything, and he worked cheap—room, board and a color TV and he was a happy man. Gert's tightfisted, and that old place of hers needs a lot of work. She figures a husband would be cheap labor, but she hasn't found any takers yet."

"Well, tempting as the idea of free room and board is, I think I can resist Gert's charms."

"Don't forget the color TV."

"That does make it harder to turn down, but I think I'll just head over to your great-aunt's mo-

tel.'' Neill bent to pick up the duffle he'd untied
from the back of the Indian. He gave David a cautious look as he straightened. ''Your aunt isn't
looking for a husband, is she?''

David grinned and shook his head. ''Nope. She
buried Uncle Leo forty years or so ago, and she's
shown no inclination to replace him. She's a bit
eccentric, but she'll treat you right. Tell her I sent
you over.''

''Thanks.'' Neill slung the duffle onto his back
and then nodded at his motorcycle. ''How long do
you figure it's going to take?''

David had already determined that the engine
had sucked a valve, but there hadn't been time to
determine the full extent of the damage. He
shrugged. ''Hard to say. I can tear down the engine
tomorrow afternoon, figure out what parts I'm going to need.''

With an inward sigh, Neill resigned himself to
the fact that he wasn't going anywhere for at least
a couple of days. It would take that long to arrange
alternate transportation if the Indian couldn't be repaired quickly, which seemed highly likely.

Following David's directions, he found The Blue
Dahlia Motel without trouble. Standing on the sidewalk, he viewed the place without favor. He'd
spent too many nights in mediocre motel room

beds to be impressed by the tidy landscaping and recent paint job. The name of the place was spelled out in blue neon script, with the dot over the 'I' formed by a multipetalled dahlia. It was a striking display, especially for a rather nondescript little building in what appeared to be a nondescript little town, but he didn't allow himself to get his hopes up.

Eccentric. Neill rolled the word over in his mind as he pushed open the door marked Office. David Freeman had said his great aunt was eccentric. Experience had taught him that the word could be used to describe a multitude of conditions from mildly unconventional to crazy as a bed bug. The woman who was watering a pair of rather sickly looking philodendrons didn't look like she fit at either end of the scale.

He guessed her age to be somewhere around seventy, but there was nothing frail about her. Her hair was an uncompromising steel gray, worn cropped short around her square face. The practical style fit the direct look in her pale blue eyes. Her short, sturdy form was clad in a denim shirt and softly faded jeans. She looked exactly as he would have imagined a farm wife would look, except for her shoes—red sneakers with gold glitter stars, worn with red and white striped socks.

Neither the shoes nor the socks would have raised an eyebrow in Seattle or Los Angeles, but he supposed in a town the size of Loving a penchant for glitter-covered sneakers was enough to get her labeled an eccentric.

"Are you Dorothy?"

"Dorothy Gale. Looking for a room?" she asked, not looking particularly pleased by the possibility.

"Yes." He offered her the smile a long ago girlfriend had told him should be registered as a lethal weapon. Unimpressed, she continued to frown at him. With a sigh, Neill abandoned charm and decided to try simple facts. "David Freeman said you might have a room available."

"No he didn't." She moved behind the desk, setting down the green plastic watering can with a thump. "No 'might' about it," she added before Neill could protest his honesty. "Pretty much always have rooms, except now and again around Christmas. David knows that." She didn't seem to expect any response, which was just as well, because Neill didn't have one. "How long are you staying?"

"I don't know. Until my motorcycle is repaired or I can make other arrangements for transportation. A couple of days. Maybe longer."

"I can let you have a room with a king-size bed and a kitchenette." She named a rate, and Neill nodded.

"Sounds fine."

"Fill this out. I'll need a credit card or cash in advance."

Neill pulled his wallet out of his back pocket and handed her a credit card before picking up a pen from the counter and pulling the file card toward him.

"We've got cable," Dorothy said, as she imprinted his credit card. Now that he'd officially become a guest, she seemed disposed toward friendliness. "Movies twenty-four hours a day. You like movies?"

"Haven't had much time for them in the past few months," Neill said absently, his attention on the card he was filling out.

"I'm not talking about the nonsense they're making these days," Dorothy said so sternly that Neill looked up. He was startled by the fierce glare she'd fixed on him. "They splatter blood and guts all over the screen and call it horror, or show a couple bouncing up and down in bed and think it's erotic. Nonsense. Pure nonsense. Not a filmmaker alive today who knows what he's doing. Know what the blue dahlia is?"

She asked the question with such ferocity that Neill couldn't help but wonder if an incorrect answer would cost him his room. Later, he decided that it must have been the pressure of the moment that dredged the faint memory to the surface of his brain.

"It was the title of a movie, wasn't it? With Alan Ladd?" He was really pushing it now, but there was a challenge in her eyes—a challenge that softened to approval at his answer.

"Alan Ladd, Veronica Lake and William Bendix. Paramount. 1946." She reeled out the information in a staccato burst. "Written by Raymond Chandler. Film noir, they call it now. We just called it a damned fine movie and left it at that. Who's your favorite actress?"

The question shot out at him, but Neill was not stupid. He abandoned Michelle Pfeiffer without a second's hesitation and searched through mental files for a more acceptable choice. An exquisite face floated into focus. "Gene Tierney."

"Made some fine movies," Dorothy admitted with grudging approval. "Can't beat *Laura* for sheer suspense."

"Dana Andrews, Clifton Webb and Vincent Price," he said, on more secure ground. He'd seen *Laura* on late-night cable just a few months ago.

He couldn't quite shake the feeling that he was being tested to see if he was worthy of having a room.

"What was the name of Clifton Webb's character?" Dorothy asked, immediately depressing any pretensions he might have had to movie buffdom.

Neill shrugged. "He typed in the bathtub. I remember that."

"Waldo Lydecker," she supplied with a friendly smile that made it clear that, if there *had* been a test, he'd passed.

Thinking about the exchange an hour later, Neill found himself grinning. Dorothy wasn't exactly warm and fuzzy but she was interesting, and there was a sparkle of humor in her eyes that suggested she hadn't come by the title of "eccentric" by accident.

The room she'd given him was larger than he'd expected. The tiny kitchenette might come in handy if he decided to wait until his bike was repaired. The decor, considering the owner, was surprisingly normal, if you didn't count the movie posters that replaced the usual innocuous prints. All in all, it seemed like a pleasant enough place to spend a couple of days. He'd liked David Freeman at first sight and saw no reason to change his opinion, and his landlady promised to provide some interesting conversation.

It was a small town. If he hung around long enough, he was likely to catch a glimpse of most of the inhabitants. Maybe he would even cross paths with that pretty little blonde with the big gray eyes. Anne. Not that he would have stayed just for that but, when life handed you lemons, you might as well try your hand at lemon meringue pie, and she had definitely looked edible.

## Chapter Three

Loving wasn't likely to turn up on anyone's list of top ten places to visit in the state of Indiana. A small farming town surrounded by corn and wheat fields, the single main street was lined with the expected assortment of businesses—a feed store, a couple of cafés, a tired-looking five-and-dime. There was a bank, and a real estate office with a sign that announced hours two days a week and gave a phone number, in case you had a sudden urge to buy or sell and couldn't wait until Tuesday or Saturday.

It was a town much like a lot of other small towns Neill had been in, a little more prosperous than some. Loving's only claim to fame was the thousands of letters that poured into the post office every St. Valentine's Day to receive an appropriate postmark. It was something of an annual event, requiring the postmistress to hire on extra help. He had this tidbit courtesy of Dorothy, who had been watering the flower beds in front of the motel when he left his room, Tuesday morning.

After a brief greeting, she'd demanded to know if he'd caught *The Prisoner of Zenda* on cable. "Didn't come on until midnight but it's worth staying up late for. Not the wussy version they made in the fifties but the original, with Ronald Coleman and Douglas Fairbanks, Jr. Now there was a man who knew how to swash and buckle."

Neill admitted that he'd been asleep at midnight but was able to say, truthfully, that he'd seen the movie and liked it. His confession that he hadn't even known there was a second version appeared to meet with her approval. She smiled, revealing a set of suspiciously perfect teeth. This morning she was wearing baggy khaki shorts that revealed knobby knees, a short-sleeved plaid shirt and another pair of red sneakers, though there was no glitter on these.

"Remakes are almost always a mistake," she said firmly. "Look at *My Man Godfrey*. Nothing against David Niven, but he just wasn't William Powell."

Neill nodded, feeling as if he was on solid ground with this. David Niven and William Powell had definitely been two different people.

"*Mutiny on the Bounty* is another one." Dorothy leaned on her rake, narrowing her eyes against the sun's glare. "Can't say the Brando version didn't have something to offer, but where was Charles Laughton?"

"Dead?" Neill offered hesitantly, when she seemed to be waiting for a response.

There was a moment of silence, then Dorothy chuckled. "Probably. You have to watch me when I get started talking about movies. Truth is, it's something of a hobby of mine."

Neill raised his brows and tried to look as if this was news to him, but she only laughed again. "Don't get smart with me." She reached into her back pocket and pulled out a battered gimme cap with the words John Deere emblazoned across the front. Tugging it on over her gray curls, she fixed him with a look of bright interest. "So, tell me about yourself."

One thing Neill had learned in the years since his first book hit the bestseller lists was the art of talking without saying much. It hadn't taken him long to figure out that successful writers tended to fall into the same category as train wrecks and alien sightings—they sparked curiosity and inspired questions he soon got tired of answering. *Where do you get your ideas? How did you get a publisher? Can you really make a living that way?* And his personal favorite: *Have I read anything of yours?* which always made him wonder if the questioner had mistaken him for a psychic. How the hell was he supposed to know what they'd read?

He'd experimented with lying—nothing killed a conversation faster than the announcement that you were a mortician, and short-order cooks generated little interest. But there was always the chance that a new acquaintance might be around long enough to find out the truth, which would lead to hurt feelings and possible recrimination. So he'd developed the ability to tell the truth—or part of it, anyway—and make it sound too dull to merit further discussion.

When he parted company with Dorothy, she knew he was a writer but was left with the vague impression that he wrote articles for technical journals. He'd told her he was taking a vacation, which was the truth, and that he had no particular schedule, also the truth. He'd also learned a considerable amount about his landlady, gotten a brief history of Loving and refused an offer to have a VCR installed in his room so he could avail himself of Dorothy's extensive collection of movies on tape.

By the time Dorothy went to answer the phone in the motel office, Neill guessed they'd been talking for close to an hour. Mostly Dorothy had talked and he'd listened, but he'd enjoyed every minute of it. Like most writers, he had an insatiable curiosity about people and places, and he enjoyed Dorothy's trenchant commentary on the town and its inhabitants. By the time they parted company, he felt as if he'd been given a crash course in local politics, and it amused him to find they were every bit as hotly debated and intrigue-filled as they were in a big city.

The Blue Dahlia Motel sat back from Signal Avenue, which was the main street in Loving. The neon sign with its multipetaled dahlia looked faintly tatty in broad daylight. There were cars parked in front of two of the dozen units, and Neill wondered if the place ever filled up completely. Christmas, maybe, he decided, when people came back to spend the holidays with family.

With nothing better to do, he wandered toward the main part of town. There wasn't enough of it to call it a downtown, he thought, walking past a hairdresser's and a drugstore. The businesses were all of the mom-and-pop type, with straightforward window displays that focused more on information than artistry. He exchanged hellos with a young mother pushing a baby carriage, a grizzled old man wearing coveralls, two young girls who looked too fresh-faced and cheerful to be teenagers, and a deep-bosomed matron wearing a floral print dress that looked like it dated to the 1940s.

Time warp, Neill decided, stopping beneath a shade tree whose branches arched over the sidewalk. That was the only possible explanation for what he was seeing. He hooked his thumbs in the front pockets of his jeans and contemplated the possibility. Smiling, friendly faces, tidy little businesses—he'd obviously passed through a time warp and landed in the fifties. Or maybe, considering his landlady, he'd fallen into an old Blondie movie.

It had just occurred to him that he was hungry when he realized that he was standing in front of a grocery store. Bill's Grocery was written in plain block letters across the front of the building. There was an appealing simplicity to that, a stolid refusal to pander to those who might want fancy names or curlicues on their letters. After two years of living in Seattle, where there was a specialty "emporium" or "market" on every other corner, there was something pleasantly honest about the chunky block of a building with its plain name.

He'd planned on eating at the diner down the street, but now he thought of the kitchenette that had come with his room. It had been awhile since he'd cooked himself a meal, unless you counted reheating Chinese take out. He liked to cook—had actually spent a few months working as a short-order cook once upon a time—and it occurred to him that it had been too long since he'd set pan to stove. Letting the impulse carry him, he pushed open the door of Bill's Grocery and went inside.

Anne hefted a cantaloupe and tried to remember the trick for telling if it was ripe. Was it supposed to have a yellow spot where it had rested on the ground and sound hollow when you thumped it? Or was that watermelons? There was something that was supposed to feel heavy for its size—lettuce or cantaloupe?

"Try smelling the stem end," a masculine voice suggested behind her. Startled, she turned and found herself staring up into smiling blue eyes. Recognition was immediate. It was the stranger from the gas station, the one she'd assumed was halfway across the country by now. Surprise had her blurting out the first thing that came to mind.

"What are you doing here?"

"Buying vegetables," he said, as if there was nothing odd in her abrupt question.

"No, I mean what are you...?" Anne stopped and bit her lip, feeling color flood her cheeks as she heard the echo of her own words. "I just...I thought you'd be...somewhere else by now."

"In the junk food aisle, maybe?" He sighed, looking regretful. "I get that a lot."

"No, I meant somewhere else." She waved one hand as if to indicate distance. "Another town or state or something. I didn't know you were staying here. In Loving."

"I hadn't planned on it, but it looks like it's going to be a few days before my bike is fixed. Your friend, David, is going to have to track down parts."

"Oh, I'm sorry. I hope you didn't have somewhere you needed to be today."

"That's what you get when you have an old bike," Neill said, shrugging. "And I'm not on any kind of schedule, so it's not a problem to hang out here for a little while."

In fact, at the moment, this unexpected stopover was starting to look rather promising. He'd thought about Anne with her big gray eyes, pretty smile and rather spectacular legs several times over the last twenty-four hours. When he'd realized that he was going to be stuck here for a while, he had wondered if their paths might cross again. It was a small town, after all, and it wasn't beyond the realm of possibility. When he'd seen her studying the cantaloupe display with such a serious expression, it seemed like his luck was running high. He decided to push it a little further.

"Lunch hour?" he asked, looking at her slim black skirt that ended several inches above her knee and lilac silk blouse whose color was reflected in her clear gray eyes. Simple black pumps with slim, tapered heels that displayed those killer legs to perfection, and her dark gold hair was pulled back in a soft twist. A few baby-fine curls had escaped to lie against her nape—a look he found ridiculously tantalizing.

"Yes. I work at the bank." Anne realized she was still clutching the cantaloupe and turned to set it back with the others, using the moment to try to gather her scattered senses. When she turned back, she felt her smile achieved just the right amount of friendly distance. "I was going to pick up groceries and run them home."

"Have lunch with me," he asked.

"What?" She stared at him, her eyes wide and startled. "I...I can't."

"Why not? You have to eat. I have to eat. Why shouldn't we eat together?"

*Why not eat together?* All the reasons why not tumbled through Anne's mind and finally came out as one simple protest. "I don't know your name."

"Neill Devlin," he said promptly.

"Anne Moore." The response was automatic, as was accepting the hand he held out, but she had to struggle not to jump at the electricity that arced from that casual touch. Her eyes shot to his face, wondering if he'd felt the same thing. The awareness in those clear blue eyes told her that the sensation had not been one-sided. Her cheeks warming, she pulled her hand back, resisting the urge to rub her fingertips against her tingling palm.

"Now that we've been introduced, have lunch with me." Neill's tone was light, easy, making it seem ridiculous to have doubts, foolish to refuse. When she still hesitated, he gave her a crooked smile. "Take pity on me. I'm a stranger in a strange land, and I hate to eat alone."

Anne's teeth worried her lower lip as she considered the idea. It was crazy, of course. She didn't do things like that—having lunch with a strange man, even if he did happen to have smiling blue eyes and a truly beautiful mouth.

"I told you how to pick out a cantaloupe," he

reminded her. "Lunch seems like the least you could do to repay the favor."

A smile tugged at the corners of her mouth. "Cantaloupe *is* one of my favorite foods."

"That makes it a debt of honor," Neill said solemnly. "You definitely have to save me from a lonely lunch."

"I...there's a diner down the street," Anne said slowly, feeling excitement curl in the pit of her stomach. It was crazy, of course. It was completely out of character. Then again, just lately, she'd started to think that her character was pretty damn dull.

Luanne's Café looked like a movie set from *American Graffiti*. Worn black-and-white checkered linoleum and red vinyl booths, patched here and there with duct tape, a long counter with a speckled gray surface and backless red stools. The walls were covered with framed photos of various sports teams, ranging from the local Little League to pro teams from all over the country and, from the look of the uniforms, dating back into the forties.

Business appeared to be good, with all the seats at the counter filled and only one booth open. Neill took it, sliding into the seat that faced the door, wondering if Anne of the pretty gray eyes was going to show up. He was inclined to think she would, but he wouldn't have bet his next royalty check on it.

She was an odd little thing, he thought, as he took a packet of crackers from the basket on the table and tore open the plastic. Not shy, exactly, but...skittish. Like a kitten who wanted to be petted but was cautious of getting too close. He hadn't imagined the way her eyes had brightened when she saw him and knew, without ego, that she'd thought of him a time or two since their brief meeting the day before. When he'd suggested lunch, she'd wanted to accept. He'd seen that in her eyes, too. Yet she'd hesitated, as if he'd suggested a torrid weekend, which, he had to admit, didn't sound half-bad.

Neill trusted his instincts. As a writer, he had to. More often that not, particularly when he was starting a new project, they were all he had. And his instincts told him that there was a lot more to Anne Moore than what you saw at first glance. They'd also told him that she'd show up, he thought, smiling as he saw her walk through the door.

Her teeth tugged at her full lower lip as her eyes skimmed the restaurant, and Neill found himself wondering how she would react if he offered to do the nibbling for her. Her eyes brightened when she saw him, and her mouth curved in a shy smile that, for some reason, made him want to drag her into the booth and kiss her senseless.

*Definitely too much time alone, Devlin,* he thought, rising as she approached.

The old-fashioned courtesy made Anne flush with pleasure, even as she wished he'd stayed seated and less noticeable. When she'd agreed to have lunch with him, she hadn't thought about the fact that there was nowhere, short of going to another town, that they could go where someone wasn't likely to recognize her and wonder who she was with. Not that there was any chance of a man who looked like he did going unnoticed unless he put a bag over his head, she admitted.

"So, is there really a Luanne?" he asked as he slid into the seat opposite hers.

"What?" The unexpected question startled her. In the ten minutes since they'd parted company at the grocery store, she'd nearly made herself sick wondering what she would say to him, what he would say to her, trying to think of witty bits of conversation. None of those fragmented scenarios had begun quite like this.

"Luanne." He tapped a finger against the name emblazoned in black script across a dog-eared red menu. "Is there such a person or did they just invent the name to give the place an air of exotic mystery?"

"Exotic mystery?" Anne's brows went up, and, catching the laughter in his eyes, she forgot to be nervous. "Y-yes, I can see how the name Luanne would conjure up images of exotic lands and sultry women. I'm sorry to disappoint you, but Luanne was the first cook here, back in the forties, and, according to what I'm told, she was a black woman, about six foot tall, skinny as a rail, chewed tobacco and had six husbands."

"All at once?" Neill's brows shot up in a look of exaggerated shock, and Anne had to struggle to hold on to her serious expression.

"Of course not. This is Indiana, and we don't permit such things. She was divorced once and widowed five times." She paused and cleared her throat, primming her mouth in a disapproving line. "There were, I believe, rumors that not all of her husbands departed the mortal coil willingly, but nothing was ever proved, and both the sheriff and the mayor were extremely fond of her chicken pot pie, so they were not, perhaps, as diligent in their investigations as they might have been."

"I knew there had to be a story behind a name like that." Neill opened his menu, then tilted it so he could look at her over the top. "What happened to her?"

"Nothing exotic, I'm afraid. She bought the place sometime in the late fifties, then sold it in the seventies and retired to Arizona where, for all I know, she's working on husband number ten."

"I hope so. I'd hate to think of a woman like that reduced to playing bingo and watching the soaps. It's important to have hobbies."

"It does sound as if her hobby might have been a little hard on her husbands," Anne pointed out.

"Yes but a really exceptional pot pie is worth a few risks," he said thoughtfully and was pleased with himself when she laughed.

She'd looked nervous edging toward frightened when she first walked in, her eyes skittering away from his. But, despite her uneasiness, she'd come to meet him, and he found that interesting. He wanted to believe it was his irresistible charm that had brought her, but he had a feeling she was proving something, whether to herself or someone else, he couldn't be sure. And why he should care one way or another was beyond him. She...intrigued him. For the moment, that was answer enough.

Neill glanced up as a waitress in a pink uniform stopped next to the table. Somewhere in her mid-twenties, with brassy blond hair and a thin, angular frame, she wore a small diamond solitaire and plain gold wedding ring on her ring finger, but, judging from the blatant invitation in her heavily made-up eyes, she didn't believe in letting marriage restrict her. Their eyes met, and she gave him a sultry smile.

"See anything you like, sugar?"

As passes went, he'd heard worse, Neill decided dispassionately. Fifteen years ago, he'd probably *delivered* worse lines himself. Hell, fifteen years ago, he might have been flattered, might even have been tempted, though he liked to think that, even at twenty, his taste had been a little more discriminating. As it was, he couldn't help but find such a blatant come-on just a little pathetic and, considering the woman sitting across from him, certainly lacking in manners.

"I think we need another minute or two." He flicked an impassive look over what she was offering and then glanced across the table. "Anne?"

Out the corner of his eye, Neill saw the waitress slant a look of studied indifference across the table. Her head was already turning back in his direction when she registered who he was with. She nearly gave herself whiplash when she jerked around to gape at his companion.

"Anne?" The husky purr vanished in a disbelieving squeak. "Anne Moore?"

"Hello, DeDe." It was only sheer willpower that kept the color from flooding Anne's cheeks. Aware of Neill's interested look, she forced what she hoped was an easy smile. "How are you?"

"Fine." DeDe continued to stare, her eyes wide with disbelief. "You're here with him?" she asked, as if she needed verbal reassurance before she could believe what she was seeing.

"Yes." Seeing that the simple affirmative wasn't going to be enough, she nodded in Neill's direction. "This is Neill Devlin. Neill, this is DeDe Carmichael. We went to school together."

Neill acknowledged the introduction with a polite smile, but he might as well not have bothered. A moment ago she'd been looking at him like a cat looking at a particularly plump canary. Now she was staring at him with the same expression she might previously have reserved for a two-headed alien. Neill wondered if he should be offended but decided he was more interested in knowing just why the fact that he and Anne were together should strike her as so extraordinary.

"We went to school together," DeDe parroted, her head bobbing up and down as her eyes shifted from Neill to Anne, then back again. The silence stretched. DeDe's pink sneakers appeared to be glued to the linoleum. Neill was just about to remind her that they needed more time to order when the annoyed jangle of a bell cut into her stupefied silence.

"You gone deaf, DeDe?" an irascible voice demanded from behind the counter. "Order up!"

DeDe jolted and frowned. "I'm coming," she called over her shoulder. She gave Neill and Anne another speculative look and flashed a quick smile. "I'll be back to get your order," she promised, and Anne told herself it was just imagination that made the words sound like a threat.

She caught the question in Neill's eyes and knew he had to be wondering at DeDe's astonishment over the fact that they were together. She briefly considered telling him that she never dated, which was more or less true. But it wasn't the whole truth, or even the most important part of it, and it didn't exactly paint her in a flattering light, so she settled for what she hoped was a casual smile and opened her menu.

"The hamburgers are excellent here."

She waited for him to ask a question she didn't want to answer, but he simply raised his brows in surprise and asked, "What? No chicken pot pie?"

Neill would have given a great deal to know what was behind DeDe's reaction, but he couldn't ignore the look in Anne's eyes, the plea she probably hadn't been aware of making. So he tamped down the curiosity—a writer's curse—pretended that DeDe's slack-jawed disbelief had been nothing out of the ordinary and set out to coax a genuine smile out of his companion.

"So, what's a nice girl like you doing in a place like this?"

Her eyes widened a little, surprise and something that might have been gratitude flickering through the clear gray depths. Neill thought he'd never known anyone whose emotions were so transparent. Everything was reflected in those eyes.

"I was born and raised here." She folded her menu and set it on top of his, carefully aligning their edges, keeping her eyes on the task because it was safer than looking at her companion. "How about yourself?"

"I wasn't born and raised here," he said, shaking his head.

His serious tone startled her into looking at him. Catching the laughter in those impossibly blue eyes, she found herself smiling easily. Despite the nerves jangling in the pit of her stomach, Anne made up her mind that she was going to enjoy the next hour without giving so much as a thought to the fact that DeDe Carmichael was a world-class gossip, which meant that, by the end of the day, everybody who was interested—and quite a few who weren't—would know that Anne Moore had been seen having lunch with a total stranger.

"And here I was, thinking you were a native."

"I think it's important to try to blend in with the native culture whenever possible," he said pedantically.

"You're doing a fine job," she assured him. "Where are you from?"

"Most recently? Seattle, for the last couple of years."

"Is the Pacific Northwest as beautiful as it looks in pictures?"

"There's lots of green stuff," Neill said, without enthusiasm. "I haven't figured out how it manages to grow when there's never any sunlight. If it ever got warm, it would be like living in a sauna. As it is, it's just chilly and damp and...green."

"So why did you live there for two years?" Anne asked, smiling at his bleak description.

"Work," he said, glancing around for DeDe and her pink uniform, hoping she would provide a distraction before Anne asked what he did. But DeDe was on the other side of the counter, arguing with the cook over an order. And Anne was already asking the obvious.

"What kind of work do you do?"

"I'm a writer," he said, tossing the word out with a verbal shrug. He didn't want to talk about his work.

"Really?" Startled, Anne looked at him. "You don't look like a writer."

The comment surprised him. "What does a writer look like?"

"More...writerly." The smile in those impossibly blue eyes deepened and she shrugged, smiling self-consciously. "Glasses, maybe. Stooped shoulders. A little vague."

"I think you've got writers confused with absent-minded professors," Neill said, grinning.

"Could be." Certainly the man sitting across from her was about as far from that image as it was possible to get, Anne thought, letting her eyes skim over those broad shoulders. She wondered what he looked like without a shirt. Was his chest smooth or covered in dark, curling hair? She could see the ripple of muscles under the thin cotton of his T-shirt, and she wondered what those muscles would feel like under her hands. Catching his questioning look, Anne felt her cheeks warm and cursed her fair complexion that made it impossible to hide a blush. To distract him—and her own wayward thoughts—she rushed into speech.

"So, what do you write?"

Neill hesitated a moment over the answer. If he told her what he wrote, there was a chance she would connect N. C. Devlin, the bestselling writer, with Neill Devlin, stranded motorcycle rider. Then things would change. She didn't strike him as the sort to start scrabbling for a pen so she could get his autograph, but fame always changed things. And, although he couldn't have said why it mattered, he didn't want to see the look in her eyes shift from interest to curiosity.

"I write nonfiction," he said, shrugging lightly. "I've done articles on a lot of different things, how to plant a rosebush, ten tips for buying a ladder—that sort of thing."

It was true enough, as far as it went. He'd spent a couple of years scrabbling as a freelance writer, working at odd jobs while he used his spare time to write *The Stranger Next Door,* his first book and, as luck and the vagaries of the publishing world would have it, his first bestseller. He hadn't lied, he reminded himself in answer to a twinge of conscience, but he was grateful for the distraction provided by DeDe's sudden arrival, pink uniform, blue eyeshadow and all.

"What can I get for you two?" she asked, pencil poised over her order pad, eyes avid with curiosity.

Anne ordered a salad and then listened wistfully as Neill ordered a hamburger, fries and a shake. It was one of the great injustices of the world that men could so often stuff their face full of zillions of calories and never gain an ounce, while most women had only to walk past a Danish to gain weight.

He didn't want to talk about his writing, she thought, lifting her water glass to sip. It wasn't hard to understand. She'd never known any writers, but she knew most of them were lucky if they made a bare living wage. It was pretty clear that he was just scraping by. The faded jeans could have been just a matter of style, but he'd mentioned that his bike was old, old enough that he was going to have to wait for parts to be found. Her mother would have said he was a failure, but Anne admired anyone who had a dream they were willing to work for.

"I've heard that publishing is a very competitive field," she said when DeDe had reluctantly departed with their order.

"It can be."

"But it's worth it, if you're doing what you love."

Her tone was encouraging, the look in her eyes sympathetic, and Neill felt a vicious little pinch from his conscience. Obviously she'd jumped to the conclusion that he was a struggling freelance writer—a conclusion he'd nudged her toward. He nearly told her the truth right then but caught himself at the last minute. What difference did it make what she believed? He was going to be gone in a couple of days anyway, and if he told her now she would probably end up feeling foolish for having tried to encourage him.

"So, where did you live before Seattle?" Anne asked, thinking a change of topic was in order, since he was so obviously self-conscious about his lack of material success in his chosen field. The vulnerability that revealed made him seem just a little less overwhelming. She settled back against the booth and smiled, suddenly almost comfortable with him.

Anne had eaten at Luanne's more times than she could count. She could remember her father bringing her here when she was a little girl, in the days before he'd withdrawn so completely into himself. They would sit at a booth, and the meal was always punctuated by people stopping to say hello to Doc Moore. On rare occasions her mother would join them, though never without mentioning some restaurant she'd known in Atlanta and how much better the food and atmosphere had been there. Fewer people stopped to say hello when Olivia was there.

When she was a little older, Jack had sometimes condescended to take his baby sister out for a hamburger or a piece of pie. He'd preferred to sit at the counter, the better to flirt with any girls who happened to be there. He never scolded her for spinning round and round on her stool, and he always let her order whatever she wanted, without telling her that her eyes were bigger than her stomach.

The few dates she'd had in high school had, often as not, ended up at Luanne's. Lacking a mall or a McDonald's restaurant, it was the hangout of choice for local teenagers. The first time Frank Miller asked her out, a little less than a year ago, he'd brought her to Luanne's. Since then, with the precision of a metronome, their weekly dates had alternated between Luanne's and Barney's Bar and Grill.

In all the times she'd been here, Anne couldn't ever remember really talking to whoever she was with. Her father had always been a man of few words, her brother had been more interested in flirting with the girls, and Frank... Well, Frank just wasn't much of a conversationalist.

In one forty-five minute lunch, she talked more to Neill Devlin than she had in the last six months' worth of dinners with Frank. He made her laugh with his stories about the horrors of a cross-country road trip, like the motel in Wyoming where he'd awakened in the middle of the night when one of his neighbors put a fist through the wall next to Neill's bed. And the one in Nebraska where the pipes had been so rusty that the shower water had made him feel like he was an extra in a horror movie.

Laughing, Anne shook her head. "You won't have to worry about that while you're here."

"The fights or the rust?" Neill asked as he poured ketchup over his French fries.

"Either one." Anne pushed a fork into her salad and tried not to think about how good his fries and burger looked. "Dorothy runs a tight ship. No rust or fist fights allowed."

"When I checked in, I felt like I was on *Jeopardy*. What's with the movie trivia?"

"Oh." Laughter sparkled in her eyes. "The shoes should give you a clue."

"Shoes?" Neill cocked one brow. "Red sneakers with or without glitter?"

"All her shoes are red. And of course there's her name. Dorothy Gale." He gave her a blank look and she shook her head disapprovingly. "Obviously you don't know your *Wizard of Oz.*"

"*Wizard of…*" Neill started to grin. "You're kidding, right?"

"Absolutely not. The movie opened on Dorothy's eighth birthday. They had the same name, and Dorothy even had an Aunt Em. The similarities had a powerful influence. As far as I know, she's worn red shoes ever since."

"Tell me she has a dog named Toto," Neill begged.

"A cat, actually." Anne grinned when he laughed. "She doesn't like dogs, but, over the years, she's had a whole series of cats, all of them named Toto."

"I love it." He saw her eyeing his plate and, picking up a French fry, offered it across the table. "Have a bite."

She leaned forward without thinking, only becoming aware of the casual intimacy of the moment when the crisp fry brushed her lips. *Idiot,* she thought. *He expected you to take it from him, not to feed it to you. Now he's going to think you're a total moron.* But it was too late to pull back gracefully, so she opened her mouth and took the fry with as much grace as she could manage.

Despite her determination not to, she looked at him as she drew back, and the heat in his eyes made it clear that his thoughts were not on her I.Q. or lack thereof. No one had ever looked at her like that, as if they were contemplating the possibility of nibbling on any part of her that might be within reach. Her pulse skittering, she lowered her eyes, staring blindly down at her salad while she tried to think of something casual to say.

"When you think of it, it's a really good thing that Dorothy didn't share a name with Bela Lugosi," Neill said, breaking the silence before it could become uncomfortable. "Red shoes are a minor eccentricity, but it would be pretty hard to carry off a cape in this kind of weather."

Anne laughed a little more than the comment warranted and hoped he wouldn't notice that her cheeks were flushed.

That was how David Freeman saw her as he walked up to the table—laughing, her face delicately flushed. He hesitated, his expression suddenly still. He'd known Anne her whole life, and he'd never seen her look like that. Looking at the man with her, he had no trouble guessing the reason for the extra color in her cheeks and the sparkle in her eyes. She looked…happy, he thought, and it was only seeing her that way that made him aware of the shadows that were usually in her eyes.

His expression thoughtful, he walked up to the table. "Hey, Anne."

"David!" Her smile changed, became self-conscious. "I didn't see you there."

"Just came in to pick up lunch." He nodded to Neill. "I was going to head over to the motel later, tell you what I found out about your bike."

Neill grimaced. "That sounds ominous."

"Good grief, I didn't realize how late it was." Anne glanced at her watch and immediately began sliding out of the booth. "I was due back at work twenty minutes ago." She hesitated long enough to give Neill a quick, shy smile. "It was nice talking to you. Good luck with your bike."

Before he could say something casual—like "How about dinner tonight?" or "Would you like to bear my children?"—she was hurrying toward the door. The strength of his urge to follow her kept Neill where he was. He was leaving, he reminded himself. Leaving. Going to Florida to soak up the sun. No plans. No commitments. Most especially no commitments.

"So, what's the story on the parts?" he asked

David as he slid out of the booth and reached for his wallet.

The other man had turned to watch Anne leave. When he turned back, there was an expression in his eyes that Neill couldn't read—an odd kind of watchfulness and something that might have been a question.

"It...may take a while," he said slowly. "Parts for Indian motorcycles aren't all that common. I have a couple of sources. One of them thinks he'll be able to lay his hands on what you need, but it could be a few days before he knows for sure."

"A few days?" Neill looked over his shoulder and out the big windows at the street. *Mayberry,* he thought, watching an ancient blue pickup rattle past. *I've landed in Mayberry.*

"Is that a problem?" David asked. "Do you need to get somewhere in a hurry?"

Anne had asked him the same thing, Neill remembered.

"No." He shook his head slowly. "No, I was more or less killing time." He didn't have to stay, he reminded himself. All it would take was a phone call and he could have a car sent to get him. His brother was in Chicago, just a few hours away. If he had any trouble arranging a car, Tony could probably be persuaded to come to his rescue. A few hours—tomorrow at the latest—and he could be on his way. He didn't have to stay.

"It's no problem," he heard himself say. "I guess I can kill time here as well as anywhere."

# *Chapter Four*

"**Y**ou had lunch with the hunk?" Lisa dropped the length of purple velvet ribbon she'd just picked up and stared at Anne in shock. "You actually had lunch with him?"

"At Luanne's," Anne confirmed, trying to look casual.

The two of them were sitting in Lisa's studio, which was a small storefront wedged between Betty's Best Bet for Hair and the newspaper office. She could have worked out of the little house she'd rented when she moved back to Loving, but she'd decided that if she was going to turn her knack for decorative hats and accessories into a business, she should have a place in which to do business. She used the narrow sliver of a shop as a studio, working regular business hours, and though she didn't run it as a retail business, the door was usually open, and several times a day she could count on someone wandering in to see what new flight of fancy she was concocting.

She liked the company, she'd said when Anne asked her how she could work with someone watching her, talking to her, marveling over the fact that there were people who would pay good money for a hat they weren't even going to wear. Now and again someone brought in some item they'd found in the attic or stored away in a cupboard—plastic fruit, flocked artificial flowers, pine cones glued together to form some barely recognizable animal. Lisa cheerfully accepted all donations, finding a place for them on the filled to overflowing shelving that lined three sides of the studio. Ribbons, laces, old prescription bottles filled with beads, baskets of feathers, stacks of vintage fabric and ancient canning jars full of buttons jostled each other in cheerful chaos, but, despite the lack of anything resembling organization, Lisa could usually lay her hands on any particular item.

The colorful clutter was so typically Lisa, Anne thought. Tonight the other woman was wearing jeans so old that the holes in the knees had nothing to do with fashion and a billowy silk shirt that swirled with mad splashes of color. Her feet were bare, revealing scarlet toenails. Her bright red hair was caught up on top of her head in a careless bun that was held in place with a yellow pencil. Big gold hoops hung from her ears, and a pair of blue rhinestone trimmed reading glasses were perched on the end of her nose. She looked like a cross between a gypsy and a school teacher. In the trim jeans and plain white shirt she'd changed into after work, Anne felt like a sepia-toned photo next to a film done in living Technicolor processing.

"You want to run that by me again?" Lisa asked, peering at her over the top of her glasses.

"I had lunch with the hunk from the gas station." A grin spoiled her attempt to look blasé. "I was squeezing cantaloupes at Bill's, and he came up behind me and said I should try sniffing the stem end to find a ripe one."

"A hunk who knows produce. Wow." Lisa looked suitably impressed. "So you sniffed a couple of melons together and then just went off to lunch with him?"

"Actually, I gave up on the melon," Anne said. Not even to Lisa would she admit that, standing there, with Neill Devlin's impossibly blue eyes on her, she would have been hard pressed to remember what a melon was.

"I can't believe you didn't call to let me know." Lisa gave her a reproachful look. "I could have wandered into Luanne's accidentally on purpose and gotten a good look at the guy."

"It was lunch, not a spectator sport," Anne said, caught off guard by a twinge of irritation.

"But he's so spectate-able," Lisa purred, and the irritation vanished in a laugh.

"DeDe Carmichael certainly thought so." Anne selected a jelly bean from the glass bowl that sat on the table counter between them and popped it into her mouth.

"Did she do the eye thing?" Lisa tilted her head back and did a creditable imitation of DeDe's sultry look.

"And the hip thing." Anne slid off her stool and fell into a semislouch, one hip cocked forward.

"Yeah, that's the one." Lisa nodded and reached for the ribbon she'd dropped. "I don't know where she got the idea that she looks sexy when she does that. I think she looks like an arthritic camel."

Anne shook her head "No camel would wear that much makeup."

"A camel wouldn't *need* that much makeup."

They looked at each other and started to giggle.

"Nothing like a little old-fashioned cattiness to work up an appetite," Lisa said, scooping up half a dozen jelly beans. "So, what's the hunk doing still in town? And does he have a name?"

"His name's Neill, and apparently his motorcycle is pretty old. I don't know what's wrong with it, but David's going to have to track down parts." Anne leaned forward to select a grape-flavored jelly bean. She bit it carefully in half before continuing. "He's staying at The Blue Dahlia."

"It's pretty much that or sleep in a ditch." Lisa began pleating the purple velvet ribbon, basting each pleat flat with silk thread before moving on to the next. "So what's he like on closer acquaintance?"

What was he like? Anne hesitated over the answer. She could hardly say that he was the most attractive man she'd ever met, or that, when he looked at her, she felt a funny shivery sensation run up her spine. Lisa was bound to jump to the wrong conclusions if she said either of those things. She would probably jump to them anyway, but there was no sense in helping her get there.

"He's...nice," she said finally, then laughed at the disgusted look the other woman shot her. "Okay, he has a great smile and impossibly blue eyes, and he's really sexy, if you like the tall, lean, broad-shouldered type.''

''Is there a living, breathing female who doesn't like that type?''

''Probably not. But he's also nice, and he has a good sense of humor. We laughed a lot. He's a good storyteller. Oh, and he's a writer,'' she added, remembering. Frowning a little, she nibbled the other half of her jelly bean. ''I don't think he's terribly successful at it, because he seemed uncomfortable when it came up, like he didn't want to talk about it. And usually, when a man has a successful career, he can't wait to tell you about it.''

''Or tell you a few lies about it,'' Lisa agreed. ''So, how long is he going to be in town?''

''I have no idea.'' Anne wasn't in the least fooled by the casual tone of the question. ''And, before you ask, I don't know if I'll be seeing him again, either. He didn't say anything about it.''

Of course, she hadn't given him a chance to, the way she'd rushed away from the table. But he probably wouldn't have mentioned seeing her again even if she hadn't left so abruptly, Anne told herself. She wasn't exactly the kind of woman that Neill Devlin was going to be desperate to see again. Not that she wasn't reasonably attractive in a wholesome sort of way, but a man like that was going to be looking for something more than a short, slightly too curvy dishwater blonde with a friendly smile and better than average legs. With an unconscious sigh, she selected another purple jelly bean and bit it in half.

Lisa had been watching the expressions flit across Anne's face and following her thought process with reasonable accuracy. Like Neill, she'd never known anyone whose emotions were so easily read. Or who underrated themselves so completely.

"So why don't you go by the motel and see him?" she suggested casually, keeping her eyes on the ribbon.

"I can't do that," Anne said, startled. "I don't want him to think I'm…"

"Interested?" Lisa lifted an eyebrow. "You think he'll be offended?"

"Yes. No. How should I know what he'd be?" she demanded crossly. "I don't even know the man."

"And you probably won't get to know him if you don't let him know you're interested."

"What's the point, when he'll be leaving as soon as David gets the parts he needs to fix his bike?"

"So? Ouch, damn!" Lisa lifted her thumb to her mouth to suck at the spot where the needle had jabbed. She glared at Anne across the wounded digit, her green eyes sharp with impatience. "I'm not suggesting that you sleep with him," she said, talking around her thumb. "I'm just suggesting that you could drop in at the motel, maybe offer to show him the sights."

"There are no sights," Anne pointed out dryly.

"Make up a few." Satisfied that the bleeding had stopped, Lisa lowered her hand from her mouth. "The point is, it wouldn't hurt you to spend a couple of days in the company of an attractive man who was not born and raised within a twenty-mile radius of this town. The fact that he'll be gone soon is probably a good thing, since he won't have a chance to get boring."

Remembering the way her lunch hour had flown by, Anne found it difficult to imagine that Neill would become boring on closer acquaintance. She had an uneasy feeling that the real problem might be just the opposite.

"If you don't watch out, you're going to end up marrying Frank Miller by default," Lisa continued, frowning at her over the top of her glasses. "That's where he's headed, you know. In his methodical, dull-as-ditch-water way, Frank is courting you. Another three or four years of dating and he'll probably be ready to propose. And if you don't do something about it, you'll end up accepting just because he's there and you can't think of a good reason not to say yes.''

"There's nothing wrong with Frank." Anne's protest was halfhearted. The truth was, she'd had the same thought herself.

Lisa nodded. "Frank is a decent man, and Jack says he's a decent cop. He's also more predictable than an atomic clock, and just about as entertaining to talk to. He's the sort of worthy guy who should marry a worthy woman someday and raise lots of worthy little children who are every bit as deadly dull as he is. I'd hate to see you fall into that trap."

"Not worthy enough?" Anne asked, her smile concealing the fear she felt listening to Lisa's tart-tongued picture. It was a little too easy to picture herself standing in a neatly-decorated little house with three or four neatly-dressed little Franks lined up before her, all looking at her with the same calm expression. It was not a reassuring image. She shook her head as if to physically shake it away and decided that a change of subject was in order.

"Speaking of worthy marriages, are you and Jack going to risk an actual engagement or do the smart thing and run off to Vegas?" Lisa had told her that the two of them had been discussing marriage, and Anne had been expecting an announcement or an elopement any time. It had seemed like a reasonable question, but she regretted it when she saw hurt flit across Lisa's eyes in the instant before her expression closed up.

"Maybe neither one. I'm not sure there is an engagement." Lisa jerked a shoulder to show how little it mattered. She reached for the length of velvet ribbon, but her hands weren't quite steady, and she let them drop into her lap.

Anne looked at her uncertainly. She'd never seen Lisa look so...defeated.

"I...it's none of my business but, if you want to talk about it... Jack is my brother, but you're my best friend. If it would help to talk... If you quarreled..."

"Quarreled?" Lisa arched her brows. "You don't know your brother very well if you think it's possible to quarrel with him. He just slides away, neither agreeing or disagreeing, leaving you to either drop the subject or argue with yourself."

Anne shifted uncomfortably and tried to think of something to say. She could have pointed out that, if Jack did what Lisa was describing, maybe it was because it was the easiest way to deal with their mother, but she wasn't comfortable saying as much.

"I told him I thought he had a drinking problem," Lisa said abruptly.

"A..." Anne stared at her in shock. Whatever she'd thought the quarrel could have been about, it hadn't been this. "Jack doesn't have... I can't imagine why you'd think he did," she finally managed.

"My ex-husband was an alcoholic." Now that she'd gotten the words out, Lisa seemed preternaturally calm. "I know the signs, and your brother has most of them."

"I haven't noticed anything unusual." Too upset to stay still, Anne slid off her stool and walked a little way away, staring at the tumble of ribbons on a shelf. "Maybe the fact that your ex had a problem is making you paranoid."

"How much wine did you drink last night at dinner?" Lisa asked.

"None. I don't care for it."

"I didn't have any, and neither did your father. Your mother had one glass. Jack finished the bottle. He had a couple shots of Johnnie Walker before dinner. For that matter, I suspect he had a couple before he left home—to fortify himself for the ordeal."

Anne stared blankly at an impossibly bright embroidered fish that was nestled in amongst several lengths of ribbon and a handful of empty walnut shells. She didn't want to believe what Lisa was saying, not just for her brother's sake but because of what it said about her relationship with him. *You don't know your brother very well,* Lisa had said. Maybe she was right.

"Maybe he drank a little bit too much last night, but you know what my mother is like. She hates it that he's a cop and that he's—"

"Seeing me," Lisa finished when she stumbled. She smiled ruefully when Anne turned to give her an apologetic look. "It's not like she makes a secret of it. Lucky for me, I have very few sensibilities, so most if it rolls right off my back."

"She doesn't mean—"

"Yes she does." Lisa waved her hand. "Your mother's opinion has never been a big concern of mine."

*Which is probably one of the reasons she hates you,* Anne thought. Lisa's indifference was much harder to deal with than her antipathy would have been.

"Maybe Jack was drinking to drown out your mother, but that doesn't make it okay. And that's not the only time he drinks, either."

"He'd never drink on duty," Anne protested, shocked that Lisa could think he would.

"Maybe not yet," Lisa conceded. "But that's the direction he's headed. I've talked to him about it before, but on the way home last night I got a little more firm about it. That's one mistake I'm not repeating."

"No, of course not." Anne walked back to the counter, her expression thoughtful. She wasn't convinced Lisa was right. If she was... Well, maybe there were reasons. Not excuses, exactly, but explanations.

"*If* Jack does have a drinking problem," she said, laying careful emphasis on the "if," "maybe there's a reason. You know, after Brooke——"

"Don't say it." Startled by the sharp interruption, Anne looked up and met the kindled fire in Lisa's green eyes. "Does it ever occur to anyone that, if Brooke was still alive, she couldn't possibly dominate your lives the way she has since she's been dead?"

The silence was so profound that the sound of a car door shutting somewhere on the street outside seemed loud as gunfire. Looking at Anne, seeing the shock on her face, Lisa closed her eyes a moment and reminded herself that it wasn't Anne's fault. Of all of them, Anne was the only one who bore no blame.

"I'm sorry." She huffed out a sigh and reached

over to put her hand on Anne's where it lay on the counter. "Jack and I will be fine. It's not like we're breaking up. I'm just frustrated and worried but I didn't mean to snarl at you. I didn't mean to bring any of this up at all. Chalk it up to PMS and over-work weakening my already scattered brain cells."

"Lisa..."

"No." Lisa shook her head, her smile wavery around the edges. "Let's not and say we did. I really am tired, and I'm probably not entirely ra-tional." She ran her fingers through her hair, dis-lodging the pencil, which clattered to the floor and rolled under the edge of the work counter. "This is the last time I take a commission from someone who wants the work last week."

Looking at her friend, it struck Anne that she really did look tired, her usual sparkle dulled. Her mind still reeling with all that had been said, she struggled to conjure up a smile. "That's what you get for letting greed overrule artistic integrity."

"I guess." Lisa looked down at the piles of rib-bon and buttons scattered across the work surface and sighed. "Maybe this will all make sense in the morning, but at the moment it looks like Jackson Pollack threw up here. Time to go home."

Anne waited while Lisa found her shoes and the keys and turned out lights. She was vaguely surprised to see that it was only twilight. It felt as if it should be much later. The air was still warm, but it carried the sweet promise of the rain that was supposed to come overnight. The street was almost empty, most of the businesses long since closed, but there was a smattering of cars angled into the curb in front of the bar down the street, a few more parked in front of Luanne's on the opposite side.

Looking at the café reminded Anne of her lunch with Neill Devlin. It seemed a long time ago.

"All set," Lisa said as she locked the door. She turned and, though the light was poor, Anne could feel her searching look. "I didn't mean to upset you."

"That's okay." Anne glanced past her at the light spilling through the window of the café. "Maybe I haven't been paying enough attention lately—to a lot of things." Because she could sense that Lisa was still worried, she gave her more. "You know, it just occurred to me that I didn't pay my share of the lunch bill today. I was in such a hurry to get back to work that I forgot all about it and left Neill stuck with the check."

Lisa's smile was slow. "Good heavens, you'll have him thinking that Hoosiers don't pay their own way. Something like that could do irreparable damage to the reputation of the entire state."

"Maybe I should go over to The Blue Dahlia and settle up with him." Anne felt a little curl of excitement in the pit of her stomach.

Neill pushed his chair back from the table and looked at the words displayed on the laptop computer's screen with baffled surprise. Where the hell had *this* come from? He hadn't been thinking about starting another book, not this soon and maybe not ever. And, if he had given another book any thought, it certainly hadn't been this. What the hell was he doing writing a western? He didn't even write fiction, for chrissake.

But the words were there, neat black text on a white screen, unmistakably the opening scene of a novel—a man, alone and wounded, left for dead by the man who'd been his partner. Now he stood surrounded by sky and prairie, with nothing but wits and luck to keep him alive. And there was a woman, not pretty, but with strong features marked by the struggle to survive in a land of stark beauty and little mercy. Their paths were going to intersect, though Neill wasn't sure just how or when.

"I'll be damned," he muttered, pushing the chair back and standing up. The light had faded while he worked, and he switched on a couple of lamps to banish the gloom before getting a beer out of the tiny refrigerator in the kitchenette. He twisted off the top and took a healthy swallow, his eyes settling on the glowing screen across the room.

When he was packing for the trip, he'd thrown the computer in more out of habit than anything else. The laptop was the high-tech equivalent of the yellow notepad he'd relied on when he first started writing, but, other than the half-formed thought of turning the trip into some sort of travelogue, he hadn't planned on doing any writing. In fact, after finishing this last book, he hadn't been at all sure he had another book in him. He sure as hell hadn't given any thought to writing a novel.

Neill took another swig of beer and grinned. It was good, he thought, looking at the first couple of paragraphs. Maybe he wasn't quite ready to send Larry McMurtry running for cover, but he'd made a good start on...whatever it turned out to be. It had been a long time since he'd written something for the pure pleasure of it. Too long.

He was debating whether to write some more or fix himself a sandwich from the groceries he'd bought earlier when someone knocked on the door. Dorothy, he thought, come to remind him of some not-to-be-missed old movie showing on cable at two in the morning. He'd been known to get hostile with people who interrupted him when he was working, but he was feeling so good about his unexpected venture into nineteenth-century Wyoming that he was smiling as he set down the beer bottle and went to answer the door.

The smile shifted, warmed, became subtly more intimate, when he saw Anne standing on the little concrete step outside his door. He'd thought about her, debated the best way to go about seeing her again. He'd pretty much settled on catching her at work, coaxing her into having lunch with him again. And now, here she was.

"Hi."

"H-hi." Anne had to clear her throat to get the word out. "I...Dorothy told me what room you were in." She had to resist the urge to fidget with the collar of her shirt. On the short drive over here, she'd nearly managed to convince herself that she knew what she was doing. That conviction faltered badly when she found herself standing outside his room, and it was only stubborn pride that had made her knock on the door. And now he was standing there, looking large and very male, and she had to admit that, when it came to this man, she didn't have the slightest idea of what she was doing.

"Come in." Neill stepped back, gesturing an invitation.

Anne hesitated, nerves fluttering in the pit of her stomach. But she could hardly stand on the doorstep and thrust a handful of money at him, even if that was the only reason she'd come—which, of course, it wasn't. Besides, Dorothy knew where she was, and he knew that she knew and, oh God, she was losing her mind.

With a sigh for her rapidly receding sanity, Anne walked past him into the room.

"I hope this isn't a bad time," she said, acutely aware of the click as the door closed behind her.

"Well, I did have an appointment with destiny, but I think I can reschedule."

"Do you think that's wise?" she asked as he walked past her into the room. "Isn't there some rule about destiny only knocking once?"

"That's opportunity. I don't think destiny knocks. I think it just hits you right between the eyes."

"Sounds painful." Standing just inside the door, Anne tried to figure out what to do with her hands. Shoving them in her pockets seemed contrived, and crossing her arms over her chest would be even worse. They hadn't always seemed so...in the way, had they? She settled for linking her fingers together in front of her.

"Can I get you something to drink? I've got beer and water—not exactly an abundance of choices."

"I'm fine, thanks." Her eyes skittered around the room, looking everywhere but at him. They lit on the glowing screen of the laptop and widened in dismay. "Were you working?"

"Not really." Neill shrugged. He wasn't ready to label what he was doing as work. "Just something I was dabbling with." Reaching down, he saved the file and then closed the lid. The soft whir of the computer's fan, barely noticeable a moment ago, seemed to leave a large silence behind when it stopped.

"If you're sure. I wouldn't want to interrupt."

In her tidy white shirt tucked into trim jeans, with her honey-gold hair still caught up in that neat little bun and her fingers linked together in front of her, she looked as prim and proper as a kindergarten teacher. Or maybe a student expecting a scolding from the principal, Neill thought with a tangled mix of amusement and lust.

"I don't bite," he said softly. "Not unless you ask me to."

Startled, Anne's eyes shot to his face. He looked as if he would like to nibble on her, she thought, and, despite the butterflies doing a jig in her stomach, she wasn't sure she would object if he did just that. Flushing, she looked away and rushed into speech.

"I forgot to pay you today." Out the corner of her eye, she saw his brows go up, and she felt her color deepen. "For lunch, I mean. My share of the bill." He started toward her, and her thoughts scattered like baby chicks spilled from a farm wife's apron. "I...I didn't want you to think that I was...that I expected you to... That I...oh."

Anne hadn't realized she was moving until the door came up against her back. Neill stopped in front of her. The light was behind him, casting him in silhouette, and she felt her breath catch a little as she stared up at him. She'd never been so conscious of her own lack of inches, never felt so vulnerable because of it. It flashed through her mind that she'd been crazy to come here. So what if Dorothy knew where she was? She was too far away to hear a scream.

"Maybe we should get this over with," Neill murmured.

"Get what over with?" Anne asked, staring up at him with huge eyes.

"This," he whispered, and, bracing one hand on the door beside her head, he lowered his mouth to hers.

His mouth was warm and firm, holding the faint

yeasty tang of the beer he'd been drinking. She'd been kissed before. She was nearly sure of it. Frank kissed her after every date. Standing on the front porch of her little cottage, he would put his arms around her, holding her as gently as if she were made of bone china, and then he would kiss her—gently, carefully, never asking more than she wanted to give. Never asking anything at all, in fact.

Neill didn't ask, either. He simply took. And as the ground fell out from under her feet, Anne could only give.

He'd wondered how she would taste, had allowed himself to imagine, but the reality was so much more. Her mouth was soft, welcoming, eager. She tasted of lip balm and jelly beans—an innocent combination that suddenly struck Neill as wildly erotic. He hadn't planned on this—on kissing her, on wanting so much more. But she'd stood there looking at him with those big gray eyes, like Red Riding Hood in her grandmother's bedroom, and he'd suddenly felt just like the Big Bad Wolf, wanting to devour her in one gulp. He contented himself with nibbling on her lower lip, taking advantage of her shallow gasp of surprise, his tongue sliding inside, finding hers.

A soft, startled whimper caught in the back of

her throat as her head tilted in an unconscious plea for him to deepen the kiss. She'd never imagined it could be like this. That there could be colors and lights and this smokey sense that she was floating somewhere outside herself. Her hands came up between them, her fingers curling into the thin cotton of his T-shirt, holding on to him as the only solid thing in her universe.

Her surrender flashed through Neill, making his blood sizzle with the need to have more—more of her sweet taste, more of her soft sighs. She swayed toward him, and his hand flattened on the small of her back, drawing her away from the door as his other hand burrowed into her hair, scattering pins until it tumbled over his fingers in a honey-colored wave of silk and curls.

*More,* he thought, dragging her closer, feeling the soft swell of her breasts against the width of his chest. He could have it all. She was as pliant as a willow wand, trembling in his arms. His, all his.

The very strength of his need to possess her set warning bells jangling. It was too much, too soon. He'd never wanted like this, hungered like this. Not for a woman he'd met barely twenty-four hours ago. Not for any woman. Ever. A man didn't get to thirty-five without some experience of desire, but he'd never been fond of one-night stands and faceless sex. He liked to know a woman before they became lovers. Yet here he was, teetering on the brink of taking this woman where they stood, her back against the door, her legs around his waist. The image had him rock hard even as he forced himself to ease back, ignoring the blood thundering in his ears, the primitive voice urging him to take what could be his.

Anne felt her heels settled back on the ground, then the solid panel of the door against her back. He kept his hands on her shoulders, steadying her, as if she might tip over without that touch. And she just might, she decided, feeling her mind spin in lazy circles. So that's what it was all about, she thought. Her tongue came out, brushing across her lower lip as if the taste of him still lingered there. Neill groaned, his hands tightening almost painfully for an instant before releasing her completely. She felt him step back and forced her eyes open, staring at him.

"I didn't mean for that to happen," he said. The words were edgy with surprise and sexual frustration.

"You didn't mean to kiss me?" She should be upset or embarrassed or outraged or...something. She didn't know what, but she was sure that she should feel something besides this pleasant floating sensation.

"I meant to kiss you. I just didn't mean to take it so far so fast." *And not half as far as I'd like to take it,* he thought, looking at that soft mouth and those big gray eyes. "You're too trusting," he muttered.

Anne hit the ground with a thud. Too trusting? He had no way of knowing just how wrong he was. How could he, when she'd walked into his motel room as casually as if she did this sort of thing every day? She thought of her mother's constant harping on the potential evils that lurked, ready to devour unsuspecting females without warning. She thought of all the dates she hadn't gone on, all the kisses she'd never had, all the nights she'd spent alone because she wasn't trusting enough, and she didn't know whether to laugh or scream.

Neill watched the emotions flicker over her face—surprise, annoyance and something that could have been bitter humor. He didn't know what he'd said, but he regretted that it had erased that look of dazed awareness from her eyes. On the other hand, maybe it was just as well, he thought. If she'd continued to look at him like that, he might not have been able to resist the urge to take things quite a few steps beyond where they'd stopped.

"Anne, I—damn." The jangle of the phone cut him off. "That's probably my brother," he said. "I left a message for him earlier today, and he always did have lousy timing. Hang on and I'll get rid of him."

"That's okay." Anne groped behind her for the doorknob and gave him a quick, impersonal smile. "I should be going anyway."

"I want to—" The phone rang again and Neill glared at the plain beige instrument.

"No, really. I have to go." Without giving him a chance to say anything else, Anne slipped out the door, pulling it quietly shut behind her.

It was only as she slid behind Lucy's wheel that she realized she'd forgotten all about paying him for her half of lunch.

# Chapter Five

Anne's fingers moved steadily over the keyboard, her eyes on the notepad propped up beside the computer monitor as she transcribed her employer's handwritten notes. She'd worked as a secretary to the bank's vice-president, Richard Lawrence, for almost four years, and today was the first time she'd had cause to regret that he was both neat and a creature of habit. Today she would have welcomed the distraction provided by having to decipher an illegible scrawl or being kept on her toes by unreasonable demands. But her day was following its usual placid pattern, and the closest she'd come to a challenge was rescheduling an appointment.

It allowed her too much time to think, and what she kept thinking about was the scene in Neill's motel room the night before. She'd already spent a good part of the night thinking about it, finally falling asleep long after midnight. When the alarm went off, she woke heavy eyed, unrested and irritated with herself. It was just a kiss, she reminded herself as she showered. Never mind that she'd never been kissed like that, had never really believed that kisses like that existed outside the pages of a novel; it was still just a kiss. And she was old enough, if not experienced enough, not to turn a brief encounter into a major experience. She'd thought about it enough, she decided as she poured herself a bowl of cereal. Now she was just going to put it right out of her head.

Easier said than done, she admitted three hours later, as she hit the backspace key to correct her thousandth typing error of the morning. It wasn't just the kiss. It was the knowledge that she'd gone to his motel room, tracking him down like a teenager stalking a rock star, and then used a pathetic excuse like forgetting to pay her half of the lunch tab. The memory of it was enough to make her want to bang her head on the keyboard. As if that wasn't humiliating enough, she hadn't even given him the damned money. He probably thought she'd just been angling to be kissed. And, God help her, maybe she had been. Worse, she was aware of an undeniable regret that it wasn't likely to happen again.

Anne stared unseeingly at the monitor, her fingers lax on the keyboard. It didn't seem fair, she thought wistfully. Last night, when Neill kissed her, she'd understood for the first time what all the fuss was about. She'd found Frank's kisses mildly pleasant—or at least not objectionable—but they'd been forgotten as soon as they were over, just as Frank was pretty much forgotten as soon as he was out of sight. Months ago, she'd come to the conclusion that her tepid reaction was probably an indication that there was something wrong with her. Who was she kidding? She *knew* there was something wrong with her. How else to explain the fact that she was twenty-five years old and had never had so much as a close encounter with lust?

Until last night.

Last night she'd finally gotten a glimpse of what all the shouting was about. And it had to happen with a man who was going to be gone in a matter of days. Was already gone, for all she knew. David could have gotten the motorcycle fixed, or Neill could have caught a ride with someone, or even hitchhiked. From some of the things he'd said at lunch, it was clear he'd traveled a lot. It didn't seem likely that a man who'd been to Paris and Budapest and who knew where else would find much to interest him in Loving, Indiana.

Anne both underestimated her own appeal and overestimated life on the road. Neill had already decided that he'd had enough of the latter, but the former...the former definitely had some potential. Being a man, he didn't spend as much time analyzing those moments in his motel room as Anne did, but, unlike Anne, he didn't even bother telling himself that it had been "just a kiss." He was thirty-five years old, more than passably good-looking, and, also unlike Anne, he'd had more than a few close encounters with lust. But not since his hormone-driven teenage days had a single kiss left him with barely a fingernail hold on his self-control.

The unexpected strength of his reaction caught him off guard, left him aching and aroused his curiosity, which his mother had often told him was his besetting sin and sure to get him in trouble one day. He'd lain awake nearly as long as Anne had, hands behind his head, his eyes on the opposite wall, where he could just make out the faint gleam of Bela Lugosi's teeth, and considered the possibility that his mother might be right. Certainly a cautious man might have made arrangements to beat a hasty retreat. But cautious men led such boring lives, and he was enough of a fatalist to feel compelled to stick around and see what happened.

Despite the fact that it was late when he finally went to sleep, Neill woke early. After one look at the clock, he closed his eyes again and pulled the pillow over his head. He'd never been a morning person, and he had no desire to start now. But after fifteen minutes it was obvious that, like it or not, he was awake. Cursing halfheartedly, he crawled out of bed. Maybe it was because he was in the middle of farm country, he thought as he stumbled over to the kitchenette to start water boiling for coffee. Probably some undiscovered neurotoxin drifting in from the cornfields, enforcing farmers' hours on an unsuspecting citizenry.

By the time he'd splashed water on his face, finger-combed his hair and taken his first sip of scalding instant coffee, he was resigned to being awake, if not particularly happy about it. He thought about turning on the TV to watch one of the morning news shows but didn't reach for the remote. He wasn't in the mood to hear a rundown of the latest wars, murders and political misdoings. Instead, he flipped open the laptop and began skimming the pages he'd written the night before, half expecting to find them absolute trash.

The next time he looked up, there was an unappetizing oily film floating on top of the nearly untouched coffee in the cup next to him. His shoulders and neck ached from hunching over the keyboard, and he had to blink several times before he could focus his eyes on the clock next to the bed. It was almost eleven, which would account for the hollow where his stomach used to be.

Groaning, he shoved his chair back from the table and stood up. God, he couldn't ever remember working like this—with the words pouring out of him nearly as fast as he could type. The story was still barely begun, but it was starting to take shape both in his mind and on the page. He still didn't know where it was going or what he would do with it when it got there, but the story was there, and he didn't think it was going to go away until he'd given it a voice.

The words tugged at him, tempting him to continue, but his head was buzzing a little from the long hours of concentration, and his stomach was sending up polite enquiries about the condition of his throat. Besides, he'd had plans for lunch, he remembered.

By lunchtime, Anne had managed to accomplish roughly half as much as she usually did. As a bonus, she'd also snagged her hose on the corner of her desk, broken a fingernail and absentmindedly entered the same report into the computer twice, under two different names.

"Having one of those mornings?" Marge Lancaster stopped next to her desk and gave her a sympathetic look.

"Is it still morning? Are you sure it isn't time to go home?" Anne asked ruefully.

"Sorry." Marge leaned one plump hip against Anne's desk, easing the weight on her feet. Her corns were killing her, and new shoes weren't helping any, though they were pretty as all get out, she thought, tilting her head slightly to admire the navy pumps with their pretty blue-and-white bows.

"New shoes?" Anne asked, following the older woman's gaze.

"Got them mail order last week." Marge said, smiling down at them.

"They're very pretty."

"Aren't they?" Marge sighed and flexed her toes, barely restraining a wince. "Of course, they're uncomfortable as the dickens, but I never could resist a pretty pair of shoes. At my age, you'd think common sense would overrule vanity, but it doesn't work that way. Harold and I have been married forty years, come December and, truth to tell, I could probably wear a couple of cow pies on my feet and he wouldn't notice but for the smell, so I can't pretend I torture myself to give him pleasure."

Anne laughed. When she came to work at the bank, Marge had been the one to show her the ropes. Officially, she was secretary to the president, but everyone, from the janitor to the president himself, knew she could just as easily have run the place herself. She was on the far side of fifty, frankly gray, plump, matronly, with a heart of gold and a mind like a steel trap.

"Oh, now if that doesn't make me wish I was thirty years younger," Marge said with a sigh, looking toward the front of the bank.

Anne turned to follow her gaze and felt her heart thud painfully against her breastbone. Neill was standing near the glass doors, talking to the guard.

She'd spent the entire morning and most of the night trying to convince herself that she'd exaggerated his looks, exaggerated her attraction to him and, most of all, exaggerated that kiss. Given another week or two, she might even have believed herself, and then he walked in and just looking at him scattered all her calm, logical thoughts to hell and gone.

"Now there's a man I wouldn't mind offering a loan," Marge said, watching Neill's progress across the bank. After that first glance, Anne didn't look. She couldn't.

"I think he's coming this way." Marge sounded surprised and curious. She straightened away from Anne's desk, sliding her feet back into her shoes as Neill stopped at the low wooden railing that separated the bank offices from the main lobby. "Can I help you?"

"I was hoping to talk to Anne Moore." There was a questioning note in his voice, and Anne realized that, between the computer monitor and Marge's somewhat substantial figure, he couldn't see her. For a split second, sheer nerves had her thinking about ducking under her desk, but, considering the way her day had been going, she probably wouldn't fit.

"Of course. She's right here." Marge turned, her eyes bright with questions Anne pretended not to see. Since Marge was perfectly capable of asking them out loud, it seemed like divine providence when Marge's phone began to ring and she went—reluctantly—to answer it, leaving Anne more or less alone with Neill, unless you wanted to count the three tellers and half a dozen customers standing in plain sight behind him, which Anne didn't, because she'd forgotten their existence.

Neill stood on the other side of the railing, smiling at her, and if a tuba-playing brontosaurus had marched through the bank, she wouldn't have noticed. He was wearing jeans again—probably all he had with him, she thought. But when a man looked as wickedly good in faded denim as Neill Devlin did, he didn't need anything else. Another T-shirt—this one sky blue—clung to the muscled width of his chest. Looking at him, Anne couldn't help but remember the feel of those muscles under her hands, and the memory made her knees feel a little weak.

She would have been horrified to know how clearly Neill read her thoughts, gratified to know that he had to slide his hands in his pockets as protection against the urge to step over the railing and drag her out from behind her desk and kiss her senseless. Slowly, he reminded himself. He'd made up his mind to take this slowly. He didn't know what they had beyond a physical attraction like nothing he'd ever experienced, but whatever it was, he'd made up his mind that he wasn't going to rush things.

So he smiled and tried not to groan when she flicked her tongue nervously over her lower lip.

"How do you feel about picnics?"

"Picnics?" Anne repeated blankly. She'd spent more time than she cared to admit imagining what their next encounter might be like, picturing herself acting with a sophistication she felt had been sorely lacking in their previous encounters, but none of the scenarios she'd imagined had involved him asking her opinion of picnics. "I...I like them just fine."

"Are you busy for lunch?"

Anne felt her uncertainties dissolving beneath the warmth of his smile. She suddenly felt foolish for spending so much time analyzing something that another woman would have taken in stride. Last night he'd kissed her. Today he was asking her to have lunch with him. It was a perfectly normal progression of events. It was only her own inexperience that had turned it into something else.

"No plans," she said, smiling up at him. "I was just sitting here thinking how much I'd like to go on a picnic."

"And they say there's no such thing as coincidence." He flicked a glance at the big round clock that hung on the back wall of the bank. "How soon can you blow this joint?"

Anne resisted the urge to get up and walk out the door with him. No one would object if she took her lunch hour early, but there would be questions, explanations. Not that there wouldn't be anyway. Already she could feel Marge's eyes boring a hole in her back.

"Half an hour?"

"Perfect." Smiling, Neill straightened away from the railing. "I'll go see what I can do about putting together something to eat."


"Dorothy seemed to approve of the picnic idea," Neill said as he spread a blanket on the grass beneath the shade of an ancient maple. "She said Humphrey Bogart took Greta Garbo on a picnic in *Mogambo*." He frowned and shook his head as he sat down. "Or maybe it was Clarke Gable and Ginger Rogers in *Duck Soup*."

"I think you've got your movies and actors mixed up. A lot." Anne sank down on the blanket, curling her legs beneath her, grateful that she was wearing a full skirt. "Wasn't *Duck Soup* a Marx Brothers movie?"

"Then maybe Gable was taking Groucho on a picnic," Neill said, unconcerned. He glanced at her, his eyes gleaming with laughter. "Wasn't that an advertisement campaign—Gable's back and Groucho's got him?"

"I think that was *Garson's* got him."

"Garson. Groucho." Neill shrugged. "Who can tell the difference?"

"I'm pretty sure Groucho was the one with the mustache."

There was a small bronze plaque near the park's entrance that said it had been created to honor those who had died in World War II, followed by a list of names—husbands, sons and fathers who hadn't come home. The peaceful sweep of sun-warmed grass and spreading shade trees was worlds away from the sights and sounds of battle, which was probably the point, Neill thought idly.

In the middle of the week, they had the park almost to themselves. A few children played in the

sand near the swings, and, though he couldn't see
the players, Neill could hear the ragged rhythm of
a basketball hitting concrete. There was a peace-
fulness here that seeped bone deep. This was what
he'd been looking for when he left Seattle, Neill
thought. This sense of time not just standing still,
but ceasing to exist.

They'd eaten sandwiches and potato salad, talking as easily as if they'd know each other for years
rather than a handful of days. He'd learned that she
liked old movies, mystery novels and yellow roses.
She hated doing laundry, had nearly flunked math
in high school and considered the pocket calculator
one of man's greatest inventions, rivaled only by
the CD player "because, sooner or later, tapes are
bound to be eaten by a tape player." They shared
a fondness for old rock and roll but divided sharply
on the question of country music, with Neill claim-
ing that, other than opera, it was the only musical
medium that encouraged great storytelling and
Anne wrinkling her nose at the thought of twanging
guitars and nasal laments about cheating wives and
love gone sour.

"You obviously haven't listened to country music in the last twenty years," Neill told her sternly
and she conceded that it had been a while. From

music, the talk shifted to authors they both admired. By the time they'd agreed that Hemingway was vastly overrated and that neither of them liked horror novels, the sandwiches were gone and the crumpled containers had been disposed of.

Pleasantly full and vaguely somnolent, Neill was relieved that she didn't feel the need to break the comfortable silence that fell between them. Most people viewed silence as either a threat or a challenge.

But Anne sat across from him, leaning back on her hands, her legs stretched out in front of her, head tilted back and eyes closed. The innocent sensuality of the pose tied Neill's stomach in knots. He wanted to reach out and bury his hand in the honey-colored hair that spilled down her back, wanted to nibble his way down the delicate arch of her throat. He didn't know what it was about her that made him want her like this. It wasn't as if she dressed to drive a man wild. The sunshine-colored short-sleeved dress, with its full skirt and V-neckline, was hardly designed with seduction in mind, but his fingers itched with the urge to unfasten the prim little row of buttons that marched from neckline to hem.

If he leaned over and kissed her now, would she

respond the way she had last night, all trembling arousal and uncertain response? And what was she wearing under that prim little dress? Silk and lace, or plain cotton?

He wasn't aware of moving until he felt his hand slide into that thick fall of hair, cupping the back of her head. Anne didn't start but only opened her eyes slowly, as if she'd been expecting him, waiting for him.

"I just have to see if I imagined it," he whispered.

"Imagined what?"

"The way you taste." The last word was murmured against her mouth.

It was different this time, Anne thought. Last night she'd been startled, a little frightened and completely unprepared for the wave of heat that rolled through her when he touched her. Since then, she'd spent a lot of time remembering, imagining, hoping. And now, here it was happening again, only better. So much better.

With a sigh, she opened her mouth to him, her tongue coming up to fence with his. He tasted of root beer and smelled of soap and aftershave. When she felt his arm come around her back, lifting her closer, she brought her arms up to circle his neck, indulging the urge to slide her fingers into his hair. It felt like warm black silk, she thought, and then whimpered softly as his teeth scraped along her bottom lip.

It was like the first time, Neill thought, dazed by the power and speed of it. One touch, one kiss, and he wanted so much more. And he could have it, he knew. He could have her. If they were alone, he could slide all those tantalizing buttons loose and take what she was so sweetly offering.

But they weren't alone, and it was too soon, even if it felt like he'd been wanting her forever. She would have regrets. He didn't question that knowledge but accepted it, just as he'd accepted the need to see her again, to touch her again. He had time, he reminded himself. He wasn't going anywhere until he'd figured out this...whatever it was between them.

Reluctantly, he eased back until he was looking down at her. She opened her eyes so slowly that they might have been weighted and stared at him with a look of staggered arousal that tested his already shaky control to the limits.

"I'd better get you back," he said, indulging the need to taste the delicate arch of her throat.

"Back where?" she whispered, her senses swimming with the feel of him, the taste of him.

"To work." He touched the tip of his tongue to the pulse that beat at the base of her throat and felt it jump.

"Work." Anne struggled with the concept. She was nearly sure that the word meant something to her, but, at the moment, she couldn't seem to recall what.

"The bank." He pressed a quick, hard kiss on her mouth before easing away. "Your job, remember?"

"Yes." It seemed the appropriate answer, but the truth was that she could barely remember her own name. Anne lifted an unsteady hand to smooth her hair as she tried to grab hold of her spinning thoughts. She was grateful when Neill stood and, picking up the bag that held the remnants of their meal, carried it to the nearest trash can. It was impossible to think with him so close, barely possible to think when he wasn't.

A kiss, she reminded herself. Still just a kiss. This sort of thing happened every day, all over the world. People kissed each other and their brains continued to function. It seemed incredible, but she was nearly sure it could be done.

When Neill returned, Anne was upright, standing on legs that were almost steady. She smoothed her hand over her skirt as he bent to pick up the blanket. He gave it a quick shake before folding it roughly. Still without speaking, they turned toward the park entrance. The silence that had been so comfortable a few minutes ago now seemed fraught with tension, and she wracked her brain for something innocuous to say.

"So where were you going when your motorcycle broke down?" Anne asked and then nearly winced at the brightness of her tone. She just didn't have any experience with making conversation with a man who'd just melted her bones with a kiss.

"Ft. Lauderdale, more or less." Neill seized gratefully on the distraction and expanded on it. "My parents retired there a couple of years ago."

"Where did they live before?" she asked.

"Wisconsin. Before that it was Denver, and before that, Texas, Los Angeles and Michigan. I was born in South Dakota."

"You moved around a lot."

"More than most families, I guess. Not as much as we would have if Dad had been in the military." A teenager on a skateboard zoomed toward them, and Neill took Anne's arm to pull her out of the way. He didn't release her when the boy passed but simply slid his hand down to link with hers.

"What did your father do?" Anne was pleased with the steadiness of her voice. No one would ever have guessed that her heart was bumping up against her breastbone.

"A little of everything. Managed restaurants, owned a dry cleaners, worked construction now and again. He had a butcher shop in Denver and even did a brief stint as a disc jockey in L.A."

"I know it's difficult to get a small business off the ground," Anne said diplomatically, thinking that his father sounded less than stable.

Neill shook his head with a smile. "Dad didn't have any problem getting a business off the ground. He just got bored once he had it in the air. It was the challenge of it that he loved. As soon as things were on an even keel, he'd sell it and start over again somewhere else."

"Wasn't it very difficult for you—always moving like that?"

"Not that I recall. We'd have a family meeting and discuss where to go next. We all got input. We moved to Denver because my older brother was thirteen and desperately wanted to be a cowboy."

"Did he manage it?"

"Not so's you'd notice. He learned to ride pretty well, but he wasn't so good at getting off. He kept getting thrown. The third time he broke a bone, my mother put her foot down and Tony had to turn in his spurs. I think he was getting a little sick of spending time in a cast, anyway."

"That's understandable." Distracted by the conversation, she forgot to feel self-conscious about holding hands with him. "Do you have just the one brother?"

"And two sisters—one older, one younger. Darcy is the oldest. She's a sergeant with the Denver Police. Tony gave up horses for pizza. He and his wife run a restaurant in Chicago where they serve fancy pizzas and pasta. Maggie's the baby of the family. She's a hotshot attorney and lives in New York City."

"So you're pretty well scattered across the country."

"We don't manage to get together all that often," Neill said. "But we keep in touch by phone and, for the last couple of years, we usually manage to connect over the holidays."

"It sounds like you're close," Anne said, feeling a twinge of envy.

"I guess we are. Maybe that's one result of moving so often. Or maybe that's what made it easy to move. It might be a new town, but we always had each other."

"I've never lived anywhere but here," Anne commented, looking at the familiar street and trying to imagine what it looked like to someone who'd spent time in so many different places. "I've never even traveled anywhere else, unless you count a trip to Disney World amusement park when I was eight." She sighed. "I used to think it would be such fun to see the world."

Neill slanted her a questioning look, wondering what was behind the wistful tone. "Last I looked, the world was still out there, and you're not exactly tottering on the edge of the grave. There's still time to see at least some of it."

"I... Yes, I suppose I could," she said after a moment, and Neill wondered why the idea should seem so startling.

He drew her to a halt and answered her look of inquiry by nodding at the building behind her. "The bank." And then told himself it was ridiculous to feel flattered by her obvious surprise.

"I had a nice time," she said.

"What are you doing for dinner Friday?" he

asked, tightening his hand on hers when she started to pull away.

"Dinner?" Anne felt a pleasant little flutter in the vicinity of her heart. He wanted to see her again. "I...oh, I can't. Actually, I have a...a prior commitment."

What she had was a date with Frank Miller, and, while she'd never been particularly excited by the idea, she found herself suddenly annoyed with poor Frank for asking her out, which was not only illogical but unfair.

"I want to see you again," Neill said and, for an instant Anne teetered on the edge of telling him she would break her date. He was only here for a little while, her heart whispered. But it would be unfair to Frank, who had never been anything but kind to her, and maybe it would be better—safer— if she didn't see Neill for a day or two. Her emotions were already tangled where he was concerned.

"There's a movie at the Roxy Saturday night," she suggested.

"They actually play movies in that old place?" Neill asked in surprise. He'd seen the old movie house but assumed it was long closed down.

"Dorothy runs it every other Saturday. She shows old movies."

"*Wizard of Oz?*" he asked, cocking one brow.

"Every year at Easter and Christmas," she said solemnly, but with a tuck in her cheek that made Neill want to pull her into his arms and kiss her right there in front of God and half of Loving, Indiana.

Anne must have read something of his thoughts, because her breath caught and her big gray eyes widened. Neill tugged her a heartbeat closer, halfway to forgetting everything but the need to taste her again.

"Anne?"

The sound of her name jolted her out of the sensual haze that had begun to drift through her mind. Anne turned to see her brother standing just a few feet away, looking at her with both surprise and questions in his eyes. She felt herself flush as she pulled her hand from Neill's and was immediately annoyed with herself for the quick surge of guilt that washed over her. Even more annoyed with Jack for standing there looking as if the sight of his sister holding hands with an attractive man was worthy of inclusion in Ripley's. Never mind that this was the first time she'd done such a thing. Did he have to look so astonished?

Neill eyed the other man with barely veiled hostility. Was this Anne's "other commitment?" The local law enforcement? There was no denying he was attractive, if you liked the tall, fair-haired Greek god sort, and some women were ridiculously susceptible when it came to uniforms.

"Jack. I didn't see you there," Anne said, striving for casual and coming up with something closer to guilty.

"So I gathered." Jack's tone was dry as he closed the gap between them. He glanced at his sister, his eyes lingering a moment on her mouth before he shifted his attention to the man with her.

Neill wasn't fooled by the look of mild inquiry in the other man's eyes. He shifted unconsciously, balancing his weight evenly, wondering what the penalty might be for hitting an officer of the law if he threw the first punch.

"Neill, this is my brother, Jack," Anne said, unaware of the subtle masculine byplay going on over her head. "Jack, this is Neill Devlin."

*Brother?* It was only when he felt it loosen that Neill became aware of the solid knot of jealousy that had lodged in his gut.

"The guy with the motorcycle?" Jack asked, remembering the conversation at his parents' house.

Anne remembered it, too, and rushed into speech before her brother could say something indiscreet. The last thing she wanted was for Neill to find out that Lisa had dubbed him the Hunk.

"David's working on the motorcycle, or waiting for a part so he can work on it," she said hastily. "Neill and I were...um...we just..."

"Had a picnic," Neill finished for her, wondering why she was suddenly so nervous. True, older brothers could be a pain in the butt when it came to their sister's boyfriends. God knew, he'd gone out of his way to make Maggie's life a living hell when they were younger. She was over thirty now, and he still preferred not to think too closely about the fact that his baby sister actually had a love life.

"Nice day for a picnic," Jack said mildly.

Anne nodded, all out of clever conversational gambits. She was aware of Neill looking from her to Jack and wondered what he was thinking. It shouldn't be awkward, she thought angrily. There was nothing for her to feel awkward about. She was twenty-five years old, self-supporting, single and uncommitted, and there was no reason on earth for this niggling feeling that she'd committed some sort of crime.

Sensing her distress, even if he couldn't pin down the reason for it, Neill decided that the best thing he could do would be to leave the two of them to say whatever it was that they were so obviously not saying in his presence.

"I've got…things to do," he said. He brushed his fingertips lightly over Anne's cheek. "I'll see you Saturday?" She nodded jerkily, and, with a nod in the other man's direction, he left them.

"Saturday?" Jack asked as soon as Neill was out of earshot.

There was nothing challenging in the soft question, but Anne's chin rose a notch as she looked at him. "We're going to the movies."

He nodded slowly, his eyes skimming from her to Neill's receding figure and then back again. There were questions in his eyes, but all he said was, "I hope you know what you're doing."

"I do," she said firmly, wishing she felt half as sure as she sounded.

# Chapter Six

Whoever had said that the only certain things in life were death and taxes hadn't known Frank Miller. When it came to predictability, he made death and taxes look like roulette wheels.

He drove a sedate black sedan, which he washed every Sunday morning. He got his hair cut the first Thursday of every month, went grocery shopping every Tuesday and always came to a full stop at every stop sign. He'd been born and raised in Loving, and had attended the same high school as Anne, where he'd played solid, if unspectacular, football before going on to college, where he'd earned solid, if unspectacular, grades. He'd returned to his hometown after college, become a sheriff's deputy and had settled immediately into the rut he'd remained in for the last ten years.

Sitting across the table from him at Barney's Bar and Grill, Loving's one concession to fine dining, Anne watched him cut his steak into neat pieces and reminded herself that he had many good qualities. He was a good-looking man, in a square-jawed, Dick Tracy kind of way, with neatly combed dark hair, worn short but not too short, and dark eyes that rarely seemed to change expression. He was solid and responsible. She was willing to bet that he never misplaced a bill or forgot to water a houseplant. He was always on time, he never failed to remember his mother's birthday, and he probably helped little old ladies across the street, even when he wasn't on duty. He was kind, considerate and...deadly dull.

"I think this is a better steak than the one I got last week," he commented, chewing thoughtfully. "How's your chicken?"

"It's very good." Anne cut a sliver off her herbed chicken breast, put it in her mouth and tried to look as if she would actually taste it.

"You must have pretty well worked your way through the menu." Frank's smile held a touch of indulgence.

"Umm." Anne settled on a noncommittal noise as the best response. Every other Friday night, Frank brought her here for dinner. They arrived promptly at seven. He ordered the porterhouse, well done, with a baked potato, one pat of butter, no sour cream, and steamed vegetables. He drank a single glass of red wine with dinner and a single cup of coffee afterward. After a month, Anne had been able to recite the order by heart; after two months, she suggested maybe he would like to try something new. But he simply smiled and shook his head.

"I know what I like, and I've never seen much point in change purely for the sake of change."

He obviously didn't see the point in change for the sake of variety, either, Anne thought, taking another bite of chicken. He seemed to think the fact that she ordered something different every week was a harmless eccentricity. She viewed it as a sanity saver. Working her way through the menu was the most entertaining thing about her dates with Frank. Shamed by the sheer bitchiness of the thought, Anne forced herself to focus on her companion. He really was a nice man, she reminded herself. It wasn't his fault that, somehow, over the last few days, "nice" no longer seemed quite enough.

For the next half hour she made an effort to keep her attention focused on the man sitting across the table from her. And it *was* an effort. Conversation had never been Frank's strong suit. She'd always known that, but now, after meeting Neill, the contrast between the two men was painful. It wasn't fair to compare then, she reminded herself as she struggled to look interested in Frank's story of a prowler call that had turned up nothing more interesting than a stray dog. But how could she avoid comparing the two men? If Neill told the same story, he would find the humor in it, make her laugh over the idea of grown men creeping through the bushes in search of a nonexistent bad guy. Frank's dry recitation was about as interesting as the official report he'd filed on the incident.

Annoyed with herself for not being able to put Neill out of her mind, Anne pinned a bright, interested look on her face and smiled as he finished the story. "Was Mr. Koshnitzki embarrassed when you told him it was his own dog?"

"I don't think so." Frank seemed surprised by the suggestion. "He couldn't have known it wasn't a prowler, and I'd certainly rather he called us than try to deal with it on his own."

"Don't you ever get tired of Loving?" Anne asked impulsively. "Don't you wonder what it would be like to live somewhere else, or what it would be like to be a cop in a town that actually has prowlers and crimes more serious than shoplifting?"

Frank had just picked up his wine glass, but he stopped, the glass suspended in midair, his dark eyes widening in surprise as he looked at her. For Frank, it was a strong expression, and Anne waited to see what might follow. But, after a moment, he shook his head slightly, took a sip of his wine and set the glass down.

"I'm a little too old to be looking for excitement."

*Well,* I'm *not,* Anne thought, only to feel the quick little spurt of resentment vanish as quickly as it had come as Frank continued.

"Besides, you, of all people, should know that violent crime doesn't confine itself to the city." It was said in his usual, calm way, but the reminder sent a chill through her.

Yes, she did know that violence could strike

anywhere, destroying lives without warning, leaving nothing but wreckage in its wake.

"No, it doesn't, does it?" she murmured, lowering her eyes to her plate.

"Anne." There was an unaccustomed note of urgency in Frank's voice, but, before he could continue, Jack and Lisa were stopping by their table, smiling and exchanging greetings.

"I thought the two of you might be here," Lisa said. "I was pretty sure it was Luanne's last week." Her tone was bland, her eyes sharp with friendly teasing as she looked at Anne.

"We're just finishing up," Frank said, rising politely. "But you're welcome to join us for a nightcap."

"We were just leaving," Jack said. "Better to have a nightcap at home."

Something in his voice had Anne looking at him, remembering what Lisa had said about his drinking. His eyes seemed a little too bright, not quite focused. He wasn't swaying, but something in the way he rested his hand on the back of a chair made her wonder if it was there for balance. Or was she just imagining it because Lisa had put the thought in her head?

When she glanced at her friend, she saw that

Lisa's green eyes were bright with anger, her wide mouth held tight, her shoulders rigid when Jack slung one arm around them. With affection or for support? Anne wondered, aware of a panicky little knot forming in the pit of her stomach.

She had no idea what was said in the minute or two that the other couple lingered by the table and could only assume that she'd made the appropriate responses. She refused to watch them walk away, not wanting to see if her brother's steps were less than steady.

Just because he'd had too much to drink tonight, that didn't mean he had a drinking problem, she told herself fiercely. But what if he did? What if Lisa was right? Shouldn't she do something? Say something? Wasn't it her duty as his sister to talk to him? Help him? Her mind boggled at the idea. She loved her brother, but she realized suddenly that she didn't really know him. They'd never talked, never shared more than the most commonplace of conversations. She didn't know what was in his heart any more than he could know what was in hers.

She thought suddenly of Neill's comment that his family's frequent moves had never bothered them because, no matter what, they had each other, and she tried to imagine feeling that way about her own family; tried to imagine them sitting down to plan where they should live; tried to imagine her parents agreeing to move to Denver for no better reason than that a thirteen-year-old boy wanted to be a cowboy. The picture wouldn't come clear, not simply because there had never been any question of them living anywhere but here in Loving, but because she couldn't imagine that it would occur to either of her parents to consult their children on anything as fundamentally important as moving across country. She didn't have to know Neill's family to picture them sitting around a table, a map spread out in front of them, arguing about their next move. So easy to remember the affection in his voice when he talked about them. And, in the reflection of that, so easy to see the distance that separated her own family, one from another.

"Anne?"

She started, suddenly aware that it wasn't the first time he'd said her name. Their waitress was standing next to the table, her expression politely inquiring.

"Sorry. What did you say?"

"I was just asking if you'd like dessert."

"No, not tonight, thank you. Actually, I have a

bit of a headache,'' she added quickly before he could order his usual slice of apple pie, slightly warmed, with a single scoop of vanilla ice cream— in a separate bowl rather than on the pie. She just couldn't sit here and watch him eat his dessert, alternating bites of pie and ice cream and, in some way she'd never been able to understand, always managing to end up with exactly the right amount of each.

"I knew you didn't seem quite yourself," Frank said, looking almost pleased to have a simple explanation for her behavior.

He didn't say anything else as he paid the bill and they left the restaurant. The short drive to her cottage was equally quiet. Anne didn't know whether it was in deference to her supposed headache or just because this was Frank, who rarely had much to say, but, whatever the reason, she was too grateful for the silence to feel much guilt over the small lie.

When they got to the cottage, Frank walked her to the door, just as he always did. He never asked to come in, never lingered in anticipation that she might invite him in. He waited while she took the key from her purse and opened the door. Following the pattern that had been set, Anne turned and lifted her face for his kiss. When it came, it was as quiet and undemanding as it always was. He didn't seem to expect much by way of response and, though she tried to block it from her mind, Anne couldn't help but remember how she'd felt when Neill kissed her—the way her knees weakened and her skin seemed to heat beneath his hands.

She sighed softly when Frank lifted his head and looked down at her with a faint smile.

"Good night, Anne. A good night's sleep is the best thing for a headache."

"Thank you for dinner, Frank. It was lovely."

Her smile faded as she slipped inside and closed the door behind her, leaning back against it as she listened to Frank's footsteps receding down the path and then the polite hum of his car's engine as it backed out into the street. The last time, she admitted with a sigh. No more Friday nights spent trying to convince herself that the fact that she and Frank had grown up in the same town created some sort of lasting bond between them.

A week ago, she'd actually wondered what she might do if Frank ever asked her to marry him, had half thought she might say yes. She wanted a home, a family, and she had no doubt that he would make a dependable husband and father. For someone else. Because now she knew beyond the shadow of a doubt that she couldn't marry him. Not ever.

And it had nothing to do with Neill Devlin—not directly, anyway. But talking with him, laughing with him, had made her see how completely impossible it would be for her to marry a man who rarely strung more than two sentences together at a time and who thought the world began and ended at the city-limit sign.

Sighing again, Anne pushed herself away from the door. It was more than a little frightening to realize that her brief acquaintance with Neill had actually changed her life in such a fundamental way. Whether he stayed around for a while or disappeared tomorrow, he'd shown her that she could never settle for the sort of lukewarm affection that was all she could feel for Frank Miller.

She wanted more. Needed more. Maybe— though it was a revolutionary thought—she even deserved more.

The five-day work week must have been invented by the Puritans, Anne thought as she pulled a load of wet clothes out of the washer and threw them in the dryer. Five days of work, one day to catch up on all the things you couldn't fit in during the rest of week, and one day left for worship. If idle hands were the devil's playground, he must really hate the typical nine-to-five schedule.

She punched the button to start the dryer and reached up to smooth back a strand of hair that had escaped from her ponytail. How did single parents manage? she wondered as she went to the broom closet and pulled the vacuum out. Or double parents, for that matter? She couldn't really complain. Living in a small town meant that she could do most of her errands during the week, either during her lunch hour or after work. That left Saturday morning for cleaning house and most of Saturday afternoons free for doing anything or nothing at all. That was a luxury a woman with a family wouldn't have.

But there would be compensations. Anne leaned on the vacuum and allowed herself to dream a little. Leisurely bubble baths would give way to rubber duckies and babies splashing in the tub. Reading Dr. Seuss instead of Robert Parker. Planning trips to Disney World amusement park rather than creating elaborate itineraries for exotic vacations she would never take. Sharing her bed with someone more exciting than her childhood stuffed toys.

There would definitely be compensations.

Sighing, she bent to unwind the vacuum cleaner's cord from where it looped around the handle. If she wanted a home and a family of her own, she could always marry good old Frank. It was pretty clear he was headed in that direction, and she could probably nudge him along a bit. Then she could have the rubber duckies and Dr. Seuss and the trip to Disney World amusement park. She wouldn't be surprised if the stuffed toys won out over Frank in the excitement department, though.

Wincing a little at the bitchiness of that thought, Anne went to plug the vacuum in, only to be brought up short when someone knocked on the front door. A glance through the frosted glass window pane showed a familiar, trim figure and her brows rose in surprise. Though the cottage was barely a hundred yards from her childhood home, her mother rarely visited. Olivia had disapproved of the whole idea of Anne living on her own. When Anne had refused to give in to either rational arguments or tears, Olivia had dealt with the situation in her own way. By keeping her distance, she could, in a sense, refuse to acknowledge that it had happened at all.

On those occasions when she did visit, she had no hesitation about expressing her displeasure about anything and everything, so Anne was hardly surprised when her mother's first words were a complaint.

"I don't know what you were thinking of when you came up with this ridiculous color scheme." She looked at the narrow porch with obvious distaste. "Yellow with pink trim. It's absurd."

"Good morning, Mom." Anne stepped back to allow her mother to enter, trying not to sigh with envy over the casual elegance of her mother's clothing. Putty-colored cotton slacks and a simple rose-colored blouse worn with canvas espadrilles, and just a few discreet touches of gold at ears and wrist. Next to her, the pink shorts and tank top that Anne had thought looked cheery when she put them on suddenly became annoyingly perky. Well, she'd figured out a long time ago that, when it came time to hand out the gene for elegance, she'd obviously been somewhere else.

"The whole place is absurd," she said, responding to her mother's comment. "It seemed to call for a paint job to match."

"You might have been able to tone it down a bit with a more conservative color scheme. Not that anything could make it look anything but what it is, which is a ridiculous little building with Victorian pretensions. All that gingerbread and carved moldings."

"Umm." Anne had heard this particular speech often enough to tune it out.

Olivia's description was accurate enough. Rose Cottage had been built by Anne's great-grandfather, back in the 1920s. The family had been quite well-to-do at that time, and he'd considered himself something of an architectural buff. The main house had been designed with Tudor pretensions that would have looked perfectly at home hunched over some English moor. The fact that it hardly suited Indiana farm country hadn't bothered Hiram Moore in the least. Nor had he hesitated to jump an ocean and several centuries when it came to choosing a style for the cottage he built to serve as a studio for his wife's painting hobby.

Rose Cottage was all Victorian gingerbread and beveled glass outside, oak floors, crown moldings and a hideously impractical but charming curved staircase inside. Anne could remember a time when the cottage had been pressed into service as a guest house two or three times a year. Her mother's friends would come up from Atlanta, all soft drawls, pastel dresses and big hair. But that had changed fifteen years ago, just like so many other things, Anne thought, and was caught off guard by the sharp nip of resentment.

"Can I get you a cup of coffee?" she asked when Olivia had run out of negative things to say about her home.

Olivia hesitated and then nodded. "Thank you." She followed Anne into the small, sunny kitchen. "Bacon and eggs for breakfast?" she asked, looking at the pan left to cool on the stove.

"Yes." Opening a cupboard, Anne went up on her toes to reach a bone china floral cup and saucer. She generally used a mug but knew that her mother would prefer something more delicate.

"I hope you're watching your diet," Olivia said behind her. "You know how easily you tend to put on weight." Anne set the cup down with exaggerated care and closed her eyes. "At your age, a few extra pounds probably don't seem like much of a problem, but it's very easy to let it get away from you. Look at your grandmother—she went from being a plump girl to downright obese by the time she hit her forties. And you're short, just the way she was. If you were a little taller, you wouldn't have to worry about it quite so much.''

Anne dug her fingers into the edge of the counter and let the words roll over her, trying not to listen. Determined not to care. She'd heard it all before, starting when she was an adolescent. Underlying everything her mother said was the unspoken thought that it was a shame she wasn't more like her sister had been. Brooke had never gone through an awkward puppy fat stage. Brooke had been tall and slim and beautiful.

With a skill born of years of practice, Anne shoved the hurt and resentment into a dark corner of her mind and slammed a door on them. Her mother meant well, she told herself as she moved to pour Olivia's coffee. She was pleased to see that her hand was steady when she lifted the cup. There had been a time when her mother's not-so-veiled criticisms would have left her shaken and trembling.

''I hardly think that an occasional breakfast of bacon and eggs is going to send me to a fat farm,'' she said lightly. ''Why don't you tell me why you're here? I know you didn't walk down here just to tell me that I have lousy taste in paint and to warn me against the evils of excess fat.''

Olivia's mouth tightened as she took the cup from her daughter. She hadn't intended to set Anne's back up about irrelevant issues. Not that she regretted anything she'd said. The paint was absurd, and it was certainly her right—even her duty—as a mother to warn her daughter of potential future dangers, which was exactly why she was here. Except that the reason she'd come had nothing to do with nutrition, and she was mildly annoyed that she'd let herself get distracted. Even more annoyed that Anne had bluntly asked why she was here, making it impossible to approach the subject with any delicacy.

"I was talking to Betty Hardeman yesterday. She's heading the committee to try to fund a restoration of the old courthouse, and she wondered if I'd be interested in participating."

"I'd heard someone was looking into it."

To give herself something to do with her hands, Anne poured coffee into a mug decorated with a whimsical scene of mice having a picnic. She was fairly sure she knew what was behind her mother's visit now. Betty Hardeman just happened to be DeDe Carmichael's aunt. The two of them didn't have much to do with one another, since Betty made no secret of thinking that her niece was no better than she ought to be, but DeDe was sure to have told her mother that Anne Moore had had lunch with a stranger at Luanne's. Lissy Raybourne wouldn't have let her shirttail hit her skinny butt before she picked up the phone to call Betty.

Well, she'd known this was coming, Anne reminded herself as she stirred sugar into her coffee. You couldn't keep secrets in a town the size of Loving. If her mother hadn't made it such a point to remain aloof from the community for the last thirty-odd years, it wouldn't have taken four days for her to get the news. Anne decided to look on the bright side and view the delay as a breathing space. Maybe it was that breathing space that gave her the courage to take the control out of her mother's hands.

"So I suppose Betty told you that I had lunch with a man none of them could identify," she said casually and had the rare satisfaction of seeing her mother thrown off balance.

It was only momentary, but the unexpected admission, as well as the hint of steel in her daughter's usually soft gray eyes, made Olivia decide to take a different tack than she'd originally planned. Anne was generally quite willing to do whatever it took to keep the peace but she did sometimes show an odd stubborn streak—such as when she'd decided to move into this absurd cottage.

"Actually, by the time Betty told me about your lunch, she was able to tell me quite a bit about your companion," Olivia said lightly. "A Neill Devlin, I think it was. A writer, apparently, whose motorcycle broke down somewhere outside of town? I assume this is the gentleman you met at David Freeman's garage last week?"

"Yes." Anne's response was wary. She knew her mother too well to take this easy acceptance at face value. A week ago the idea that her daughter had so much as spoken to a stranger had been enough to send her into near hysterics. Now she brought it up as if there was nothing unusual about it at all. "I've seen him a couple of times," Anne admitted, feeling as if they might as well have everything out in the open.

"Have you?" Olivia kept her smile in place, but her fingers tightened on the delicate little cup. She hadn't known that, and the new knowledge confirmed what her instincts had told her, which was that this man was a danger that needed to be dealt with as quickly as possible.

"He's taking me to the movie tonight." Anne tilted her chin and met her mother's eyes. "I like him. I like him a lot. He's done a lot of traveling, and he's interesting to talk to, and has a great sense of humor.''

"And if I can believe Betty, he's also attractive.''

"Yes." Anne couldn't prevent the color from creeping into her face. "He's very attractive.''

Olivia nodded and lowered her gaze to her cup, while she debated on the right approach. She allowed her voice and expression to soften, become more vulnerable. "I know I...overreacted last week when you mentioned him. I suppose it seems silly to you. After all, it's been fif—fifteen years.'' There was a subtle hitch in the words. "That's a lifetime to someone your age, but I've never been able to forget what happened.''

"None of us have." Anne reached out to touch her mother's arm. "I haven't forgotten.''

"Then maybe you can understand why I worry so much about you.''

"I—of course I do." Anne stumbled over the agreement, not quite able to forget her mother's ruthless ability to manipulate those around her to get what she wanted. Or what she'd decided they should want.

If Olivia heard her hesitation, she chose to ignore

it. "I was wondering if perhaps your...Mr. Devlin would like to come to dinner tomorrow night," she suggested. She read the shocked surprise in Anne's face and continued quickly. "I know I'm being overprotective, but I'd feel much better if I—if we—met this man you're seeing."

"I don't know that I'm actually 'seeing' him," Anne protested. "For all I know, he may be leaving for...wherever tomorrow. He's only here until David can get parts for his bike."

Well, if he's already left, then we won't either of us have anything to worry about, will we?" Olivia said, smiling a little. "But if he's still here, I'd very much like it if you'd bring him to dinner." Her mouth tilted self-deprecatingly. "I'd feel much better if I had a chance to meet him."

"I...I'll ask him," Anne said, trying to conceal her reluctance. She didn't want to bring Neill to dinner tomorrow night. The time she'd spent with him had been something apart from her real life. To him, she was just Anne Moore, who worked in a bank and drove a car named Lucy. He didn't know anything beyond what she chose to tell him. When he looked at her, he didn't see dark tragedy and loss. He just saw...her. She hadn't realized until now how much that meant to her.

But she couldn't refuse her mother's request. Because, no matter what, Olivia's loss was real. Maybe she was using it to manipulate, but that didn't make the worry any less valid.

"I'll ask him to dinner," Anne repeated, forcing a half smile.

"Thank you." Olivia's smile was warm.

And why shouldn't it be? Anne thought ruefully as she saw her mother out the door. She'd just gotten exactly what she wanted—as usual.

She bent to pick up the vacuum cleaner cord that she'd dropped when her mother arrived. Plugging it into the wall socket, she wondered what Neill was going to think of the invitation she'd promised to deliver.

"The man took male chauvinist piggery to new heights," Anne said firmly. "Or depths."

"I don't think male chauvinist pigs existed in the nineteenth century," Neill argued, frowning. "I don't think the species appeared until sometime in the sixties. Besides, you've got to give a man credit for strong family feeling. He could have just ignored his brothers' emotional pain, but instead, he took action and did what he could to alleviate their suffering. When you think about it, he was really a man ahead of his time—sensitive and caring."

Anne stopped dead on the sidewalk and turned to look at him. "Kidnapping six terrified girls and deliberately stranding them in the mountains with a bunch of illiterate, uncouth louts was sensitive and caring?"

"Okay, so maybe he was a little...impetuous," Neill conceded. Another couple walked past, eyeing them curiously. "But those illiterate, uncouth louts were his brothers, and it was his deep concern for their happiness that led him astray."

"Led him astray?" Anne choked on a gurgle of laughter. "Next you'll be telling me that he was really the innocent party in the whole movie."

"Well..." Neill stretched the word out consideringly. "I don't know that I'd go quite that far, but I do think there was a certain...nobility of spirit about his actions that—" He broke off when Anne laughed. It was such a young, happy sound that it made it difficult for him to hold on to his serious expression. "I thought we were having a deep, intellectual discussion about the social relevance of the film we just saw."

"I bet it's the first time anyone's tried to find social relevance in *Seven Brides for Seven Brothers.*"

He arched his eyebrows and looked down his

nose at her. "Then it's past time someone recognized its true value. For example, how can you fail to miss the deeply layered meaning in lyrics like, 'I'm a lonesome polecat'?"

"Or the profound melancholy underlying the surface of a song like 'Bless Your Beautiful Hide'?"

"I'm not too sure about that one," Neill said, frowning thoughtfully. "I think that may be nothing more than a demonstration of complete male chauvinist piggery."

Their laughter drew several glances and a few sympathetic smiles. Most of the week, the sidewalks in Loving were pretty well rolled up by nine o'clock. Other than the restaurants and a couple of bars, the businesses closed up shop. Saturday nights were different. Saturday was date night or take the family out for a hamburger night and, every other week, catch a movie night. When the movie ended, the small crowd left the shabby theater and, on a warm summer night, took their time heading home.

They passed an elderly couple walking slowly, matching shuffling step to shuffling step and holding hands like your lovers. Up ahead was a young couple, a child between them who picked up his feet and swung on his parents' hands every few feet.

"Mayberry," Neill muttered, and then was surprised that he'd spoken the thought out loud. He caught Anne's questioning look and shrugged. "This town. It makes me feel like I just fell into a movie set. I keep expecting Barney Fife to come swaggering down the street or Aunt Bea to toddle out of the beauty parlor."

Anne looked around, trying to see the scene through his eyes. To her, it was simply the town where she'd grown up. She knew it was small and rural, even out of date, but she'd never really given it much thought. It simply was what it was.

"Does it bother you?" she asked curiously.

"No. It makes a nice change." Neill reached out to take her hand, linking his fingers with hers, and Anne felt her heart bump with pleasure at the casual intimacy. "It's certainly got its advantages. People smile at you. You don't have to worry about finding a parking place, and the crime rate is probably too low to measure."

Anne shivered despite the warmth of the night air. "It's not paradise," she murmured. "Crime isn't limited to big cities."

"No, but it doesn't measure into the triple digits

in a place like this.'' He saw her face as they stepped beneath a streetlamp, and his fingers tightened over hers. ''What's wrong?''

''Nothing.'' Anne smiled with an effort, deliberately closing the door on the memories that tried to slip through. She glanced up at him, her smile taking on an edge of mischief. ''I was just thinking that I never did pay my share of lunch that first day. How about if I buy you an ice cream sundae to make us even?''

''I wouldn't mind an ice cream sundae.'' His voice slowed to a drawl. ''But I have to tell you that I think your first offer was more than adequate compensation.''

She gave him a questioning look, saw the warmth in his eyes and realized he was talking about the kiss they'd shared that first night when she'd come to his motel room. Color warmed her cheeks, and she looked away, half afraid of what he might see in her eyes. Wholly afraid of the emotion fluttering in her chest.

*A movie, ice cream sundaes and walking a girl to her car on a warm summer's night.* Neill tried to remember the last time he'd spent such an innocent, enjoyable and sexually frustrating evening and decided it had to have been when he was in high school.

They'd laughed over the movie, then sat talking over a pair of ice cream sundaes until Luanne's owner announced that it was closing time and shooed the last of her customers out the door. And all the time, under the laughter and the conversation, he was aware of a low hum of awareness, a hunger. A need. She felt it, too. He caught glimpses of it in her eyes, those clear gray eyes that did such a poor job of hiding her thoughts. He could feel it in the little jolt that went through her when he took her hand or reached out to brush her hair back from her face.

Because he was a man, he couldn't help but wonder if he could talk her into coming back to his motel room. He thought the odds were pretty good. But because he wanted something more from her than a quick roll in the sack, he'd made up his mind not to try. He wasn't sure just what that something more might be, and that scared him a little. It also made it easier to rein in his baser instincts. Until he understood what he was feeling, he didn't want to rush into anything.

"I had a lovely time tonight." They'd reached her car, parked in front of Lisa's tiny shop. Stopping by the driver's door, she turned to look up at him. "Thank you, Neill."

"My pleasure." She was so pretty standing there in her tidy blue and white striped shirt and trim jeans, her hair caught back from her face with a pair of simple gold clips, thanking him as politely as a little girl after a birthday party.

Her eyes widened a little when he stepped close and braced one hand on the roof of her silly little car. Her breath caught raggedly, and her eyes widened on his. What was it about her? Neill wondered half-angrily. She wasn't at all his type. He liked long, leggy brunettes with eyes that said they knew a lot about the way the world worked. Not women like this curvy little blonde with innocent gray eyes and, God help him, the most kissable mouth he'd ever seen in his life.

Anne's breath sighed out as his mouth closed over hers. This was what she'd been wanting all night. No, if she were honest, she had to admit that she'd been thinking about this since he'd kissed her in the park two days ago. She'd half convinced herself that she'd dreamed it—the way the world dipped and swirled and filled with light and color. The way her blood seemed to thicken even as her pulse rocketed.

The keys she'd taken from her purse dropped to the pavement as she clutched at Neill's arms for balance, feeling the ripple of muscle and sinew as he pulled her closer, shifting the angle of the kiss to deepen it. His mouth opened over hers, tasting her shivering response.

With an effort, Neill dragged his mouth away from Anne's. Staring down at her, he tried to figure out what it was about this woman that tried his self-control like no one else had. One kiss—in public again, dammit—and he was rock hard and ready to pull her into some dark alley and take her. And she just might let him, he thought, seeing the stunned arousal in her eyes. She was quivering under his hands, and his fingers tightened on her shoulders for an instant before he released her and took a cautious step back.

Goddamn scruples and common sense, he thought savagely. Bending, he scooped her keys up off the pavement.

"You'd better go," he said, pressing them into her hand.

"Y-yes." She stared down at the keys for a moment as if she wasn't quite sure of their purpose. After a moment's fumbling, she managed to sort out the right key and open the car door. Neill shoved his hands in his pockets and stood watching her, his expression brooding. Before sliding into the seat, she turned and looked at him, her eyes wide and uncertain, her teeth tugging nervously at her lower lip. "Do you...can I give you a ride back to the motel?"

"Thanks, but I think I'll walk. I can use the exercise." And he didn't trust himself to spend another minute with her. But when she turned to get into the car, he reached out and caught the top of the door, stopping her. "Dinner tomorrow night?"

"Oh." Anne bit her lip, remembering her promise to her mother. "I'd like to but I—we—my brother Jack and I always have dinner at my parents' house on Sundays. Actually, my mother asked me if I'd invite you."

"Your mother?" Neill's brows rose, and Anne felt herself flushing.

"She heard...I mean, I...ah...mentioned that we'd met, and she wanted to meet you." Her face felt as if it was on fire. She was so accustomed to the fact that her family—her mother—felt the right to oversee her life that it wasn't until she was offering the invitation that the strangeness of it struck her. This wasn't the way it was done in the real world, she thought. In the real world, a woman of twenty-five did not bring home a man she'd known less than a week for her parents to inspect.

Neill considered the invitation for a moment. Times might have changed a lot in recent years, but meeting a girl's parents still held an ominous ring of possible commitment. But he was curious, he realized. He'd told her all about his family, but Anne rarely spoke of hers. He'd met the brother. It might be interesting to meet her parents.

"Sure," he said slowly. "Sunday supper sounds good."

## Chapter Seven

A week, Neill thought, staring out at the sporadic Sunday afternoon traffic going past the gas station. A week ago he'd been limping along a dusty road, fantasizing about hopping on the first plane that would take him a thousand miles from the nearest cornfield. Now he had only to turn his head to see the cornfields that hovered at a polite distance from the edge of town, and the view didn't bother him at all. He was even willing to concede that there was something rather majestic about the endless rows of dusty green leaves and golden tassels.

The air was hot and still, the sun beating down out of a cloudless sky. He'd spent a couple of evenings in one of the local bars, nursing a beer and listening to the regulars talk. There was some concern about rain—would they get enough of it and would it come at the right time? You couldn't discount the possibility of hail, either. 'Course the corn was nearly ready to harvest, so hail wouldn't be the disaster it would have been earlier in the season. He'd heard about Milt Bowdrie's prostate surgery and that it looked like the youngest Lewis girl had herself a scholarship to some fancy college back East, and had listened to idle speculation on the possibility that Sally Ann Weaver's recent trip to see her family in Bismark had been a cover-up for the fact that she was having breast implants.

Anyone who thought gossip was a woman's game should spend an afternoon in a pool hall, Neill thought, remembering. He watched a faded blue station wagon slow to let a shaggy gray mutt trot across the street and lifted a hand to return the driver's wave. He didn't have the slightest idea who she was and wondered if she thought she knew him or was just being friendly.

Contentment. That was what he was feeling right now. It wasn't something he'd had much contact with, particularly not in the last few years. He'd known some dizzying heights—selling his first book, watching it creep onto the bottom of the *New*

*York Times* list, then selling the second book and proving to himself that it hadn't been a fluke, that he might finally have found something he could do for the rest of his life.

He couldn't say he'd been unhappy, but lately he'd been aware of a niggling feeling that something was missing. Like the old song, he'd found himself wondering, is that all there is? And then he had cursed himself for being a greedy bastard for asking. This last week had made him realize that it wasn't that he wanted more. It was that he wanted something else, maybe even less than what he'd had, at least in terms of conventional success. He'd remembered something he'd almost forgotten—how much he loved to write.

The story he'd started that first afternoon was still there, pulling at him, giving him no choice but to write it. He didn't have the slightest idea what he was going to do with it when it was done, and he didn't care. For the moment, it was enough to simply enjoy the process.

"Can you give me a hand here?" David said behind him.

Neill turned away from the door and walked over to where David was working on an ancient black pickup truck. A newly rebuilt engine hung suspended over the engine compartment, ready to be lowered in place.

"Steady it on the side while I lower it."

"Got it." This was something else he'd missed—the smell of grease and exhaust fumes, the satisfaction to be found in building and repairing, creating something with his hands rather than his head. After spending his mornings writing, he'd gotten into the habit of wandering by the garage and lending a hand with whatever needed done, including pumping gas for the handful of drivers willing to pay a higher price for the extra service. If David Freeman thought there was anything odd about his sudden acquisition of an assistant, he didn't say anything. Once he was satisfied that Neill knew the difference between a carburetor and a fuel pump, he left him alone.

"At a guess, I'd say this truck is older than my grandfather," Neill commented as they eased the engine down. "Wouldn't it make more sense just to run a new chassis in under the engine?"

"Bill Brent bought this truck brand new back in '55. Probably paid a couple thousand for it. According to my dad, he bitched about the price for the first fifteen years, then put a new engine in it and bitched about the fact that the old one had only lasted a hundred and fifty thousand miles. Since then, he's complained about every repair he's had done on it, first with my father, then when I took over the shop. He just kept bringing it in and complaining. Fact is, he cares a lot more about this truck than he does about his wife. Not that I can entirely blame him," David added in the interest of fairness. "Roberta Blair has a face that looks like she fell out of an ugly tree and hit every branch on the way down, a voice that could shatter glass at fifty yards, and she's usually complaining about something."

"Sounds like a match made in heaven."

"Probably, but at least Bill doesn't sound like fingernails on a chalkboard."

They worked in easy silence after that. When he was in high school, Neill had spent one summer working for a mechanic, earning enough money to buy his first car—a wreck of a Camaro coupe that he'd restored himself. He couldn't think of anything he'd owned before or since that had filled him with the same sense of pride. The engine in place, he picked up an orange rag from the top of a tool chest and wiped the grease from his hands. Maybe he should sell the Indian, buy something he could fix up.

"Hear you've been seeing quite a bit of Anne Moore," David said. He didn't look up, and Neill couldn't read anything in his voice.

"I guess, in a town this size there isn't much that doesn't get noticed."

"Not much," David agreed. He straightened and looked across the body of the truck at Neill. "I've known Anne pretty much her whole life. I'd hate to see her hurt."

The veiled warning prodded Neill's temper—all the more so because he'd worried about the same thing. It didn't take a lifetime of knowing her to recognize Anne's vulnerability. There was no guile in her, no games, none of the brittle shields most people erected to protect themselves.

David must have seen the quick flare of temper, but his gaze remained steady. Questioning.

"I didn't realize she had more than one brother," Neill said edgily.

"When it comes to Anne, she's got a whole town full of brothers. She's had enough hurt in her life."

Neill's head snapped up, his eyes sharp with question. The idea of someone hurting Anne sent a wave of pure rage licking through his system.

"Who hurt her?" The question was soft. Dangerous.

"It was a long time ago. Best forgotten." David shook his head and frowned down at the engine, and Neill had the feeling that whatever he saw there, it wasn't forgetfulness. When he looked up, his expression was rueful. "It's none of my business," he admitted. "I just can't help feeling responsible in a way, for you being stuck in town so long, meeting Anne."

"You can't do much without parts."

"No, I guess not." But he still seemed uneasy.

Neill felt the quick surge of anger vanish as quickly as it had come. He couldn't fault the other man for caring about Anne.

"I don't know where Anne and I are headed," he said at last. "But I won't hurt her if I can help it."

"Fair enough." David nodded, then grinned crookedly. "I guess you'd rather have popped me on the jaw."

"Actually, I prefer to go for the nose. It makes a much more satisfying crunch." He laughed when David winced. His good mood restored, Neill leaned against the truck's fender and decided to do a little probing for information himself. "So tell me about Anne's family. I'm having dinner with them tonight," he said, and saw David's eyes go wide with shock.

"Bring a flak jacket," David blurted, and then looked as if he wished the words unsaid.

"A flak jacket?" Neill's brows rose. Of all the answers he might have expected, this wasn't one of them. "Am I likely to be facing a hostile father with a shotgun full of buckshot?"

"I doubt if Doc Moore knows one end of a shotgun from the other. The only thing you have to worry about from him is that he may forget you're there."

"Well, I've already met the brother, and I'll admit that the uniform and the big shiny gun were a little intimidating, but he didn't look like the sort to shoot first and ask questions later."

"Jack's okay," David said slowly, frowning down at the engine. "We went to school together. He's...changed a lot over the years, but he's okay."

"That pretty much leaves Anne's mother." Intrigued, Neill leaned forward. "So what's with the mother? Does she prowl the cornfields when the moon is full? Chew tobacco and pick her teeth with a knife?"

"Not that I've ever seen." David hesitated and then shrugged. "She's lived here almost forty years, and I don't think she's on a first-name basis with more than two or three people."

"Interesting." Neill rocked back on his heels and considered. In a town the size of Loving, almost everyone was on a first-name basis with everyone else. If Anne's mother had managed to remain aloof from that for four decades, it was quite an accomplishment. The comment about taking a flak jacket made it clear it wasn't shyness that had kept her on formal terms with her neighbors. So what kind of a woman could both set an entire town at a distance and raise a daughter as warm and open as Anne? Definitely an interesting question.

"I probably shouldn't have said anything," David said uncomfortably.

"I asked." Neill straightened away from the truck and changed the subject. "I don't suppose there's any place in town that rents cars, is there?"

"Not that I know of. Not much call for car rentals. You need a ride somewhere?"

"Nowhere in particular. I'm just getting a little tired of hoofing it everywhere."

And, stupid as it was, he didn't like the idea of

Anne picking him up to take him to her parents' house for dinner. It was an outdated notion, but he couldn't quite shake the idea that he should be picking her up, not the other way around. A perfect example of what she would call male chauvinist piggery. And rightly so, he admitted ruefully.

David straightened and reached back to pull a rag out of his pocket. Wiping his hands, he contemplated Neill thoughtfully.

"I've got something I could loan you," he said slowly. "Hasn't been driven in a while, but I keep it in shape."

"I'm not picky," Neill assured him. "Any old clunker will do."

David laughed. "I don't think I'd call it a clunker."

"David loaned you his Corvette coupe?" Anne stared at the low-slung car in disbelief. When she'd seen the car pull up in front of the cottage, there had been one heart stopping moment when she thought David had come to tell her that Neill had left town. Even when she saw Neill's tall frame unfolding from beneath the steering wheel, it had taken her a moment to grasp the reality of it.

"David doesn't loan anyone this car," she said

positively. "He doesn't even drive it much himself."

"Yeah, that's what he said." He ran his hand down the fender, his expression rapt, and Anne couldn't help but wonder what it would be like to have him touch her like that. "Said he got it for a song from some old lady in Arkansas whose husband bought it and then ran off with a kindergarten teacher a couple of years later. She left it to sit in the yard for thirty-some-odd years. Can you imagine just leaving an original '65 Stingray coupe sitting out like that?"

He sounded so appalled that Anne bit her lip to hold back a smile. What was it about men and cars? Not that she could throw stones, not with Lucy sitting there smiling at her.

"It was pretty scruffy looking when he towed it home. I thought he'd be better off junking it," she couldn't resist adding and nearly laughed out loud at his horrified look.

"Are you kidding? Do you know what this is? This is the roadster model with both tops. It has the Turbo-Jet V-8 engine—396 cubic-inch big block, 425 horsepower, close ratio four-speed, solid valve lifters and disc brakes. There were only a few hundred of them made. The body's straight, and the tranny was still—''

Neill caught the glazed look in Anne's eyes and broke off, grinning a little sheepishly. "Sorry. I guess I got carried away."

"That's okay. I understood the part about it having both tops, because it's a convertible, but you lost me after that," she admitted. "I assume it all boils down to the fact that it will go really fast."

"Pretty much. I thought maybe we'd take it out on the road sometime this next week, put the top down and let the engine unwind a bit, see what it can do."

Anne smiled. She liked the sound of that—not so much putting the top down and letting the wind turn her hair into a rat's nest. But she liked the fact that he planned on being around next week, and liked even more his casual assumption that they would be seeing each other. It made her feel...couple-ish.

"So, where do your parents live, and do we drive or walk?"

"Walk. It's just up the driveway. Let me grab my keys and lock up." She'd been so amazed to see that he was driving David's precious Corvette that she hadn't waited for him to walk to the door but had come out to meet him.

Neill watched her hurry up the walkway. She was wearing another of the simple little dresses she seemed to favor—this one was summer sky blue, sleeveless with a modest scoop neck and a flippy little skirt. It was so sweet and innocent that it was practically wholesome. And all he could think about was how much he wanted to find out what she had on under it.

Annoyed to find that just thinking about it was making him ache, Neill shoved his hands in his pockets and crossed his legs at the ankles as he leaned back against the coupe and tried to think of something else. Something besides those long, slim legs wrapping around his waist or the way her breasts—

Cursing under his breath, he straightened away from the car. Arriving with a hard-on was not likely to make a real favorable first impression on a girl's family, especially one whose brother carried a gun. With a determined effort, he focused his attention on the house in front of him. It was certainly unusual enough to provide a distraction. Two stories of gingerbread and spindles, painted a soft pink with yellow shutters, it was a toy box version of San Francisco's great painted ladies. There was a white picket fence with an arbor and a gate beneath it, and the area from the fence to the house was filled with rose bushes. They covered the arbor and scrambled up the porch pillars. There were roses of every color and size, and the air carried the soft weight of their perfume. It was like looking at an enchanted cottage in a picture book. And, when Anne left the house and came down the walkway toward him, he thought she fit the image. There was something of the fairy-tale princess about her—a certain unawakened quality, as if she were just awaiting a kiss to awaken her to happiness.

Without thinking, he moved forward, meeting her as she reached the end of the walkway. She stopped on the other side of the gate, looking up at him, her eyes questioning. Neill wasn't sure what the question was, and he sure as hell didn't know the answer. All he knew was that he had to taste her, here beneath an arbor covered in roses the color of ripe apricots, with the sleepy drone of a bumble bee in the background and only the two of them in all the world.

He saw her eyes widen as he cupped his hands around her face, saw the smokey-gray awareness come up in them, and then watched her lashes drift slowly shut as he lowered his mouth to hers.

It was a kiss of such bone-melting tenderness that Anne felt her heart stop as her knees turned to water. She brought her hands up to catch hold of his wrists, clinging to him as the world dissolved around them.

It ended as slowly as it had begun, and Anne opened her eyes slowly, reluctant to return to reality. Neill was looking down at her, his blue eyes dark with something she couldn't quite read. It seemed almost a question, but whether he was asking it of her or of himself, she couldn't guess. They stood there for what seemed like a long time but could only have been moments, his hands cupping her face, his eyes searching hers. Then his expression shifted, his eyes warming with a smile. He brushed his thumb across her cheek and let his hands fall away, leaving her momentarily staggered by a sense of loss.

Without a word, he pushed open the little gate and, taking her hand, pulled her into the twilight beyond the arbor.

Sunday supper in farm country—the phrase conjured up a certain image. The family crowding around the big oak table, laughing and talking as they passed heaping platters of crisp fried chicken, fluffy white biscuits and bowls of creamy country gravy. Red-and-white gingham curtains fluttering in the warm breeze, the sound of birds chirping and cattle lowing, a long wide porch with rocking chairs and maybe a swing where everyone sat after supper, sipping lemonade and contemplating the amber waves of grain and maybe even a purple-majesty-cloaked mountain or two.

There were, Neill decided, more than a few gaps between that fantasy and reality. The table was polished mahogany rather than oak; the dining room, beautifully decorated in cool shades of gray and blue, was more funereal than homey; and central air conditioning effectively eliminated the warm breeze, the chirping birds and the lowing cattle. There was a front porch, but it wasn't the swings and rockers sort of porch, which was probably just as well, because Neill couldn't imagine the Moore family sitting together, sipping lemonade and chatting.

By the time the meal was served, they seemed to have run out of conversation. A question or two about how each of them had spent the week, a brief discussion of the weather, mention that Dr.

Moore's receptionist was thinking of retiring, and no one seemed to have anything else to say. Neill couldn't help but compare it to his own family get-togethers, with everyone talking at once, conversations started and abandoned when a new topic came up, arguments and laughter. He wondered if anyone had ever laughed in this coolly elegant room. Certainly not without Olivia Moore's permission, he decided, glancing at his hostess.

Until his talk with David at the garage this morning, he hadn't given much thought to Anne's family. He'd met her brother, and he knew her parents lived in Loving, but he'd had no reason to think of them beyond that. David's assessment of them had been interesting, but he hadn't taken it as the last word, preferring to make up his own mind. But it was pretty obvious that David knew the family very well indeed.

Anne's father was a little above average height, with a slightly stoop-shouldered posture and a thick shock of gray hair. He looked like a stereotype of the country doctor. He shook hands politely when Anne introduced them, poured Neill a predinner drink, sat down in a softly upholstered chair and, by some means Neill couldn't quite define, managed to absent himself from the proceedings.

Since Neill had already met his hostess, this didn't seem as odd as it might have. Even on brief acquaintance, it was fairly obvious that Dr. Moore's retreat was probably based on survival instincts honed over more than thirty years of marriage.

Despite David's comments, Neill had still pictured Anne's mother as an older version of her daughter, but, other than their gender, it was difficult to find any similarity between the two of them. Olivia Moore was taller and more slender. Her hair was an ashy blonde that successfully concealed any hint of gray, and she dressed with the same cool elegance with which she decorated her home. Though he knew she must have been in her mid-fifties, she could easily have passed for ten years younger. In the battle against age, she was more than holding her own. He didn't doubt that, when she was younger, she had been strikingly beautiful. In middle age, she was still a lovely woman—if you could ignore the icy coldness of her eyes, a chill that seemed reflective of her personality.

When Anne introduced them, Olivia managed to convey—with utmost courtesy—that he was as welcome as a case of hives.

"Mr. Devlin. How nice to meet you," she said insincerely. "I understand you're waiting for repairs to your motorcycle. Do you know yet how long it will be before you're able to get on your way again?"

*Here's your hat and what's your hurry,* Neill thought, surprised and a little amused. He wondered if she'd invited him solely to make it clear that he was unwelcome. Looking into those cool, ice blue eyes, he decided that she had and wondered if she'd found the technique effective in the past.

"Hard to say," he said, answering her question. "The parts could get here tomorrow or next week. Could be another month." He smiled cheerfully. "Lucky for me, I can stay just as long as it takes."

"Don't you have a family member or a friend who would be willing to...assist you in getting home?"

"Mom." Anne's voice was stifled with embarrassment.

"What?" Olivia's brows arched in question. "I'm just suggesting something Mr. Devlin might not have thought of. It isn't as if there's any reason for him to stay in Loving if he doesn't have to."

Her meaning was clear—he couldn't possibly be interested in staying because of her daughter.

Color rose in Anne's face, and Neill forgot to be amused. He reached out to catch her hand, feeling her start with surprise. "Actually, I don't have any immediate plans to leave, even if David gets the parts in right away."

Olivia's mouth curved in a tight little smile. "It will be interesting to see how you feel when your motorcycle is actually in working order again."

"I guess it will," Neill said, giving her a friendly smile.

He thought she might have pursued the conversation, but Anne's brother arrived just then, and she turned to greet him. The woman with him was stunningly out of place amid the elegant decor and muted colors. Tall and slim, with a mass of flaming red hair and a narrow face that was more interesting than pretty, she was wearing a pair of neon orange leggings and an oversized silk shirt in eye-searing lime green. Big gold hoops dangled from her ears, and her feet were thrust into a pair of rhinestone studded gold sandals, revealing irides-cent lavender polish on her toenails.

Introductions were made, and he learned that her name was Lisa Remington, and that she'd returned to her hometown two years ago after spending nearly a decade in California. Neill liked her on sight. Particularly when Olivia accorded her a welcome every bit as chilly as his own. Anyone she disliked was bound to be worth knowing.

It soon became apparent that the two women were old adversaries. Olivia inquired after Lisa's "little business," which Neill gathered had something to do with making hats. Lisa mentioned an ad she'd seen for a product guaranteed to minimize fine lines and wrinkling in middle-aged skin. Olivia commented on how charmingly bright Lisa's outfit was. Lisa thanked her and mentioned how much she envied the older woman's ability to look good in insipid colors.

It was like attending Wimbledon, watching them lob insults rather than tennis balls. It was a far cry from the happy family get-together Neill had envisioned, but he had to admit that it had a certain entertainment value. The two women were well matched, neither giving an inch. If he had to choose, he would have put Lisa a bit ahead, because it was obvious that, like him, she saw the humor in the situation. Meeting her eyes across the table, Neill barely restrained a grin. Yeah, this was definitely someone he could come to like. He wondered what she had in common with the man beside her, other than the fact that they'd grown up in the same town.

Jack didn't contribute much more to the conversation than his father did, though Neill was fairly sure he was listening, which was more than could be said for the older man, who sat at the end of the table but might as well have been sitting in Katmandu. Jack was there. Watching, listening—and putting away most of a bottle of wine, Neill noted as the other man refilled his glass. Added to the Jack Daniel's whiskey he'd downed before dinner, it would be interesting to see whether he was actually able to get out of his chair or if he simply slid under the table.

The writer in Neill was fascinated by the dynamics of the family. The man in him was aware that Anne was not enjoying the polite warfare being waged between the other two women. Sensing her distress, he reached for her hand under the table, smiling when she looked up. Her answering smile was a little lopsided.

Catching the exchange, Olivia's mouth tightened. She'd suggested that Anne bring Neill to dinner because she'd wanted a chance to assess him. She'd had a pretty good idea of what he would be before she'd met him, and she hadn't seen anything to make her revise her opinion. A man with no commitments, no responsibilities. He probably didn't own anything more than what he could carry on his motorcycle. A writer, for heaven's sake. What was this fatal attraction her children had for creative types? There was no denying the fact that he was very attractive. She could see why Anne would be attracted to him, but no good could come of the relationship. She didn't want to see her daughter hurt when he left, as he surely would. Perhaps it would be possible to open Anne's eyes a bit.

"So, Mr. Devlin, Anne tells me you're a writer."

"That's right." She was smiling, and Neill found himself remembering a nature film he'd seen on cable. It had been on crocodiles, and he seemed to recall that they had a similar look right before they grabbed an unsuspecting antelope and dragged it under.

"That must be an interesting profession."

"It has its moments," he admitted.

"Like Lisa's little hats, it must be difficult to earn a decent wage."

Neill thought of his last advance, which could

have bought this house and its contents two or three times over, and gave his hostess a friendly smile. "It's not easy, but I've been pretty lucky. I don't go hungry more than three, maybe four weeks out of the year," he said cheerfully. "And I can always move back in with my parents if things get really ugly."

Olivia's mouth tightened with disapproval, her pale blue eyes freezing over. "I hope you'll forgive me for saying so, but it seems odd that a man of your age should be less than self-supporting."

Briefly, Neill considered the possibility of telling her that he thought it was damned ballsy of her to criticize his supposed lifestyle, but he couldn't resist the wicked little voice that prompted him to play the scene out.

"My older brother thinks the same thing," he said, widening his eyes a little at this seeming coincidence.

"He's more settled then?"

"Like he was cast in concrete. Wife, couple of kids, a mortgage. Like having anvils tied around his neck." He shuddered, throwing his sister-in-law, niece and nephew to the wolves without a second's hesitation. He felt Anne twitch but kept his attention on the woman at the end of the table. She was looking at him as if she'd just discovered a slug in her salad.

"Not everyone considers a family a burden, Mr. Devlin."

"I guess not." His slightly puzzled tone carried the suggestion that there was no accounting for taste.

"Your brother sounds like a responsible adult," she added, apparently in an attempt to bring him to a sense of his own unworthiness.

"That's Tony, all right." Neill shook his head regretfully. "He's responsible, but he doesn't have much time for fun. You know, throwing back a few brewskis with the guys and watching football on Sunday, cruising for chicks on Friday night."

Across the table, Jack seemed to choke on his wine. Ignoring him, Neill continued in the same cheerful tone.

"Tony's always after me to get a real job. But the way I look at it, you're only young once, and you might as well play while you can. I figure another four, five years and I'll start thinking about settling down, get myself a cheap little apartment somewhere, maybe find myself a wife with a nice steady job. Not that I'd expect her to support me," he said earnestly. "But, like you said, it's tough for a writer to earn a living, and we'll need a dependable income, especially when the kids start coming.''

Ignoring his hostess's outraged expression, he forked up the last bite of peach cobbler.

For the space of several heartbeats, no one said a word. Glancing across the table, Neill caught a gleam of something that might have been amusement in Jack's eyes and barely suppressed laughter in Lisa's. Beside him, Anne seemed to be hardly breathing, and he felt a twinge of regret that he'd let his temper get the better of him. But Olivia Moore's silk-gloved tyranny flicked him on the raw.

It didn't bother him for himself. The older woman's opinion of him and his profession meant less than nothing. As near as he could tell, her husband had managed to divorce himself from his wife's petty tyranny, if not from the woman herself, and, if tonight was anything to go by, her son drowned her out with whiskey. Lisa seemed more amused than offended by the delicately sharpened barbs that came her way. But Anne was neither amused nor drunk, nor did she share her father's ability to absent herself from what was going on around her.

She hadn't said anything, but he could feel the tension in her and was irritated with himself for letting her mother's acid-dipped tongue prod him into playing her game. Any satisfaction he might have gained from the older woman's horrified expression was hardly worth the distress it so clearly caused Anne.

Seeking something to break the sudden silence before it could become uncomfortable, Neill's eyes fell on the cluster of pictures that sat on the buffet. The largest of the group was of a very pretty blonde who looked to be in her late teens. There was a picture of the same girl in the living room. The one in the living room was a formal portrait, showing just her head and shoulders, and he'd thought it was a picture of Anne's mother in her youth. But this was a candid photo, with the girl in jeans and a tank top, laughing into the camera, and, while the resemblance between her and Olivia was marked, it was obvious that they were not one and the same.

"Who is that?" he asked, nodding to the picture.

Anne's eyes followed his, and she felt her heart stop for a moment when she realized who he was asking about. Though her sister's portrait was always there, no one ever mentioned her. Her mother might allude to her, usually when speaking of how much she'd lost, but no one ever said her name or openly acknowledged that she'd ever existed. The pattern had been set in the first terrible months after Brooke's death and had simply never been broken.

But Neill couldn't know that, and he'd asked who the girl in the photo was. Anne couldn't bring herself to look at her mother—couldn't, in fact, look away from the laughing girl in the photo. The silence had already stretched too long. She couldn't just sit there like a lump, as if Neill hadn't spoken.

"That's Brooke," her father said calmly, speaking for the first time since the meal had begun. Anne was nearly as shocked by the fact that he'd responded to something that hadn't been addressed directly to him as she had been by Neill's unexpected question. He was looking at Neill, a small, sad smile curving his mouth. "Our older daughter. She…died some years ago, just a short time after that picture was taken, in fact."

"I'm sorry," Neill said sincerely and wondered what was behind the sudden, painful tension his question had evoked.

"I should probably apologize for baiting your mother," Neill said, sliding his hand down Anne's arm until he could link his fingers with hers. "I let my temper get the better of me."

It had been twilight when they walked up the long drive between Anne's cottage and the main house. Now it was full dark, with only the lamps that lined the driveway to light their way. The day's heat lingered to warm the night air, and crickets scratched out a ragged concerto somewhere in the darkness.

"My mother can be...difficult," Anne said, choosing her words carefully to tread the fine line between honesty and loyalty. "She's just...protective of me, I guess. Worried that I'll..."

"Fall in with bad company?" he finished so dryly that she laughed a little.

"I guess." She didn't want to talk about her mother, not when it felt so pleasant to be alone with him like this. The darkness fell like a cloak around them, blocking out the real world, leaving only the two of them to listen to the cricket song and breathe the rose-scented air.

"What happened to your sister?" Neill asked, and Anne felt the peaceful illusion tremble, as if reality were a hammer, tapping to get inside.

"She died," she said, after a long moment. "That's all."

Neill hesitated and then decided not to push, though instinct told him there was a great deal more to be said. There was something there—something about Brooke or about her death, so that, years later, even the mention of her could fill a room with tension.

But, for now, he was more interested in the fact that he was alone with a pretty girl who fit in his arms as if made to be there.

## Chapter Eight

"You know, after spending ten years in L.A., rain in the summer still seems a little miraculous," Lisa commented as she held open the shop door for Anne to come in. "Since I grew up here, you'd think all this would seem normal, but what sticks is those ten years in the middle."

"I think I read somewhere that a person's weather imprint is established in their twenties," Anne said. She slipped off her jacket and hung it over the back of a chair, then combed her fingers through her damp hair.

"Weather imprint?" Lisa arched a disbelieving brow. "There is no such thing."

"If there isn't now, I bet I could get a government grant to prove it exists."

"Probably. As near as I can tell, the stupider the idea, the more money they're likely to cough up." Lisa locked the front door and threaded her way past several laundry baskets heaped with ribbons, a box full of fabric remnants and a giant pretzel can with lace spilling over the top, until she reached her work counter, where the beginnings of a new hat were spread out.

"I got this idea last night. I'm designing a hat for Titania."

Anne settled on a stool across from her friend and reached absently for a jelly bean. "Titania? You're making a hat for a sunken ship? What's the theme—flippers and a scuba tank?"

"That was the Titanic," Lisa said, grinning. "I'm talking about Titania—you know, queen of the fairies. Married to Oberon. I went to the library yesterday and looked them up."

Anne nibbled a jelly bean and considered the array of silk flowers and ribbons heaped together on the counter. "Do fairy queens wear hats? I have this vague idea that they run around naked a lot. Isn't she going to look kind of odd wearing nothing but a hat?"

"I should have said I was making a hat *inspired*

by Titania," Lisa said oppressively. "I don't actually expect her to show up to wear it."

Anne considered this while she ate another jelly bean. "I like the scuba theme better. You could maybe have an iceberg in the center and a miniature replica of the ship sailing along the brim, or maybe just half the ship dangling off the brim—to represent the sinking."

"Pearls before swine," Lisa muttered in disgust.

Anne frowned a little. "Were there pigs onboard, too?"

They grinned at each other, well pleased by the absurdity of the exchange.

One of the things Anne enjoyed most about her friendship with Lisa was that they shared a sense of humor. It wasn't until Lisa had moved back to Loving and they'd become friends that she'd realized how seldom anyone in her family laughed. Brooke had laughed a lot, she thought, caught off guard by the sudden memory of it.

"So, tell me about your Neill," Lisa said, and Anne pushed Brooke's image away.

"He's not my Neill," she protested halfheartedly. "He's just... We've only gone out together a few times. That's all. There's nothing... I mean, as soon as his bike is fixed, he'll probably leave. Certainly leave. It's not as if there's anything between us.... Nothing serious, anyway.'' She realized she was babbling and drew a slow, shallow breath before finishing with what she hoped was a plausible note of amusement. ''I've only known him a week, for heaven's sake.''

''And that's relevant because…?'' Lisa glanced at her, her thin brows arched in question.

''Because no one falls in… I mean, gets serious about someone else in a week.''

''There's a law prohibiting it?''

''Common sense prohibits it.'' Emotions churning, Anne slid off the stool. She might have paced, but boxes and baskets turned the shop into an obstacle course, so she settled for sifting restlessly through the weird assortment of items on one of the shelves. Shells, plastic hula dancers and tiny wooden clogs jostled for space with a slightly balding flocked reindeer, a miniature Easter basket and a ceramic bowl full of fake grapes.

When Lisa didn't say anything, Anne turned to look at her. ''Well? Aren't you going to tell me I'm wrong?''

''Do you want me to tell you you're wrong?'' Lisa asked mildly.

''Of course not. Because I'm not. I'm right.''

She picked up a plastic windup penguin and turned the knob absently. "He's only been here a week. He could leave any minute. I'd be crazy to let myself forget that."

"No one said you should forget it. I'm just wondering how relevant it is." Lisa's long fingers moved among the flowers and ribbons, pairing, separating, pairing them again. "Not every relationship has to lead to something permanent, you know."

Anne did know, but she was starting to think that there was nothing she wanted more than for Neill Devlin to be a permanent part of her life. She set the penguin on the counter and watched him waddle along for a few inches until one foot landed on a piece of red velvet ribbon. Off balance, he tilted, seemed to almost right himself, and then fell nose-first onto the table. His legs churned uselessly until he wound down.

Anne thought she knew just how he felt. She'd been waddling along, feeling as if she had her life fairly well in order. Maybe she'd had a few doubts, wondered where she was heading, but still, she'd been steady on her feet. Then Neill Devlin walked into her life and—bam!—she was suddenly in danger of falling flat on her face. Just like that penguin.

"So, are you seeing Neill tonight?" Lisa asked casually.

"We're having dinner at Luanne's." Anne disentangled the little toy from the lace and set him back on the shelf, next to a life-sized stuffed chicken.

"If it makes you feel any better, I liked him," Lisa said.

"It's not a question of liking him. It's just that...I don't know." Anne groped for the words to explain what she was feeling. "For a long time, my life has been pretty smooth. And now, suddenly, things are changing—or I feel like they are."

"And it scares you," Lisa finished for her.

"It scares the hell out of me," Anne admitted with a sigh. "I don't know how he feels about me. I don't know how I feel about him. I don't know what's going to happen tomorrow or next week. It's scary."

Lisa let her hands fall idle amid the flowers and ribbon as she looked at Anne seriously. "Nobody knows what's going to happen tomorrow or next week. No matter how safe and settled your life seems, everything can change in the blink of an eye. You should know that better than most." She didn't wait for a response but continued, one corner of her wide mouth tilting in a half smile. "Let me give you the benefit of my eight extra years on the planet and tell you that I think Neill Devlin is the best thing that could possibly have happened to you, even if he ends up breaking your heart."

Anne gave her a startled look. "Thanks!"

"You're twenty-five," Lisa said, ignoring the interruption. "And you've been settled in the same rut for the last six years. Nineteen to twenty-five, Anne. Those are the crazy years. That's when you're supposed to have mad affairs and stay up all night talking with a man who might be—but probably isn't—the love of your life. That's when you try weird clothes and change your hairstyle half a dozen times a month, and you go to keg parties and drink too much, then throw up on your shoes."

"Sounds lovely," Anne said dryly.

"Not all of it. You get hurt, and you think your life is over, and then you figure out it isn't and you move on." Lisa reached out and set her hand over Anne's. "This last week, you've done more living than you have in the two years since I came home. Maybe Neill Devlin's going to ride out of town like Shane the minute his bike is fixed. Or maybe the two of you will fall madly in love and live happily ever after. Either way, you're finally waking up a little.''

''What if I fall madly in love with him and he still rides away like Shane?'' Anne asked slowly.

''Then you'll pick up the pieces of your heart, glue them back together and move on. But at least you'll have known what it's like to love someone.''

The problem, Anne thought, was that she was more than a little afraid that she already did know what it was like. It was a terrifying thought.

Half an hour later, when she left Lisa's shop, the rain had turned to a sullen drizzle. The sidewalks were empty, traffic at a minimum. On a night like this, not even Luanne's ''guaranteed fine home cooking'' could draw many people out. Since the restaurant was only a few doors down from Lisa's studio and across the street, it hardly seemed worth driving, so Anne left Lucy where she was and started walking, her thoughts wavering between her conversation with Lisa and anticipation about seeing Neill.

And the fact that she was feeling such a bubbling sense of anticipation should be a warning, she told herself sternly. It was easy for Lisa to talk about putting the pieces of her heart back together again, but she wasn't the one who would have to find the glue with which to do it. If she had any sense, she would tell him she couldn't see him anymore. But it was hard to think sensibly when her heart was beating double time. Maybe Lisa was right. Maybe it was time for her to do something crazy.

Head down, shoulders hunched against the rain, Anne didn't notice when she crossed in front of a narrow alley, didn't see the thin figure dart from its mouth, so she was completely unprepared when something slammed into her shoulder, nearly knocking her off her feet. Startled and off balance, her hands tightened automatically on her purse when her assailant grabbed for it. Instinct had her hanging on when he jerked at it.

"Give me the fucking purse, lady." The words were spat out at her.

Anne wanted nothing more than to comply. There was nothing in her purse that couldn't be replaced, nothing worth risking her life over. But her fingers were locked in a death grip over the soft leather and didn't respond to her mental orders to let go.

Cursing, her assailant used his hold on the purse as leverage and spun her around. Anne cried out in pain as her shoulder slammed into the brick face of the building. And still she couldn't get her fingers to loosen their hold on the purse.

"Goddamn bitch. Give me the bag." She had a flashing impression of a narrow face, red-rimmed, colorless eyes and lank brown hair. And then the thin light caught on a blade and everything else vanished.

Fear clawed at her throat and blurred her vision. She was going to die. Right here, on the sidewalk, in plain sight of anyone who happened to drive by. Only it was past eight and no one was driving by, and, if they were, their attention would be focused on the wet road, on getting home in time to catch their favorite sitcom or tuck the kids in bed. And even if they glanced this way, they might not see what was happening. The light was poor, and the rain made it worse.

In some distant part of her mind she found herself thinking that she'd always known this would happen. Lightning didn't strike twice, people said, but it did. It had. And she was going to die because of it.

"Hey!" The shout barely penetrated the white hot fear that filled Anne's mind, but its effect on her attacker was immediate. Cursing viciously, he gave the bag one last frantic jerk, the force of it dropping Anne to her knees on the sidewalk. And then he was gone, swallowed almost instantly by the darkness beyond the alley's mouth. Vaguely, Anne heard someone running toward her but she could only kneel on the concrete, her fingers locked around her purse, her eyes blank with fear.

"Anne! My God, are you all right?" Neill dropped to his knees beside her, his hands trembling as he ran them over her shoulders and arms, looking for injuries, offering comfort. "Jesus, I was across the street. I saw you and was walking over to meet you when he—did he hurt you?"

It must have taken just a few seconds, she realized. From the time he grabbed her until Neill's shout made him run couldn't have been more than a few seconds. But it had seemed like hours—a lifetime.

"Anne? Honey, are you all right? Did he hurt you?"

"I'm all right." The three words seemed to come from someone else.

"Thank God." Still kneeling on the concrete sidewalk, Neill put his arms around her, dragging her against his chest, holding her tight enough to hurt. In a heartbeat, he was pushing her away, his fingers digging into her shoulders. "Goddammit, why didn't you give him the fucking purse? You could have been killed."

"That's what he called it," she murmured, blinking against the drops of rain caught in her lashes.

"What?"

"A fucking purse." Her tone was almost dreamy. "That's what he called it. It's actually a Coach purse. My parents gave it to me for Christmas last year."

Neill stared at her as if she'd lost her mind. "I don't care if it was handmade by Santa's elves and delivered to you personally by Rudolph on Christmas morning," he said, gritting the words through clenched teeth. "You should have let the little scumbag have it."

"My fingers wouldn't let go," she said simply. "They still won't."

"Jesus." Neill's anger vanished as quickly as it had come. He lowered his forehead to hers and wrapped his arms around her. "I'm sorry I yelled at you, honey. I was never so scared in my life."

Oblivious to the drizzling rain, he held her, letting the feel of her—warm and alive—seep into him. He knew he would never forget the way he'd felt when he saw that shadowy figure dart out of the alley. Rage that someone would dare to attack her. Frustration that he was too far away to stop it from happening. And fear that she might be hurt before he could get to her.

He didn't know how long they knelt there, but it was the feel of the rain on his back that finally brought him to a sense of where he was. They were both soaked to the skin. She needed a hot bath and dry clothes. He needed a chance to get his hands on the slimy little sonofabitch who'd done this to her, but he would settle for getting her warm and dry. He eased reluctantly back and looked down at her. "Are you sure he didn't hurt you?"

She nodded. Her shoulder ached where he'd slammed her into the wall, and her knees throbbed from their impact on the sidewalk, but those were minor complaints.

"I'm going to drive you to the sheriff station," Neill said, his fingers gently prying hers loose from her purse. "You need to talk to your brother, file a report."

"No!" The word exploded from her, her head jerking up so quickly that she nearly smashed into his chin. "I don't want anyone to know."

"Anne, the guy attacked you, tried to steal your purse. You can't just let him get away with it."

"He has gotten away with it," she said bluntly. "He's gone. Talking to Jack, telling him what happened, isn't going to accomplish anything." Her fingers dug into his forearm, and, even in the poor light, he could see the plea in her eyes. "Please, Neill. If I tell Jack and he files a report, everyone will know. They'll remember Br—they'll remember, and it will make them look at me again. Please, I just want to go home. Just take me home."

"Okay. It's okay." He stood, bringing her up with him. "You don't have to tell anyone." He swung her up into his arms as easily as if she were a child, cradling her against his chest. He didn't understand why she was so adamant about not talking to her brother, but she was right about it being a largely futile gesture. It wasn't worth upsetting her over. He brushed a kiss over her forehead. "I'll take you home, baby."

"Are you sure you're okay?" Neill asked as he took her keys from her and unlocked the cottage door.

She hadn't said a word during the short drive but had simply sat in the passenger seat of the

Vette, her hands lying limp in her lap, her eyes wide open and staring at nothing.

"I'm fine," she said, but he wasn't sure he believed her.

Neill pushed the door shut and guided her into the house. She would feel better now that she was home, he thought. She'd been frightened, but she wasn't really hurt. He wished she would cry. Tears would probably help. But she remained dry-eyed, looking around the small living room a little blankly.

"Is there someone you want me to call? Your friend Lisa, maybe?" He'd seen enough of her mother; guessed enough about their relationship, that he didn't bother to suggest calling Olivia.

"No." Anne shook her head slowly. "I don't want anyone. I don't want anyone to know."

"Okay." Neill set his hand gently on her shoulder, feeling the rigidity of her muscles. She was wound so tight that a wrong word might be enough to make her shatter. "Okay. I won't call anyone if you don't want me to. I'll just stay until you're settled."

His soft, soothing tone made Anne aware of her own unnatural stillness. He must think she was nuts. It wasn't as if she'd been hurt. She hadn't even lost her purse. Her fingers knotted over the soft leather until the pressure made her knuckles ache. It was stupid to be so upset. Nothing had happened. She had to pull herself together.

Reaching deep inside herself, Anne found a small pool of calm to draw on as she turned to look at him, forcing a small smile. "I'm okay. Really. You don't have to stay. I'm fine."

Looking at her, Neill thought "fine" was an overstatement. Her skin was the color of parchment, and there was a bruised look about her eyes that made his hands ache for the feel of her attacker's throat beneath his fingers. Fine? Under other circumstances it would have been funny. What she looked was fragile. Breakable. He wanted to pull her into his arms and hold her until the shadows went away, but something in the rigid way she held herself made him think that, if he touched her now, she might fall apart, and he wasn't sure that would be a kindness.

"I'm not going anywhere." He silenced her protest with a lift of his brow. "I'm not leaving you alone right now."

"Okay." She looked away before he could see how pathetically grateful she was.

"Why don't you go take a hot shower while I

see what I can come up with by way of something hot to drink?''

Anne nodded and moved toward the stairs. Her movement felt stiff and clumsy, as if her muscles weren't working quite right but she forced herself to climb the stairs, away from Neill's too-observant gaze. Panic—unreasoning and uncontrollable—was welling up inside, knotting her stomach and making her throat ache. She didn't want him to see her like this. She'd spent most of her life learning to lock the fear away in a little compartment inside herself, but now the lock was broken and it was slithering out, threatening to swallow her whole. She just needed a few minutes alone to force it back.

Neill watched her out of sight, his forehead creased. She would do better to let go of some of that damned self-control. And he wished she would let him call her brother, file a report. What was it she'd said? *Everyone will know and they'll look at me.* What the hell was that about?

The sound of a door shutting upstairs shook him out of his thoughts. Still frowning, he headed for the kitchen. For a woman who seemed as open as a book, Anne certainly had a lot of hidden corners.

He had no problem finding his way around her kitchen. It wasn't big enough to present a challenge. Small but welcoming, he decided, as he poured milk into a pan to heat for cocoa. There was a window over the sink that he guessed must look out over the rose garden and a cozy breakfast nook in one corner. The walls were a soft white and the cabinets a pale oak finish. Porcelain knobs in the shape of strawberries added a whimsical touch.

While the milk was heating, he found two mugs and made note of the fact that she had several cans of soup. He would see how she was feeling when she got out of the shower and maybe he'd be able to coax her into eating a little something. According to his mother, hot soup and a grilled-cheese sandwich were a near universal cure-all.

The milk was starting to bubble, and he reached out to turn it off, cocking his head for the sound of the shower. In a house as small as this, he should be able to hear water running. But there was nothing but the soft susurration of the rain outside. Maybe she'd finished and was drying off? But when he thought about it, he couldn't remember hearing the shower at all.

Uneasy now, Neill left the kitchen and went to the foot of the stairs. He heard nothing at first; then there was a low, keening sound that made the hair rise on the back of his neck. He took the stairs two at a time. The upper hallway was little more than a wide landing. There were three doors, but only one with light showing beneath it. The sound was clearer now, a soft whimpering that made him think of a trapped and dying animal.

"Anne?" He tapped on the door, but the whimpering continued unabated. God, had she been hurt after all? Wild visions of internal bleeding and concussion swirled through his mind. He tried the knob and cursed quietly, viciously, when he found it locked. Grabbing for control, he leaned his forehead against the door and tried to make his voice soothing, coaxing. "Anne? You've got to open the door, honey."

There was no response, only that sad, hopeless whimpering that cut through him like a knife. Frustration nearly had him putting his shoulder to the door and breaking it down, but he caught himself. She'd been through enough tonight. Having him break down the bathroom door was probably not going to do her any good. But he couldn't just stand out here like a damned statue. Listening to her was tearing holes in his gut.

*Think, Devlin. There's got to be a way to...* Grinning maniacally, Neill fished his wallet out of his back pocket. Every two-bit private detective on television could open a lock with a credit card. How hard could it be?

It was harder when your hands weren't completely steady and your pulse was beating twice as fast as it should, but, in the end, he figured it wasn't more than half a lifetime before he heard the quiet snick of the lock. His breath exploded from him as he pushed the door open and stepped into a surprisingly spacious bathroom.

He had a flashing impression of cream-colored tiles, punctuated by the hot flash of purple bath towels and curtains splashed with purple and yellow pansies. But his attention was all for the figure curled up on the floor under the window. She'd drawn herself into a tight little ball, arms wrapped around her legs, face pressed against her knees, and she was rocking back and forth and whimpering softly to herself.

"Anne?" Neill crouched next to her, his hands not quite steady as he reached for her. "What is it? Are you hurt?"

The low voice nudged against the cold white terror blanketing her mind. She'd learned a long time ago to hide from the fear, to retreat inside herself, squeeze her eyes tight shut, throw her hands over her ears and hide until it went away. It was better that way, better to deal with it alone. She was ashamed of the weakness, had always been ashamed of it. *Don't cry, Anne. How can you be so selfish? I'm the one who lost a daughter. Stop acting like a baby. Don't you care about me at all?*

The long ago words echoed in her mind, the voice sharp and angry, making her want to put her hands over her ears to block it out. But she couldn't block it out, because it was inside her head.

*Something terrible had happened to her sister. No one would tell her what. When she asked what had happened, Mama slapped her and sent her to her room. Mama had never slapped her before. She curled up in a ball on her bed, clutching her old teddy bear as a shield against the fear that beat frantic wings inside her chest. She didn't understand what had happened to Brooke, didn't understand why she couldn't walk to school anymore or even go out to play in the yard without someone coming with her, but she knew it was wrong to ask why, selfish to be so afraid. She wasn't a baby anymore. She was a big girl, and big girls weren't afraid.*

Ignoring her weak attempts to pull away, Neill wrapped his arms around her and pulled her against his chest and held her tight. "It's okay, baby. Let it out." He crooned the words, as if talking to a frightened child. "You'll feel better if you cry. Come on. Just let go. I've got you safe."

The arms around her felt strong and solid, a warm barrier against the fear. Safe, he said. *I've got you safe.* Anne shuddered once and, turning her face into his shoulder, let the tears fall.

She had no idea how long she cried, but, when the tears finally subsided to shuddering half sobs, she became aware that she was no longer on the floor but was cradled across Neill's lap, as he sat on the closed lid of the toilet. Her cheek was resting against his chest, and she could hear the solid rhythm of his heart beneath her ear.

"Feel better?" he asked quietly, and she was vaguely astonished to realize that she did. In a little while she would remember to feel embarrassed by her loss of control, but at the moment it felt so good to just lie there, with his hand stroking her hair. She had to swallow a murmur of protest when he eased her a little away and stretched out one long arm to grab a handful of tissues from the box on the counter. "Let's dry your face, and then you need to get out of those damp clothes."

Suddenly self-conscious, Anne tried to duck her

head, but Neill held her easily, mopping up the traces of tears with a kind of gentle ruthlessness that made her heart stutter in her chest. Hesitant, half afraid of what she might see, she lifted her eyes to his face. He didn't look disgusted, she thought.

"I'm so—"

"If you say you're sorry, I'm going to have to get violent," he said flatly.

"But I—" His brow arched, and she swallowed the words.

"Good choice." He brushed a kiss against one flushed cheek before setting her on her feet and standing up. "I want you to take a hot shower and get warm. You'll need a robe or something to put on," he said, glancing around the bathroom for something suitable. "Tell me where to find one."

"I can—"

"No, you can't," he said, smiling as he reached up to brush a damp curl back from her forehead. "Let me take care of you for a little while, okay?"

How could she argue with that smile? With those eyes? How could she argue when it felt so good to have him taking care of her? Giving in, she told him where to find her robe and waited while he turned on the shower and adjusted the temperature.

It was only when he reached for the buttons on her shirt that she came to life.

"I can undress myself," she said, stepping back.

"Too bad," he said huskily, and was pleased when she flushed. Smiling crookedly, he brushed his fingers over her warm cheek before leaving her alone.

When Anne went downstairs twenty minutes later, he was setting steaming bowls of soup on the tiny breakfast table in her kitchen.

"You're just in time," he said, as she hovered in the doorway. Turning off the burner, he scooped a pair of grilled-cheese sandwiches onto plates, cut each in half with a deft stroke of a knife and set them on the table next to the soup. "I hope you don't mind me raiding your cupboards. We missed dinner tonight, and I figured you might be hungry. I know I'm starving."

Anne had opened her mouth to tell him that she couldn't possibly eat anything but closed it without speaking. If he was hungry...

"I wasn't sure what you'd want to drink." He cocked an eyebrow in inquiry.

"I...water, I guess. Water would be just fine."

This domestic little scene wasn't what she'd expected. While she was in the shower, she'd had time to think. And what she'd thought about was the fact that Neill was sure to have questions. He would want to know why she didn't want to file a police report. He probably thought she'd overreacted to the attempted mugging. After all, aside from a couple of bruises, she hadn't been hurt, hadn't even lost her purse. Had she said anything about Brooke? She couldn't remember, but, if she had, he was going to want to know what the connection was. She'd come downstairs, dreading the questions, knowing she owed him truthful answers, without evasion.

And all he'd asked was what did she want to drink.

"It's not exactly gourmet," Neill said, as he set her water glass on the table. "But I did put a slice of tomato in the sandwiches before I grilled them, which is a unique little touch I invented myself."

"Maybe you should market it," Anne said, coming forward when he pulled out her chair with a flourish.

"I prefer to keep it my own little secret. Let Wolfgang Puck gnash his teeth in frustration over the superiority of my grilled cheese."

Anne was startled to hear herself chuckle. He pushed her chair in and...did she imagine it, or did he actually brush a kiss over the top of her head? Her eyes, wide and uncertain, met his as he sat down across from her, but there was nothing in his expression to suggest he'd just kissed her, and she told herself it must have been her imagination.

She was sure she wasn't hungry, but, after he'd gone to so much trouble, she felt obligated to at least eat a few bites. Twenty minutes later, she was astonished to discover that she'd eaten everything he'd given her.

"There's more soup, if you want," Neill said, the first words either of them had spoken since the meal started.

"No, thank you." She laughed a little and shook her head. "I didn't think I wanted what I had."

"No one can resist my grilled cheese," he said smugly, gathering up their plates and carrying them to the sink.

"I'll do that." She rose, intending to take the pans from the stove, only to find herself being shepherded gently but inexorably out of the kitchen.

"You're not going to do anything but go to bed." He herded her toward the stairs. "I'll clean up the kitchen, and then I'm going to sack out on the couch tonight."

"You don't have to do that." The protest was automatic, and she was desperately grateful when he shook his head.

"Yes, I do. I'm not leaving you alone tonight."

"I...thank you." Pride demanded that she send him away, but the thought of knowing he was just downstairs was too tempting. She climbed one step, then turned. "I didn't thank you. For what you did earlier. Chasing that guy off, then...after. I'm so—" She caught the warning in his arched brow and swallowed the apology. "Thank you for being there."

"You're welcome." This time, there was no question of imagining the kiss he brushed over her forehead. Anne tilted her head back, needing more, and, after a barely perceptible hesitation, Neill accepted the invitation so sweetly offered, his mouth settling on hers. It was a kiss intended to comfort rather than arouse, and Anne savored the tenderness. She couldn't remember ever feeling so thoroughly cared for and protected.

When the kiss ended, she reached out to fiddle with one of the buttons on his shirt.

"Your shirt's still damp," she murmured.

"I'll hang it somewhere to dry tonight."

The thought of him, bare chested and sleeping

just a few feet away from her own bed, made her mouth go dry.

"You don't have to sleep on the sofa," she whispered, feeling the color creep up into her cheeks.

In the silence that followed, she could hear the soft hiss of the rain outside. She waited, wondering if she'd just made a fool of herself, afraid he didn't want her anymore and was trying to think of a way to let her down gently.

"Not tonight." Neill folded his fingers over hers, drawing her hand away from his chest. "I want you so much it makes my teeth ache, but there are rules about this sort of thing. You had a bad scare, and you're grateful that I was there to help you through it." He caught her chin in his hand, tilting her face up until her eyes met the sharp, hungry blue of his. Her knees weakened, and her pulse scrambled. "When we become lovers, Anne, there's not going to be any gratitude in the mix."

Not "if" they became lovers but "when." The certainty in his voice sent a delicious little shiver up Anne's spine.

He dropped a hard kiss on her mouth, then put his hands on her shoulders and turned her around.

"Now go to bed and stop tempting me to forget my good intentions."

She climbed the stairs obediently, hugging close to herself the idea that she could tempt a man like Neill Devlin.

# Chapter Nine

Nobility had its price. There was simply no possible way for a six-foot-tall man to sleep comfortably on a five-foot-long sofa. It didn't help that, throughout the long, mostly sleepless night, Neill was acutely aware of the fact that, just up the stairs, was not only a bed but a warm and willing woman.

The damned sofa was too narrow for tossing and turning.

He fell asleep somewhere near dawn and woke barely an hour later to the discreet buzz of Anne's alarm going off upstairs. Only half-awake, he rolled and barely caught himself before he fell flat on his face on the floor. The alarm stopped in mid-beep, and he heard the floorboards creak overhead.

Work, he remembered. Anne was going to work. If he'd given it any thought, he would have guessed that she would go in as if nothing had happened.

He swung his feet to the floor and sat up, groaning as every muscle in his body expressed its displeasure at his choice of bed. *Coffee*. He all but whimpered at the thought. A cup of coffee or ten and he might actually start to feel human again. Maybe.

Before she came downstairs, Anne looked out her bedroom window and saw the red Corvette still parked in front of the house, so she knew Neill had stayed all night. She resisted the urge to creep down the stairs and steal a peek at him, like a child hoping to catch Santa putting presents under the tree.

If she chose to wear a very flattering summer sky blue silk blouse that just happened to do wonderful things for her hair and a trim gray skirt that showed off her legs, there was nothing wrong with that. She'd gone through a difficult time and needed the extra boost of knowing that she looked good. She applied her makeup carefully, lifted her purse from the dresser and took one last look in the mirror. Satisfied that she looked her best, she went downstairs. Neill wasn't on the sofa, but she could smell coffee and hear movement from the kitchen.

There was nothing to be nervous about, she told herself as she set her purse down and smoothed a very nervous hand over her skirt before walking into the kitchen. She was a mature, adult woman and he was—

Male. The sheer force of it stopped her in her tracks. Nothing had prepared her for the impact of finding all that tousled, unshaven masculinity in her tiny kitchen. He'd put on his shirt, but it hung open, framing a mat of dark curling hair that swirled across his upper chest before tapering downward to arrow across his flat stomach and disappear into the waistband of his jeans. It took a conscious effort to drag her eyes away from that intriguing line.

"Morning," he offered. "I made coffee."

"Oh, good." Her voice was a little too high and tight, but she didn't stammer, and Anne counted that as a triumph. It wasn't a good idea to look at his face, either, she decided, because the sight of those sleepy blue eyes and the shadowed darkness of his jaw seemed almost painfully intimate.

Neill sipped his coffee and wondered what she would do if he threw her down on the table and pushed that tantalizing little skirt the rest of the way up her thighs. From the hungry way she'd been looking at him a minute ago, she might not offer much argument. The thought didn't do anything to soothe the semipermanent ache in his loins.

But there was a time and a place for hot, quick sex, and this wasn't it. The first time he had Anne, he wanted a nice, wide bed and plenty of time. And he wanted to be damned sure that she wasn't thinking that she owed him anything for taking care of her the night before.

It was going to have to be soon, he told himself as he drained his coffee. He hadn't spent so much time in a state of semiarousal since he was a teenager. It just might do permanent damage to a man his age.

Since Anne's car was still parked next to the bank, Neill drove her to work. He wondered if it would occur to her that anyone seeing them would assume that he'd spent the night with her, which he had, and that they were lovers, which they weren't. Yet. If it did, it didn't stop her from kissing him in broad daylight.

The kiss, three cups of coffee and barely an

hour's sleep combined to have his nerves jangling as he drove back to the motel. Dorothy was out front on her hands and knees, weeding a flower bed. She rose as he got out of the car and ambled toward her. She was wearing navy blue shorts that revealed a pair of very knobby knees, a white man's shirt with the tails left hanging out and the expected pair of red sneakers, these decorated with white polka dots. A baseball cap was perched on her head—this one emblazoned with the New York Jets logo. She eyed him consideringly, her faded blue eyes taking in his wrinkled shirt and unshaven jaw.

"Just getting in?"

"Yeah." Neill narrowed his eyes against the dazzle of morning sunlight and looked at the bright sweep of flowers. "Snapdragons, aren't they? My mom grew them when we lived in—" The memory slid through his tired mind and back out again. He shrugged. "She grew them somewhere."

"These are the old-fashioned kind," Dorothy said, giving the flowers a satisfied look. "Not those new ones that are opened like a petunia. If I wanted to grow petunias, I'd grow 'em. Can't see the point of growing a snapdragon that doesn't snap."

"There does seem to be something contradictory about it," Neill agreed.

"Heard you've been seeing a lot of the little Moore girl."

Neill hooked his thumbs in his pockets and smiled ruefully. "I have enough respect for the grapevine in this town to bet that you know exactly how much time we've spent together and probably what we ordered for lunch."

Dorothy laughed, a sharp bark of amusement. "I wouldn't be surprised if I could find out without half trying. That's life in a small town."

"So I've discovered." He could have ended the conversation there, gone to his room, taken a much needed shower, maybe caught a couple of hours sleep. But he sensed that she had more to say, and, even in the short time he'd known her, he'd figured out that he might as well let her say it.

"Pretty girl."

"I think so."

"Sweet, too."

"That she is."

"I suppose you think I should mind my own business," she said with a touch of belligerence.

Neill widened his eyes in surprise. "No one else

in this town does. I don't see any reason why you should swim against the tide.''

She laughed again, and he grinned. He liked Dorothy Gale, with her old movies and her red shoes.

''Well, it isn't any of my business,'' she admitted generously. ''Or anyone else's, for that matter. But I suppose there's quite a few folks in this town who feel like she needs a little extra looking after.''

''Why?''

The simple question had her eyes darting to his and then away again. She pulled off her cotton garden gloves. ''They've had more than their share of trouble in that family,'' she said slowly. ''Maybe they didn't handle it as well as some would have, but I'm not one to point a finger at other folks and say they should have made a better choice.''

''What kind of trouble?'' Neill asked, his tiredness forgotten. ''Something to do with the other daughter? The one who died?''

Dorothy nodded reluctantly. ''I wasn't here then. My husband had just found out he had cancer, and we spent most of that year at a fancy clinic in Boston, getting treatments that didn't seem to do a whole lot of good. He died that summer, and I didn't pay much attention to anything for quite a while before or after." She was silent for a moment, remembering, but then she shook herself and glanced up at him. "You might want to ask my grandnephew. He was seeing the girl who died."

"Thanks. I will." He started to turn away, but she wasn't quite done.

"Before you start asking questions and opening doors that are maybe better left closed, you ought to consider whether or not you're going to like what you find."

"How will I know whether or not I'm going to like what I find until I find it?" he asked simply.

A hot shower, a couple hours' sleep, two cups of coffee, toast and three slightly overcooked eggs later, Neill left his motel room feeling, if not refreshed, at least marginally human. Briefly, he considered opening the laptop and spending a couple of hours working on the book he hadn't planned to write, but there was too much on his mind in the here and now for him to be able to focus on nineteenth-century Wyoming.

For a change, David had a fairly late model sedan up on the lift when Neill walked into the garage.

"I didn't think you worked on anything newer

than 1970," he commented, watching the other man loosening the lug nuts on one of the wheels.

"Now and again I'm forced to compromise my standards," David said, throwing him a grin. "Actually, I don't have the equipment to work on a lot of the newer cars. The way they're set up, they need a computer programmer more than a mechanic." He shook his head in disgust. "A hundred thousand dollar computer to tell you how to do a tune-up."

"I think it's called progress," Neill said dryly.

"I guess. Makes it expensive to stay in business, though. And pretty well makes it impossible for anyone who wants to do their own maintenance." The whine of the power wrench punctuated the sentence as he removed the remaining lug nuts.

Neill hooked his thumbs in his pockets, leaned back against the work bench and waited for him to finish. His motorcycle leaned in the far corner of the garage. Idly, he wondered if David had heard anything more about getting the parts he needed to repair it, but he didn't feel any urgent need to ask. Even if the Indian was repaired today, he didn't plan on going anywhere. Not until he'd worked out his feelings for Anne. And then—just maybe—he wouldn't be leaving alone.

David slid the tire off, letting it bounce gently against the concrete floor as he rolled it out of his way.

"You said you'd known Anne all her life," Neill said, as the other man picked up a box wrench and went to work on the wheel.

"That's right." David's agreement was absent, his mind on the job at hand.

"Then you must have known her sister."

The wrench clattered on the concrete floor. There was a moment of dead silence, then David bent to pick the tool up, straightening slowly to look at Neill with shuttered eyes. "I knew her. Matter of fact, we dated quite a bit through high school."

"What happened to her?" Neill asked, deciding that bluntness would serve better than subtlety. "How did she die?"

David bounced the head of the wrench lightly against his palm, considering. "Why do you want to know?"

Neill hesitated for a moment. If he told David about the attempted mugging and about Anne's near panic at the thought that people might find out and "look at her," he was fairly sure he would get the full story. But Anne had said she didn't want anyone to know about the attempted mugging, and, though he didn't understand her reasons, he had to respect her wishes. He shrugged. "It was something Anne said. It made me wonder."

"Why don't you ask her?"

"I did. She said it was a long time ago and that she didn't want to talk about it."

"But you're not willing to let it end there?" David asked, his tone neutral.

"I don't think it is ended," Neill said flatly. He didn't know why or how, but he knew that, whatever had happened to her sister, it was still very much a part of Anne's life.

David nodded slowly. "Maybe not." His eyes dropped to the wrench. He seemed to be debating with himself about something. After a long moment, he shook his head. "I don't think Anne would appreciate it if I told you."

Neill released his breath in a frustrated hiss, but he didn't offer any persuasion. In David's shoes, he would probably have made the same decision. It was a matter of loyalty. It was ironic that their mutual concern for Anne had set them at cross-purposes.

"Thanks anyway." He turned away, only to stop when David spoke again.

"It wasn't a secret when it happened." The words came slowly, as if pulled from him. "It was in the papers. Fifteen years ago come this next May."

The Loving Public Library was housed in a squat concrete building set back from the main thoroughfare by a wide sweep of well-tended lawn. A bronze plaque set in the wall beside the entrance announced that, in 1953, the building had been the generous gift of a Mr. and Mrs. Whiteberry, who believed that the joys of reading should be made freely available to all. The building itself had been designed by their son, Mr. Alvin Whiteberry. Neill appreciated their civic mindedness and thought it a pity that young Alvin had apparently taken World War II bunkers as his inspiration for the building's design.

The interior was much lighter and airier than he would have expected, with soft colors and honey-toned wood adding to the sense of spaciousness. Aside from a woman standing behind a low wooden counter and an elderly man dozing in a soft chair in the magazine area, the place appeared to be empty.

Neill stopped just inside the doors, debating the

wisdom of this expedition. He'd asked Anne about her sister and she'd said she didn't want to talk about it. Maybe that should be the end of it. If and when she wanted him to know more, she would tell him. Did the fact that he was sliding into love with her give him the right to poke around in her past? He wasn't sure, but he couldn't shake the memory of her trembling in his arms the night before, or the conviction that her fear had been caused by more than some punk trying to snatch her purse.

Besides, if whatever had happened to her sister had been in the papers, it was public knowledge, so he wasn't exactly invading her privacy, right? If he'd been around fifteen years ago, he could have read all about it, along with everyone else. And if that wasn't specious reasoning, he didn't know what was, he admitted with a sigh. But he needed to know.

As soon as he asked for copies of the local paper for the month and year David had given him, the librarian, a short, plump brunette in her late twenties, nodded.

"The Moore girl's murder," she said knowledgeably. She turned away and began scanning the shelves behind the desk. "We've got it separate from the regular files because there was so much interest in it. Not so much now, but for the first few years there was quite a demand for it. And people still come in now and again.''

She slid a thick black notebook off a shelf and carried it over to the desk. ''It was before my time, of course. I only moved here a few years ago, but my husband, Jim, he went to school with the Moore kids. He was a couple of years behind the murdered girl. He says the whole town was in an uproar for weeks. I'm from Detroit, and it seemed kind of odd to me that one murder could have such an effect on a town.'' Her shrug was self-deprecating. ''But, after you live here for a while, you start to understand.''

''Murder's a big deal in a small town,'' Neill said automatically. The word ''murder'' was spinning in his head. He'd considered the possibility, of course, but even after David had told him that Brooke's death had made the papers, he'd still thought it might have been an accident or even suicide. Suicide, especially, could certainly leave terrible scars on those left behind.

''And this was a particularly awful one,'' she said, shuddering a little. ''And I suppose it didn't help that they never caught the guy.''

"No. That makes it worse," Neill murmured, thinking of the cases he'd written about, of the survivors' need to see the killer caught and brought to justice before they could start putting together the pieces of their own shattered lives.

"It certainly doesn't help." She continued more briskly, "We don't check the book out, but you can make copies if you want. The copy machine is on the west wall, just past the children's section. We close early on Wednesdays, so you've only got about an hour."

Neill carried the notebook to one of the oak reading tables and pulled out a chair. Aside from the librarian and the elderly gentleman he'd seen earlier, who was now dozing gently, he had the library to himself. He set the notebook down but didn't immediately open it. Tapping his fingers on the cover, he thought of Dorothy's comment that he might not like what he found out. He had an uneasy feeling that her words might turn out to be prophetic.

His jaw set, he opened the notebook's cover.

Despite the volume of clippings, it really hadn't been a complicated case. Gruesome enough to provide for some extremely lurid press coverage, but the actual facts available were fairly concise.

Brooke Moore had been an eighteen-year-old high school senior. She was a cheerleader, homecoming queen, ran track and was a member of the National Honor Society—the ideal American teenager. The grainy black-and-white news photos showed her in a cheerleading costume and on prom night, on the arm of a thin, serious-faced young man who Neill could barely recognize as David Freeman. If you could believe the press, she was beloved by all her teachers, adored by her classmates, and the pride and joy of her family.

And then she disappeared.

Brooke had attended school that day, and some of her friends remembered seeing her as they left the campus. They'd offered her a lift home, but she'd told them her brother was picking her up. But he'd lost track of time and was half an hour late, and, when he got there, she was gone. Assuming she'd grown tired of waiting and had walked home, Jack had gone out for burgers with friends. Their parents had assumed that Brooke was with her brother, and it wasn't until he came home alone that anyone felt concerned.

Reading between the lines, Neill could guess that it had taken several hours for the concern to become real worry and then for the fear to come.

There would have been calls to all her friends, a check of the local hangouts—not many of those in a town the size of Loving. When that turned up blank, the fear would have begun. Some of the calls would be repeated. *Are you sure she didn't say anything about going somewhere?* Friends would be calling each other, eager to share the news that Brooke Moore was missing and where on earth could she have gone?

He imagined that, in a town like this, it would have taken awhile for the possibility of foul play to really sink in. Though it looked like the sheriff had done everything by the book, Neill was willing to bet that he'd considered it a waste of time, had been fairly sure that Brooke would turn up safe and sound sooner or later. Only as one day became two, and then three, and she was still missing, would local law enforcement have absorbed the fact that they might be dealing with a serious crime. In a big city, that would have been not only the first thing they thought of but the first thing they believed. But in a town this size, where everyone pretty well knew everyone else, major crime was fairly rare. Stolen cars, an occasional robbery, domestic violence—those were the big crimes in a town like Loving.

It was almost two weeks before there were any leads. Neill's stomach rolled as he read the account. A farmer had stopped to repair a flat tire on a road about two miles out of town and had found a girl's hand lying in the ditch. After he finished losing his lunch, he left the flat tire to mark the spot and drove straight to the sheriff's office. Brooke's father identified the hand by the ring his daughter had worn.

If they'd been clinging to any hope of seeing their daughter alive again, it must have disappeared then. It was two days before they found the next piece of her, about a mile from where the hand had been. After that, it was a matter of combing the roadside ditches, tracing the killer's path by the body parts he'd strewn behind him, like litter thrown from a passing car.

There was a big write-up on the funeral, which had been attended by nearly every citizen of Loving, as well as by press from every major wire service. Neill squinted at a fuzzy picture of the bereaved family and wondered if he was reading too much into the fact that they stood without touching each other—Olivia in a simple black dress, her spine rigid, her face absolutely still, her husband standing slumped next to her, head down, expression hidden. A younger, slighter Jack, his fair hair falling over his forehead, his face holding the blank emptiness of someone in shock.

And a ten-year-old Anne, standing at her brother's side, her eyes huge and bewildered, thin little legs sticking out from beneath the hem of a black dress. He wondered if Olivia had gone shopping for proper mourning clothes and then thought perhaps he was doing her an injustice. She seemed to be an ice-cold bitch now, but maybe Brooke's death was largely to blame for that.

The remaining clippings talked about the ongoing investigation, which had gotten nowhere. According to the police, aside from the body itself, they had nothing to go on. No one had seen anything. No one had noticed any strangers in town. They questioned everyone who knew her, but no one seemed to have a motive. Annoyance over being beaten out for Homecoming Queen rarely resulted in dismemberment.

The gaps between the clippings grew wider, until a little over a year later, when there was a flurry of new information over a murder with a similar m.o. in Oklahoma. The FBI was called in, and there was speculation that both killings were the work of a serial killer. But if they had been, he hadn't killed again—or his victims hadn't been found—and Brooke's death became another unsolved crime, the case file officially open but unofficially dropped, because the police had nowhere to go with it.

Neill sat, staring at nothing, his hand on the closed notebook. It explained a lot, of course. Anne's reaction to the attempted mugging, her near hysteria over the thought of having people looking at her, remembering. He could guess what it had been like for her. *That's the murdered girl's sister, you know. Wonder how the family is holding up? Wonder if she knows what happened, poor thing.* Most of it wouldn't have been intended unkindly, but for a sensitive little girl to suddenly find herself the cynosure of all eyes must have been painful.

Had her family understood that, in some ways, her sister's death had been hardest on her? Or had they been so absorbed in their own pain that they hadn't recognized hers?

And how was she going to react when she found out that he wasn't a struggling freelance writer but had instead made his name—and a considerable amount of money—writing books about exactly the kind of thing her family had gone through?

\* \* \*

She should have felt awkward, Anne thought, as she exchanged greetings with the bank's other employees. After the emotional storm she had gone through the night before, she should have cringed at the thought of seeing Neill again. She should have been so embarrassed by her own loss of control that she couldn't bear to speak to him, she decided, as she put her purse in the bottom desk drawer and booted up her computer. She'd sobbed in his arms like a frightened child, allowed him to see the fear she barely allowed herself to acknowledge. Then she'd all but propositioned the man, telling him that he didn't have to sleep on the sofa, inviting him into her bed. And he'd turned her down.

Oh, but the way he'd turned her down. *When we become lovers, I don't want any gratitude in the mix.* When. Not "if" but "when."

Anne's mouth curved in a secret half smile. She supposed there were women who would be offended by the arrogance of that statement, but she wasn't one of them. To her, it had been reassuring. He wanted her. He'd said so. And he cared about her, because, if he hadn't, he would have taken her up on her invitation instead of spending what she was sure must have been a mostly sleepless night on a sofa that was a good foot shorter than he was. So it was more than just desire on his part. And, heaven knew, it was so much more than that on her side. Just how much more was something she shied away from defining, even to herself.

She was half in love with him—maybe more than half. It didn't matter that she'd only known him a matter of days. She'd always pictured herself slipping slowly into love—a long, leisurely process of getting to know someone, finding out their likes and dislikes, learning their goals and dreams. In her mind, she'd seen it as if through a camera lens coated with petroleum jelly, a little out of focus, violins playing in the background—everything soft and gentle.

She hadn't expected to feel the flare of lights and colors when Neill kissed her; had never imagined the sharp bite of hunger she felt when he touched her. There was nothing soft and dreamy about what had happened between them. It was bright and brassy. Edgy and needy. Elemental and irresistible. And, for once in her cautious, safe little life, she wasn't going to try to resist.

*When we become lovers.*

Oh yes, she definitely liked the sound of that.

\* \* \*

Most days Anne's job was not particularly demanding, and this day was no different. It gave her time to think, and what she thought about was Neill. At one point she actually caught herself staring into space, fingers lax on the keyboard, her mouth curved in what she suspected was a sappy smile. Twice Marge stopped by her desk to ask her if she was feeling all right.

"'Cause you looked like you were somewhere else just now. And that's the third time today that you've watered that philodendron over by the window. One more time and the poor thing's going to float right off. And that's the second set of loan docs that you've passed on for approval with nothing but the customer's name filled out."

"I'm sorry." Anne flushed and took the paperwork from the older woman. "I guess my mind's wandering a little today."

"Well, it happens to the best of us." Marge's exasperation shifted to curiosity. "Any particular direction it's wandering? In my experience, when a woman can't think straight, more often than not it's because she's thinking about a man. I know a lot of people would call that old-fashioned nonsense, but the world hasn't changed that much since I was a girl, and there's still nothing like a man for scattering a woman's thoughts.''

"You're right, it *is* old-fashioned nonsense." Anne's smile took any possible sting out of the words. "I'm just feeling absentminded today. That's all."

"If you say so," Marge said, without any pretense of belief. She looked past Anne and smiled. "Of course, if it did happen to be a man you were thinking about, might be you're going to get a chance to talk to him."

*Neill.* Anne turned quickly, her heart fluttering in anticipation. Then had to struggle to hide her disappointment when she saw Frank Miller approaching the low rail. Frank. She'd known him all her life, had had dinner with him just a few days ago, but it seemed almost an effort to remember his name. She hadn't given him so much as a thought since that tepid kiss on her front porch on Friday night.

"Anne. Marge." He nodded to both of them.

"Hey, Frank." Marge's smile was friendly. "How's your mom doing these days? Didn't see her in church on Sunday."

"She's fine. Caught a bit of a cold. Nothing serious, but she's got a sore throat and a bit of a cough, and she decided not to risk a coughing fit in the middle of the sermon.''

"Honey and lemon in a little hot water," Marge suggested. "Best thing for a sore throat."

"I'll pass that along." Frank shifted his eyes to Anne, who still hadn't said a word. "I was wondering when you might be taking a break."

It didn't take a mind reader to guess what he wanted to talk to her about, Anne thought. Some helpful soul was sure to have mentioned seeing her with Neill. She had to squash a quick surge of guilt. They'd never made any promises to each other, she reminded herself. They weren't engaged, or even engaged to be engaged.

"Why don't you take your break now, Anne?" Marge said, a plump, smiling matchmaker in a blue-striped dress.

"I...thanks." Anne saved her work then started the screen saver, waited to see the slowly changing kaleidoscopic pattern begin and then pushed her chair back.

Ever polite, Frank moved to open the little gate for her, and she smiled a thank-you and stepped through. She could feel Marge's speculative look boring into her back.

"I thought we could sit in the patrol car and talk

for a minute, if that's all right," Frank said, pushing open the bank's outer door for her.

"As long as you don't make me sit in the backseat behind the mesh window," Anne said, trying for a touch of lightness, but one thing about Frank, he didn't have much of a sense of humor, even on a good day.

"The front seat will do just fine," he said seriously.

The cooling effect of the previous night's rain had burned off before noon, and Loving steamed gently under a cloudless blue sky. Frank opened the passenger door for her and then went around the front of the car, sliding beneath the wheel and starting the engine so that the air-conditioning would kick in.

"I wanted to talk to you about Friday night," Frank said.

"Frank, I—" Anne stopped, swallowed and stared down at her hands, which lay clasped together in her lap. She liked Frank. She didn't love him, but he was a good man, and she didn't want to hurt him. Drawing a deep breath, she lifted her eyes to his. "I don't think we should see each other anymore. At least, not the way we have been. It's not...going to take us anywhere."

If her words had any impact, she couldn't tell it by looking at him. He continued to regard her with the same calm, steady gaze he always did. And, just like always, he was in no hurry to say whatever was on his mind. Waiting, Anne found herself acutely aware of the muted hiss of the air-conditioning. People were walking past on the sidewalk, some of them eyeing the patrol car curiously.

"Is it this guy with the motorcycle? The one who's supposed to be a writer?" There was no accusation in his tone. She wasn't even sure there was curiosity.

"If you're asking if I've gone out with him, I'm sure you know the answer is yes. If you're asking if that's why I think we shouldn't date anymore, the answer is no. Neill may have been the catalyst," she added honestly. "But I've known for a long time that you and I..." She trailed off, groping for something that was honest without being hurtful. "I just don't feel for you all the things you deserve a woman to feel."

"That sort of thing grows with time."

*Or it springs up overnight.*

But she didn't say that. She wasn't sure what Frank felt for her. That was one of the problems: she'd never been sure what Frank felt about anything—or even *if* he felt anything. But, if his emotions were involved, then she didn't want to hurt him any more than she had to.

"I'm sure they can grow with time," she said honestly. "But there has to be something there to get them started—a spark, at least—and, much as I like you, I just don't feel that spark."

"That's honest enough." Frank looked away from her for a moment, and when he looked back, there was concern in his eyes—one of the few times she'd been able to read what he was feeling. "This guy is just passing through, Anne. From what I hear, he'll be hitting the road as soon as David gets the parts for that bike of his. I'd hate to see you get hurt."

"I won't be," she said, and hoped it was the truth.

He nodded. "Well, it's your business." The brief flicker of emotion was gone, and Anne wondered if she'd imagined it.

There was another short silence, this one awkward and stiff. She'd never broken up with anyone before. Was there a certain length of time you were both supposed to sit, perhaps contemplating what might have been? Was there a protocol to cover who was supposed to make the first move?

"I guess I'd better get back to work," she said finally, when the silence threatened to become unbearable. She reached for the door handle. "I...I'll see you around."

"Sure." He nodded but didn't look at her, and she slipped gratefully out of the cool car and into the steamy heat outside.

By the time she stepped onto the sidewalk, Frank was backing away from the curb. She turned to watch as he drove away and hoped she hadn't hurt anything more than his pride. But she'd done the right thing. Whatever happened between her and Neill, there was no chance of anything ever happening between her and Frank Miller.

"Oh!" Turning, she nearly walked straight into the man who'd been standing behind her. "Neill."

"That wasn't your brother," he said, his eyes on the patrol car.

"No. That was Frank Miller. He and I have...um...we've gone out a few times." She wasn't sure why she felt the necessity of offering an explanation.

"Should I be jealous?" His eyes, a sharp, questioning blue, cut to hers.

"Would you be?" she asked, and then caught her breath at the lightning-edged expression that flashed in his eyes. It was gone in an instant, and he was smiling, but, for a moment, there had been something dangerous there, something that, God help her, sent a shivery little thrill down her spine.

"Frank and I are just friends," she said breathlessly. Later she would allow herself time to consider the idea that she could make a man like this feel jealous. No doubt it was completely shameless of her, but it was a thought she had every intention of savoring.

"Friends are a good thing," Neill said. He brushed a loose tendril of hair back from her forehead. He lingered to let his fingers trail over her cheek. "I came by to see how you were feeling."

"Fine. I'm just fine." Unless you counted the fact that her knees were melting and her pulse was beating double time.

"Good." His thumb stroked across her lips, and Anne barely restrained the urge to open her mouth and draw it inside. "Come to Chicago with me."

It took a moment for the words to register. When they did, her eyes widened. "What?"

"Come to Chicago with me for the weekend. This weekend. We'll have dinner, maybe take in a show. My brother has a restaurant there. I can probably con him into feeding us at least once. If you can get off early on Friday, we can drive up Friday afternoon, come back Sunday afternoon. I'll get—''

''Yes.'' Anne didn't have to think about it. It was probably crazy to agree to spend the weekend with a man she'd known less than two weeks.

A cautious woman would take a little more time, not make any hasty decisions. But she knew from experience that cautious women led very dull lives. This one time, she was going to take a chance, ignore common sense and listen to her heart.

# Chapter Ten

Anne estimated that the hotel lobby must have contained at least an acre of plush blue carpeting. The expanse was broken up by cozy seating areas and potted plants. Over the murmur of hotel guests—arriving, leaving or just people-watching—was the muted splash of a fountain, complete with palm trees and pond. It was like walking into a movie set, and she found herself gawking shamelessly, wanting to see everything at once.

Seeing her wide-eyed pleasure, Neill chuckled, but he was aware of a slow-burning anger at the thought that she'd lived her whole life just a few hours away, yet this was the first time she'd made the trip into the city. If she'd had no interest, that would have been one thing. But the open delight she took in everything she saw, her fascination with things that should have been commonplace, left him torn between anger that her life had been so restricted and a guilty pleasure that he was the one to show her what she'd been missing.

He'd brought her here because he'd been sure she would enjoy it, but also because he thought it might be a good idea to be on neutral ground when he told her that he knew about Brooke and explained that his career was not exactly what she thought it was.

He'd spent the last two days convincing himself that there was nothing to worry about. Anne might be annoyed, maybe a little hurt—and he would much rather face the former than deal with the latter—but it wasn't as if he'd lied to her. Exactly. And what had happened to her sister was public information, so he hadn't pried into any secrets. Exactly.

So he'd brought her to the big city to dazzle her with the sights, take her to a fine restaurant, maybe ply her with a glass or two of wine, before making his confession. It was a little depressing to realize that he'd become such a manipulative bastard, he thought with a faint sigh for ethics churned to dust by need.

When she'd seen the quality of the hotel Neill had chosen, Anne had thought it was sweet that he was going to so much trouble to make the weekend special. She assumed he'd gotten one of the least expensive rooms and hoped he wasn't straining his finances too far. As they rode up in the elevator, she worried her lower lip with her teeth and wondered if she dared offer to split the expenses with him, but, even with her limited experience, something told her he wouldn't be open to that particular suggestion.

When the elevator doors opened and they stepped into a small lobby to be greeted by a smiling middle-aged man, she was mildly surprised, but she'd never stayed in a hotel and thought that perhaps, in a place like this, someone was assigned to greet guests on every floor. Even if she'd noticed the discreet brass plaque that said Concierge Level, it wouldn't have meant anything to her.

But it didn't take a seasoned traveler to recognize the luxury of the room Neill was ushering her into. Thick, pearl gray carpeting, royal blue drapes, two sofas, one upholstered in a rich floral, the other in a two-tone blue stripe. A wet bar, tasteful prints on the wall, an exquisite mixed bouquet on the table next to one of the sofas, and a second open door across the room, through which she could glimpse the corner of a bed. Not a room but a suite.

"I made reservations for an early dinner," Neill said, crossing the room to pull open the drapes and reveal a spectacular view of Lake Michigan.

Feeling as if she were caught in a dream, Anne walked to the window and looked out. Spread out below them, the city was painted in twilight shades of gray and gold. She'd never been so high before, and, for an instant, she felt a little dizzy. Or maybe it was the shock of finding herself here.

Turning slowly, she surveyed the room again. She couldn't even begin to guess what a suite like this must cost, but she knew it had to be a lot. When he'd asked her to come away with him for the weekend, she'd thought she knew what to expect. That they would become lovers was a given. If she'd given any thought to the setting, she would have guessed that Neill would choose it carefully. But this... She'd never pictured anything like this.

Watching her, Neill recognized her hesitation but mistook the cause.

"If you don't like the room, we can get something else—or go to another hotel, for that matter."

"Of course I like it. It's gorgeous." She waved one hand to encompass the luxurious setting. "It's like something out of one of Dorothy's old movies. How could I *not* like it? It's just that—" She stared at him helplessly for a moment and then decided that there was simply no tactful way to say it. "It must be costing a fortune and I don't...can you afford this?"

She was worried that he was spending more than he could afford. The realization brought a mixture of pleasure and guilt that was rapidly becoming familiar. Pleasure that she was concerned for his financial state and guilt that he'd left her with the impression that there was reason to be concerned.

*Tell her,* his conscience whispered. But he wanted to have at least this one evening with her. There was always the chance that she would be so angered by his tacit deception that she would walk out without giving him a chance to explain, which might be just as well, he thought ruefully, since he wasn't sure he had a good explanation to offer.

"I didn't think you'd mind washing a few dishes to pay for our room and board," he said lightly. She smiled, but the worry remained in her eyes, and Neill reached out to catch her hand, tugging her closer. ''A couple of nights in a fancy hotel isn't going to bankrupt me, honey. I don't exactly lead an extravagant lifestyle.''

That was true enough, he consoled himself as he saw her worried look ease.

''If you're sure.'' She looked up. ''You don't have to do this for me,'' she said shyly.

Had he thought he was sliding into love? Neill wondered. He was all the way there. Looking into Anne's big gray eyes, he thought maybe he'd fallen that first day when she'd stood there, next to that ridiculous little car of hers, and looked at him like she half expected him to pounce at any moment. He'd wanted to pounce. He'd wanted it then, and he wanted it now.

Taking a tight hold on his self-control, he lowered his head, taking her mouth in a long, drugging kiss that left her weak and clinging to his shoulders. For a moment he considered consigning their dinner reservations to hell and taking her to bed. But that wasn't the way he wanted to do things. Slow and easy, he reminded himself. This was more than a weekend fling. So much more that it scared him to think about it.

\* \* \*

It was a magical evening. The restaurant, with its white tablecloths, heavy flatware and delicate glasses, was a masterpiece of elegant understatement. At Neill's insistence, she ordered lobster. It was wonderful. And the wine was wonderful, and looking out over the waters of Lake Michigan was wonderful. Even the waiter was wonderful. But she knew the evening would have been just as wonderful if he'd taken her out for a burger and fries. It wasn't the food or the setting that made everything special. It was Neill.

She'd been lying to herself when she said she was halfway in love with him, she admitted as she sipped the delicate white wine. She was head over heels, all the way gone, heart on her sleeve in love with him. There were even moments—when he smiled at her, or kissed her with such melting tenderness—when she could almost believe he might feel the same.

And if he didn't...well, she would worry about that when the time came. She'd spent her whole life being cautious. For once—for this single weekend—she was going to live without counting the possible cost.

After dinner he took her to the Hancock Observatory, informing her as they reached the viewing platform that she was now some ninety-four stories and over one thousand feet above the ground. His pedantic, bored-tour-guide tone made her laugh, but the spectacular view of the city stretching away on every side took her breath away.

"It's beautiful," she murmured, her eyes dazzled.

"Not half as beautiful as you are." And pulling her into his arms, he kissed her until the city's twinkling lights seemed to dip and sway around her.

It was late when they returned to their hotel. Riding up in the elevator with Neill, Anne had the same delicious, floaty sensation she remembered from the one time she'd had too much to drink. But it wasn't the single glass of wine she'd had with dinner that made her feel that way, it was the man standing next to her, the man who was about to become her lover. And wasn't that a wonderful, powerful word?

By the time Neill was pushing open the door, shepherding her inside, he was aching with the need to touch her. Taste her. The kisses they'd shared, the casual little touches throughout the evening, had left him edgy with a lust that couldn't quite block out the jitter of nerves. This mattered. What happened here, tonight, with this woman was important. Important enough that he could wait.

He watched her walk into the middle of the room, then turn to look at him questioningly, and thought he'd never seen anything more beautiful than the way she looked in that simple black dress, those long legs encased in sheer black stockings, her dark gold hair caught up on top of her head in a soft twist that made his fingers twitch with the urge to pull the pins loose and watch it tumble around her face. He drew a deep breath.

"There's no obligation here, Anne. If this isn't what you want, you only have to say so."

She tilted her head curiously, attentively. "And you won't mind sleeping on the sofa?"

"I won't mind," he lied steadily.

She brushed her fingers absently along the dress's neckline, and Neill's mouth went dry as he followed the movement. "You mean I can sleep in there alone and you'll sleep out here alone?"

*Was she trying to kill him?* Her fingers slid over the soft upper swell of her breast.

"Yes. Alone." God, she'd reduced him to speaking in one-syllable sentences. Another few minutes and he would be down to inarticulate whimpers.

She let her hand fall to her side and watched him silently for a moment, then slowly—deliberately, damn her—ran her tongue over her upper lip. "Do you know what I have on under this dress?"

"W-what?" His voice stumbled, nearly cracked in a way it hadn't done in twenty years.

She pouted. "I bought some fancy lingerie out of a catalog last year. It promised to make me irresistible."

"Did...did it?"

"They guaranteed it." She slanted him a look that was pure invitation, then turned toward the bedroom. "Maybe I should return it and get my money back?"

He would not pant. Not yet. He wasn't going to drag her to the floor and ravish her, either. Not this first time. He had enough control to follow her into the bedroom without howling with pure lust. He was nearly sure of it.

Anne stopped next to the bed and linked her hands together. The courage that had been so easy to find a moment ago was suddenly shaky. She couldn't believe she'd offered such a bold invitation, didn't know where the words had come from.

She'd never played the part of a seductress. But something in the way Neill had stood there, his eyes all but burning with hunger even as he offered to let her sleep alone, had made something fierce and feminine well up inside her.

But now, here she stood, next to the bed, and she was suddenly acutely aware of the fact that he was very large and very male, and, while she wasn't afraid of him—could never be afraid of him—she was just a little nervous about what was going to happen next. Not afraid, because she knew how it worked. You didn't have to have actual experience to know what went where, but there was, she admitted reluctantly, a bit of a gap between knowing and *knowing*. She wanted Neill to help her close that gap but still...now that the moment had arrived, she was just a little uneasy.

And then she looked over her shoulder at him, saw not just hunger but a need that burned right through to her soul, and an answering need surged up inside her, swallowing the fear and nerves and giving her a slightly shaky courage.

"If you could help me with the zipper," she murmured, turning her back.

The zipper slid slowly down her spine, and she felt the brush of Neill's fingers every inch of the way. When it stopped, she could only stand there, breathing a little too quickly, wondering what she should do now. He had to know she wanted this. Wanted him. She couldn't have made it any plainer. Maybe she should lower the hand she had pressed to her chest, let the dress fall, but her courage was slipping away again.

And then she felt his breath on her skin, warm and moist. She closed her eyes on a shiver as he pressed slow, lingering kisses across her shoulders, then began working his way down her spine. Shuddering, she barely noticed when he eased the dress over her shoulders, tugging at the slim skirt until it fell away from her body, dropping to the floor. She turned blindly, obediently, in response to his hands, holding her arms stiff at her sides as she faced him.

"Jesus." The word was half prayer, half plea for mercy. "Are you trying to kill me?" he asked on a pained laugh.

"What?" Surprised by his laughter, her eyes flicked open.

"This is the kind of stuff that should be a registered weapon," he muttered as all the blood left his head and went straight to his loins. The black lace bra barely covered her nipples, and he'd seen postage stamps that covered more than the matching panties. But with them… God, with them, she was wearing a lacy garter belt to hold up cobweb-fine black stockings. And then she stood there looking at him, her pretty gray eyes full of nerves and need, and he was fairly sure that his heart was going to slam its way right out of his chest.

He flicked open the front clasp on the bra and watched the cups slide over her pale skin, stopping at the last minute, caught on the taut peaks of her nipples.

"Neill…Neill?" Her voice cracked when he traced the tip of one finger over the fine tracery of blue veins on the inside curve of her breast. "I've never done this before," she blurted.

His hand stilled, and he lifted his eyes to her face. She looked half-guilty, as if she were confessing to a crime. And half-scared, as if she wasn't quite sure how she'd come to be where she was.

"I know you haven't." He thought he'd known from the first time he kissed her, or maybe it was the innocence shining in her eyes. Whatever it was, he'd known all along, and, God help him, it only made him want her more. "We can stop if you want."

"I don't." She drew a shaky breath, and his

mouth went dry when the movement shifted the bra another half inch to the side, baring the delicate rosy circle of her aureole.

"I won't hurt you."

"I know." Her eyes still on his face, she reached up to slide the bra straps from her shoulders, letting it fall to the floor behind her. Her cheeks were flushed, but her eyes remained steady. "I want this."

She reached for the buttons on his shirt, but he caught her hands and pulled them away. If she touched him, he thought he just might explode.

"I want to see you," she said.

"There's time. All the time in the world."

"But I…" Anne's protest died on a whimper as he filled his hands with her breasts, stroking his thumbs over her nipples. She shuddered at this first touch of a man's hands on her body, felt her knees weaken as he bent to catch one taut peak in his mouth, laving, stroking, then suckling strongly. The pull of his mouth on her breast set off shock waves deep inside, making her press her thighs together in a vain attempt to ease the sudden ache there.

Neill told himself to go slow. He was the first. If he had his way, he would be the only. There was time, he'd told her. But he'd never wanted like this, never had to have. Had to have. She was so warm. So responsive. And his. Only his.

He eased her back on the bed, pausing long enough to jerk his shirt off, still in control enough to leave his jeans on, not sure how long he would be able to hold off without that barrier. And then he was stroking her. Touching. And every place he brushed seemed to catch fire.

He slid his hands over the quivering muscles of her belly, sliding his finger through the nest of soft curls at the top of her thighs, feeling her jolt as he cupped his palm over her, found her all sleek heat and moisture. Soon, he thought, his heart hammering against his breastbone. Soon. But not quite yet. Not. Quite. Ah, there. He moved his hand on her with wicked knowledge, watching her face as her eyes went blind, the breath shuddering in and out of her.

"Please. I don't— I can't—" Her hands came up, her fingernails biting into his shoulders as her body arched, trembling, caught on the sharp pinnacle.

"Let go, sweetheart. I want to watch you go over." He slid one long finger into her, at the same time brushing his thumb over the swollen nub of flesh at the top of her sex.

Her breath exploded from her on a sob as she shattered. He could feel the delicate contractions grip his finger, and he thought he'd never felt anything more exquisite. And if he didn't have her now, he was going to die.

Limp and trembling, Anne watched through dazed eyes as he rose and stripped off his jeans, his movements quick and almost clumsy. He was beautiful, she thought. His chest was broad, the muscles rippling as he shoved his jeans over his thighs. Her eyes followed that tantalizing line of dark hair as it arrowed across the washboard flatness of his stomach to join the swirling mat of hair at his loins.

Her eyes widened a little as she stared at his erection. She'd seen naked men in magazines, but nothing could have prepared her for this first sight of a fully aroused man. Neill had one knee braced on the bed, but he stopped when he saw her looking at him. He waited, wondering if she was going to change her mind, wondering if he would lose his if she did.

Then she lifted her hand and touched him, her fingertips featherlight as they trailed from base to tip and back again. Neill's teeth ground together in a desperate bid for control. He didn't want to do anything to startle her, but he was starting to think she really might be the death of him. His head fell back, his breath leaving him on a groan when her hand closed around him, testing, stroking in a way that had need clawing like daggers in his chest.

"Later," he growled, catching her hand and drawing it away from his straining flesh.

He came down onto the bed next to her, and she could feel him all along her side, his skin fever warm, his body so much harder than hers. She hadn't thought she could respond again so soon, but he was touching her, stroking, teasing, and she could feel the hunger rising again, drawing her upward, pressing her against him. She heard herself whimpering, pleading, and then he was over her, his legs sliding heavy between hers, and she was arching to meet him. Wanting. Needing.

His pulse drumming in his ears, his muscles tight with control, Neill fought the urge to drive himself into her. Her first time, he reminded himself, and felt his blood sizzle at the thought. He pressed forward, finding the slick heat of her, easing inward, testing.

"Hold on," he murmured, and bent to take her mouth even as he took her body.

There was heat, an instant of resistance, and then he was sheathed in the damp velvet warmth of her and it was better than his darkest fantasy. He pressed his forehead to hers, his muscles screaming as he struggled to give her the time she needed to accept his invasion.

Anne held herself very still beneath him. She'd thought she knew what to expect, but knowing the mechanics of it didn't tell her what it felt like to share her body with a man. There had been pain, but that had been gone in an instant. What she was left with was an aching sense of being filled, stretched almost beyond bearing, and yet there was a sense of satisfaction in the filling, a need at least partially fulfilled.

Experimentally, she contracted the muscles that held him and felt a surge of purely feminine triumph when Neill groaned. There was power in being wanted this much, a dark, primal thrill in knowing she could make him tremble. She rocked her hips, taking him deeper, urging him, wanting...more. And then he was moving on her, his hips easing back, sliding forward, back and forward, the rhythm increasing as the pressure built within her, within him.

Anne whimpered, her head tossing back and forth on the pillow as the tension grew, more powerful than it had been before. She arched to meet each powerful thrust, wanting more, her body stretched as if on a rack, needs and hunger swirling within her, driving her.

Neill wrapped his fist around her hair, stopping the restless movement of her head, pinning her with the feverish blue of his eyes.

"Look at me." He shifted the angle of his thrusts so that each stroke rubbed across the tiny knot of nerves he'd touched before. There was an instant when the tension was nearly unbearable, and then it shattered, taking her with it. She heard him groan, a harsh, guttural sound torn from his throat, and then he was shuddering in her arms.

A very long time later, his face still buried in her hair, his breathing ragged, Neill said her name.

"Anne?"

"Hmm?"

"I don't think you should ask for your money back on that fancy underwear."

And that was another thing she hadn't known— that laughter could be a part of the mix.

## Chapter Eleven

Anne came awake slowly. The first thing she noticed was that she was too warm, and she frowned fretfully at the weight of the covers around her waist and hips. Why on earth would she have piled so many covers on the bed in the middle of summer? Barely awake, she moved to push them away, but what she touched wasn't soft linen and wool but warm, hard muscle and sinew. Memory rolled over her in a wave, her breath rushing out as her eyes flew open to stare at an unfamiliar ceiling.

Neill. She was with Neill, in Chicago, in the suite he'd brought her to the day before, in the bed where he'd made love to her the night before. Several times. Cautiously, half-afraid she might have dreamed it all, she turned her head on the pillow. He was sleeping on his side, one arm thrown across her stomach, one leg resting between hers with a casual intimacy that made her flush with pleasure and a touch of embarrassment.

Not that she had any business feeling embarrassed after the night just past, she thought, her flush deepening as the memories rushed over her, warming her skin. It seemed incredible that a man like this could want her so much, but she'd had unmistakable proof in the way he'd reached for her again and again during the night. The last time had been somewhere near dawn, because she remembered the pearl gray light seeping through the windows, shadowing his face as he moved above her, the newly familiar weight of him pressing her gently back into the yielding mattress as he loved her with long, slow strokes that seemed to reach all the way to her soul, making it last until she was clinging to him with damp hands, his name leaving her on a sob as he took her over the edge, burying his face in her hair as he fell with her.

Oh yes, he definitely wanted her.

She smiled at the thought, a small, feline curve of her lips. So this was the morning after. She'd always wondered what it would be like to wake up in a man's arms, to know herself wanted. Now she knew, and it felt simply incredible. Her skin felt sensitized, as if his touch had brought new nerve endings to life. There was a delicious tenderness in her breasts and between her thighs. With every breath, she could smell the warm, musky scent of sex, a scent she knew on some primal level.

Her fingers moved gently on Neill's arm. She felt different, not just physically, but within herself. She felt...womanly. Her smile took on a sheepish edge. It seemed a ridiculously old-fashioned idea, like something out of an old novel where the heroine loses her virginity and suddenly, in an amazing transformation, changes overnight from girl to woman. But it wasn't the loss of her virginity that made her feel different. It was what this weekend represented. She'd finally stepped outside the cushioned box in which she'd spent most of her life. She was taking a chance, actually having a life. It was a heady thought.

Neill stirred beside her, and all her newfound courage vanished in a flash. A giddy wave of panic surged through her at the thought of facing those clear blue eyes this morning. Cautiously, she eased her way out from under the weight of his arm and leg, sliding toward the edge of the bed. She started to swing her legs over the edge of the bed, only to feel a hard arm slide around her waist and drag her back to land against the pillows in a flushed heap.

Sleepy, sapphire eyes smiled down at her. His voice was a husky rasp. "Where were you sneaking off to?"

"I...um...just to...I wasn't sneaking," she lied, staring at his collarbone. It had been easy to be bold last night, riding high on his kisses and maybe just a little on the wine, knowing she looked her best. It was something else altogether this morning, with the memories of the night just past tumbling through her brain and both of them naked in the sunlight that spilled through the curtains that neither of them had thought to pull.

"You were definitely sneaking," he accused. He lowered his head to nuzzle her neck. His jaw felt rough against her tender skin, a new, unfamiliar intimacy that sent a shiver up her spine. "Sneaking is a punishable crime in Chicago."

"Is it?" He was nibbling his way down her throat, sending every logical thought spinning out of her head. "Don't I...oh!" Her back arched as his mouth slid across her breast, his tongue swirling over her nipple. "Isn't there some sort of trial?" she got out breathlessly.

"In the case of sneaking, the victim gets to hand out whatever he feels is a fitting punishment." Neill's tongue probed the shallow indentation of her belly button, his mouth curving against her skin as he felt her arch, her legs parting in unconscious invitation. She was so incredibly responsive— warm and trembling and his. Only his. After the night they'd just shared, it hardly seemed possible, but he was as hard as if he'd never touched her, every muscle quivering with the need to have her again.

"What...what sort of punishment?"

"This," he whispered, lowering his head to taste her sweet, moist flesh. She jerked in shock, her breath exploding from her.

"Oh my God! Neill, you—" Her fingers slid into his hair, tensed as if to pull him away, but he lifted her, opening her more fully, his tongue stabbing into her, and her hands dropped away in mute surrender.

By the time he gave in to the howling demands of his own flesh and slid up her body, Anne was limp and trembling beneath him. Her big gray eyes held a glazed look as he positioned himself against her, entering the first tiny bit and then stopping long enough to wrap his hand in her hair, holding her eyes as he thrust his aching hardness into the yielding warmth of her.

"Mine," he whispered gutturally and bent to kiss her, letting her taste herself on his mouth as he drove her ruthlessly to climax.

It seemed a long time later when he summoned every ounce of strength left in him to roll to the side. She was definitely going to be the death of him, he decided, listening to the ragged sound of his own breathing. But what a hell of a way to go.

"If that's what I got for just *trying* to sneak out of bed," she said huskily, "I can't wait to see what happens if I actually make it out of the room."

Laughing a little shakily, Neill pulled her close against his side. "Don't make me get tough with you. At least, not until I've had time to recover."

They ordered lunch from room service. Neill grinned at Anne's obvious delight in having a white-clothed table rolled into the room with everything covered by silver-domed lids. He'd spent enough time in hotel rooms that he took such things for granted, but her pleasure made him remember the publicity tour for his first book and the wonderful novelty of having a black-jacketed waiter bring breakfast to his room.

After lunch, he resisted the urge to take her back to bed and swept her out to see something of the city. The weather was in a cooperative mood. It was summer, which meant heat, but the humidity was down and clear blue skies arched over the city.

He took her to the Miracle Mile, where they window shopped, along with hordes of tourists and residents. He bought her a bumper sticker that said ''I Love Chicago'' and a tacky plastic figure, purporting to represent Mrs. O'Leary's cow, presumably in the days before it kicked over the lamp that started the Great Chicago Fire. He saw a dozen other things he wanted to buy her—a dress she admired, a diamond bracelet that made her sigh— but, even if she would have accepted them, expensive gifts would mean explanations, and that was the last thing he wanted.

Sometime during the night, he'd decided that explanations could wait. It might have been when she'd told him she was wearing lingerie that came with a guarantee. Or maybe it was before that, when they'd stood suspended high over the city and he'd kissed her. Or maybe he'd never really intended to make explanations until the weekend was over. He was no longer sure what his thinking had been, and it didn't really matter. He didn't really care about anything right now except seeing the happy glow in Anne's eyes. The real world would simply have to wait a day or two.

Neill didn't tell Anne that they were having dinner at his brother's restaurant until he was pulling the Vette into a parking place marked Employees Only.

"I knew parking would be at a premium on Saturday night," he explained as he handed her out of the low-slung car. "But Tony promised not to have the car towed."

"I didn't expect to be meeting your family," Anne said, hanging back.

"Just my brother." He tugged on her hand. "If it was going to be the whole bunch, I'd have provided you with earplugs. We tend to be a little noisy when we get together."

"I didn't really dress for meeting people," she said uneasily. The thought of meeting Neill's family, even if it was just one member, had nerves fluttering in the pit of her stomach.

"You look great," he assured her truthfully. The apricot-colored dress, with its nipped-in waist and gentle scooped neckline, suited her. She'd pulled her hair up into a soft knot, leaving little curls free to tease the nape of her neck. It was a style that never failed to make his fingers twitch with the urge to pull the pins loose and see her hair tumble down around her face. Then again, just looking at her made him twitch with the urge to do any number of things, all of them highly unsuitable at the moment. "You'll like Tony and his family."

"I'm sure they're very nice." But she still hung back, eyeing the building nervously.

"You owe me," Neill said. "I ate dinner with your parents and survived to tell the tale."

Reluctantly, Anne let him pull her forward. She could only hope that his brother wasn't as intimidating as her mother.

The sign on the restaurant read "Devlin's" in neat black script. The interior was rough-cut wood and sawdust on the floor, but there were fresh flowers on every table, and the wait staff wore trim black trousers and crisp white shirts. It was an interesting mix of café casual and understated elegance. Judging by the fact that almost every table was full, Anne assumed that business was good.

When Neill gave his name to the girl standing behind the wooden podium near the front door, she smiled and immediately led them to a table near the kitchen door.

"Most popular table in the house," she said, running an expert eye over it to make sure everything was as it should be. "Tony had us hold it for you. I'll let him know you're here."

As they sat down, Anne gave Neill a questioning look. "Since when is a table right next to the kitchen the most popular one in the house?"

"Since you're eating at Devlin's." He pulled a long bread stick from the glass in the middle of the table, broke it in half and handed one half to her. "People don't just come here because the food's great, which it is. They come here because Tony makes them feel like their presence was the one thing he needed to make his life perfect. He makes it a point to leave the kitchen and meet the customers, talk to them about what they like, what they don't like, ask how their grandmother in Cleveland is doing and how does their daughter like the new school. He has an incredible memory, and he never forgets a face.

"This table is the best in the house because he always stops here, and, if he's working out a new dish, there's a pretty good chance that, whoever is sitting here is going to get to sample it and offer comments. Not that he pays any attention to what they say," he added with a grin. "When it comes to his food, Tony doesn't listen to anyone but himself, but it makes people feel like they're a part of things, like they're—"

"Family," Anne murmured.

"Exactly."

Before he could say anything else, the kitchen door swung open and a horde of people spilled out. Grinning, Neill shot to his feet. For a few minutes all was laughter and chaos, at least to Anne's dazzled eyes, but after a bit she managed to sort the horde into three people—four if you counted the big-eyed baby perched on the woman's hip. Neill reached out to catch her hand, drawing her out of her chair.

"Come meet the guy who made my childhood a living hell."

"That's the privilege of being an older brother." Tony Devlin smiled as he said it, but the look he gave her was assessing, questioning. "Don't believe everything he tells you," he advised. "The truth is, he was always my mother's favorite, and she spoiled him hideously. I was just trying to balance things out a little."

"Jealousy rears its ugly head," Neill said, shaking his head sadly.

Anne shook hands with Tony, his wife Mary Ellen, their daughter, Sophy, who had just celebrated her fourteenth birthday the previous month, and received a toothless smile from the baby, who was six months old and named Timothy.

"We believe in spacing our children carefully," Mary Ellen said, chuckling.

It was like being swept up in a cheerful tornado. Sentences were started, interrupted and finished later without anyone ever seeming to lose track of who was saying what. By the time Tony announced that he had to get back to the kitchen or risk ruining his business, Anne's head was spinning with a whirlwind of impressions.

The two brothers shared the same coloring but not much else. Tony was shorter and stockier, the blue of his eyes was not quite as brilliant, and his features hovered between ordinary and pleasantly homely. Until he smiled. When he smiled, you couldn't help but smile back and wonder if maybe he wasn't much better looking than you'd originally thought.

His wife was comfortably forty and comfortably plump. At Neill's insistence, she and Sophy had joined them for dinner.

"Of course, if I keep eating Tony's cooking, I'm never going to lose the extra weight I put on with the baby, but I guess that's what I get for marrying a chef," she said, patting one ample hip. "Sometimes I wish I'd fallen in love with a stockbroker, but then I figure he'd probably make enough money for me to be able to afford to buy Tony's cheesecake and I'd end up fat anyway."

"And divorced," her husband said, coming up behind her in time to catch the last comment. "Because the first time I delivered a cheesecake and saw you, I'd have to steal you away from your husband."

"You don't do deliveries," Mary Ellen pointed out, tilting her head back to look up at him. "Ernie does."

"But when Ernie told me about the beautiful, lonely woman who kept ordering my cheesecake, I'd have to meet you."

"Maybe I'd end up with Ernie instead," she said haughtily.

Since Anne had already met Ernie—a painfully thin seventeen-year-old with royal blue hair, a nose ring and sticklike arms and legs that looked too long for his body—she couldn't suppress a quick snort of laughter. Neill didn't even bother trying to suppress his own laughter, and Tony grinned down at his wife.

"You see, everyone knows we were destined to be together," he told her, pressing one hand over his heart and lowering his voice to a dramatic throb. "Nothing could keep us apart. Not a stockbroker, not even Ernie, could stand between us." Grabbing her hand, he placed a passionate kiss in her palm.

"I forgot to tell you that, right after the cowboy phase, Tony joined the drama club at school," Neill said, plucking an olive from the antipasto plate. "For weeks he went around the house with a sheet draped over his shoulder, declaiming 'a rose by any other name.' Mom was impressed that he'd suddenly become interested in the arts, but what he was really interested in was getting a chance to play Romeo to Alison Sinclair's Juliet. He spent most of that school year trying to get her to notice him."

"Alison Sinclair," Tony said reminiscently. "She looked just like Marcia Brady. Half the boys in class had the hots for her."

"Da-ad." Sophy dragged the word into two syllables. "Puh-lease."

"What?" Tony arched his brows. "You don't think I should admit to having once had my heart broken by a tempestuous beauty with hair like spun gold and eyes the color of emeralds? Your mother understands and forgives me, don't you, honey?''

''Of course I do.'' Mary Ellen patted his hand absently. ''Especially since she brought her girl-friend to your high school reunion.''

Her uncle's shout of laughter nearly drowned out Sophy's agonized plea of, ''Mo-om.''

Taking pity on her, her mother handed her the baby. ''Would you take him upstairs and change him for me, sweetheart?''

''She's at that age when just having parents is humiliating,'' Mary Ellen said as Sophy disappeared up the stairs, where Tony kept his office. ''If she could, she'd stuff us in a closet and only let us out to cook meals and pay for her clothes. When her father and I told her that we were having another baby, she seemed to think it was part of a deliberate plot to humiliate her.''

''Why would you having a baby humiliate her?'' Anne asked.

Mary Ellen raised her eyebrows in mock horror. ''The idea that her parents might actually be having sex. At our age!'' She shook her head, her soft brown eyes sparkling with laughter. ''Parents aren't supposed to have sex, you know.''

''Aren't they?'' For as long as she could remember, Anne's parents had slept in separate bedrooms. She doubted if the door between them had even been opened in her lifetime.

"Everybody goes through the same phase, I guess," Mary Ellen said comfortably. "And Sophy's very good with Timothy."

Anne let the other woman take her smile as agreement. She'd never gone through that phase. When she was Sophy's age, she could remember waking up with a knot in her stomach that didn't ease until she got to the breakfast table and saw that neither her parents nor her brother had disappeared during the night.

A waiter appeared just then, bearing plates of linguine in white clam sauce and a basket of crisp garlic toast. The first bite of garlicky sauce told Anne why Tony's restaurant was a success. When she said as much, Tony slapped Neill on the back and told him that he was glad to see his taste in women was improving.

"The last woman he introduced to the family was a brunette, about six foot tall and weighed maybe ninety pounds," he told Anne. "She ate two lettuce leaves, sipped a glass of water and said she was stuffed."

Neill considered jabbing his elbow into his

brother's stomach to shut him up. He should have known that Tony wouldn't be able to resist the chance to embarrass him, which was the price you paid for family. But he wasn't sure Anne would appreciate hearing about some woman he'd dated in the past.

"If you were cooking, then she didn't know what she was missing," Anne said, and, when her eyes met Neill's, he saw nothing to suggest that his brother's mild indiscretion had bothered her.

If he'd asked, Anne could have told him that hearing that he'd once dated a tall, slim brunette might have bothered her even yesterday, but the fact that he'd spent the whole night—and part of the morning—making love to her had made it pretty clear that—for now, at least—he wasn't thinking of another woman.

It was after ten when they left the restaurant. Anne's mood was pensive, and Neill didn't press for conversation. From the things he'd said, she'd known that his family was very different from her own. When he spoke of them, it was with affection and warmth and genuine liking—words she could never apply to her own family. She loved them, and she thought—she hoped—that they loved her, but she couldn't honestly say that she knew them.

It had taken Lisa pointing it out for her to see that Jack had a drinking problem. Once it was pointed out, she had to admit that the signs had been there, but she'd never really looked at what he was doing. Because no one in her family every really *looked* at each other. And even now that she'd seen the problem, she didn't know what to do about it. The thought of saying something to Jack about it boggled the imagination. There simply wasn't enough of a personal connection between them. He was her brother, but the ties were of blood only.

She tried to imagine what Tony would do if he thought Neill had a similar problem. Probably cuff him alongside the head and drag him to counseling, she decided, smiling a little. From what Neill had told her, she thought the rest of the family would have a similar reaction. They were…there for each other.

It hurt to realize how far short of that ideal her own family fell.

Neill watched her face as they rode up in the elevator. She was so wrapped up in her thoughts that he wasn't sure she'd even noticed that they were almost back to their room. He'd watched her tonight, too, seeing the way she opened up to the warmth of his brother's family, talking to his niece and sister-in-law, holding the baby, her eyes soft and tender as she looked down at him.

The need to see her holding his child had caught him by surprise. He'd never given much thought to having children of his own, putting it in the category of maybe, someday. But he wanted to see Anne's belly round with his baby, wanted to hold a child that had been born of the love he felt for her, the love he was nearly sure she returned.

He opened the door to their room, stepping back to let her enter first. Watching her cross the room, he thought of how pretty she looked and of how much he loved her. He opened his mouth to say one or the other and was amazed by what came out instead.

"Anne? Tell me about Brooke," he said softly.

Anne had been about to set her purse on the table. It hit the floor instead, and she stared blankly down at it for a moment, gathering her thoughts, telling herself that his question didn't really mean what it so obviously meant. She bent to pick up the purse, taking her time, trying to still the nervous chatter in her head. Setting it on the table, she turned to look at him, her expression calm, faintly surprised.

"What do you mean?"

"I know what happened to her, Anne."

Shock flared in her eyes, and her head jerked back as if recoiling from a physical blow. There was a thick, painful silence, and, when she spoke, her voice sounded thin in her own ears. "What do you...how did you find out?"

"I looked it up at the library."

"The library?" It seemed ridiculous that he could have learned about her sister's murder in such a prosaic way. "Were you looking for something else?"

For an instant Neill considered letting her believe that. She could hardly blame him for stumbling across the information, could she? But he wasn't going to lie to her about something that was so important to her.

"I went there to find out what had happened to your sister," he admitted steadily and felt something twist in his chest at the hurt in her eyes. He wanted to go to her, put his arms around her and hold her until that look went away. But this time, he was the one who'd caused her pain, and he was just going to have to live with that guilt.

"Why?" She sounded bewildered. "Why would

you want to know about something that happened so long ago?''

Neill slid his hands into the pockets of his jeans as protection against the urge to take hold of her. ''It was obvious that whatever happened to her was still very much a part of your life. When that guy tried to mug you, you were more terrified that people would find out than you were by what had happened. You said that you didn't want anyone to know, because they'd remember and look at you. You even started to say Brooke's name.'' He shrugged. ''It wasn't hard to guess that whatever you were afraid of had something to do with her death.''

''Why didn't you ask me about it?'' Anne's mouth felt numb, the words hard to shape. She hadn't realized until now how much she'd counted on him not knowing about her sister's murder. Freed of the burden of his knowledge, she had been able to be someone else, someone whose life wasn't defined by her sister's death. Finding out that he knew about the murder made her feel like she'd been caught out in a lie, as if he must have known all along that she wasn't what she was pretending to be.

''I did ask,'' he reminded her gently. ''You said

she was dead and that it was a long time ago. You told me you didn't want to talk about it, so I went looking. I'm a writer, Anne. Research is a big part of what I do for a living.''

"And you felt you had the right to pry into my private life?''

Neill's brows rose at the sharpness of her tone. He wasn't sure what he'd expected, but it wasn't the anger that darkened her eyes to storm gray. Then again, he would rather deal with anger than tears.

"Since it was in all the papers at the time, it wasn't exactly private," he said evenly. "And it was obvious that, whatever had happened, it was still very much a part of your life, a part of who you are. I wanted to know what it was.''

"Did it ever occur to you that it was none of your business?'' Rage bubbled up in Anne's chest, a sharp acid heat. His knowledge was a betrayal. "You had no right.'' Her voice cracked on the last word, and she spun away, hands clenched at her sides. "No right.''

Looking at her rigid back, Neill searched for the right words to make her understand why he'd felt as if he did have the right to know what had happened to Brooke. Before he could formulate them, Anne spoke again.

"She was murdered, but we never use that word," she said casually, the way she might have commented that it looked like rain. "My family, I mean. When it comes up, which it almost never does, no one ever says, 'Brooke was murdered.' We just say she died." She swung around to face him, her mouth quirked in a humorless little smile. "You know that routine George Carlin does about the seven dirty words? In my family, murder is number eight." She looked down, smoothing her fingers over an invisible wrinkle in her skirt. "Funny, isn't it? As if using a different word changes what happened."

"What did happen?" Neill resisted the urge to go to her, to pull her into his arms and tell her not to talk about it anymore, not to even think about it. There had already been too much of that in her life.

"You read the newspaper reports. You already know what happened."

"I'd rather hear it from you."

She hesitated, then shrugged, as if it didn't matter to her. "The papers were pretty accurate. Jack was supposed to pick her up after school, but he was late. When he got there, she was gone. He figured she'd gotten a ride home with someone else. He and some friends went out for hamburgers. My parents thought Brooke was with him, so no one knew she was missing until Jack got home.'' Anne folded a series of tiny pleats in the fabric of her skirt, then smoothed them out again. ''I was ten when it happened. I remember my father started making phone calls. I can still hear the strain in his voice, and I couldn't understand why he was so upset, because Brooke was all the time spending the night with a friend. When I asked if something was wrong, my mother hushed me and sent me to bed.

''It was two weeks before they...found her. I was so scared but no one would tell me anything. And then, suddenly my parents were saying Brooke was dead, but no one would tell me what had happened to her. Just that she'd died. I suppose they thought I was too young to be told what had really happened.''

So instead they'd left her at the mercy of her imagination, Neill thought. And their well-intentioned silence had probably frightened her more than the truth could have.

"It must have been terrifying for you," he said, keeping his tone neutral.

"I suppose." Anne moved over to the window, staring blindly out at the lights of the city as she tried to order her thoughts. She'd never talked about this. The topic had been forbidden in her family, buried away like a guilty secret. It was only in the last couple of years, after she'd moved into the cottage, away from her mother's control, that she'd even let herself think about it.

"They quarreled the day before it happened," she murmured, almost as if talking to herself. "My mother and Brooke. They were always quarreling about something. When I got older, I could look back and see that it was because they were so much alike. My mother is the original steel magnolia, velvet over pure steel. Brooke didn't bother to coat the steel in quite such a pretty cover. My mother wanted her to be a debutante—all virginal dresses and soft voice. Brooke wore red spandex and blue jeans.

"They clashed constantly, especially after Brooke started dating. I didn't understand much of it at the time but, over the years, I've pieced together what was happening. Brooke was sleeping around—or my mother thought she was. My room was next door to Brooke's, and I remember hearing them fight over the fact that Brooke was taking birth control pills. It was just after her sixteenth birthday. She was furious that Mom had gone through her room, and Mom was saying that she wasn't going to let her daughter act like a slut.

"They went back and forth, and Brooke finally shouted that if Mom didn't get off her back, she was going to go fuck the whole football team. It was the first time I'd ever heard anyone say that word," she mused. "I didn't even really know what it meant, but I looked it up in the dictionary afterwards."

Anne fingered the edge of the drape, her eyes distant, focused on the past. "Mom slapped her. It was such an ugly sound. I wanted to put my hands over my ears, but I just sat there, frozen in place, afraid to move. Afraid to breathe. Brooke didn't cry. I don't think she said anything at all. She just left. She didn't come back that night, and I heard Mom and Dad arguing in their room. I couldn't hear what they were saying. I didn't want to hear. I remember lying in bed, wondering if Brooke had run away, wondering if Mom would love me more if Brooke wasn't there anymore. But Brooke came home the next day, and everything went back to the way it was before, except that, after that, she and Mom fought constantly. They fought about Brooke's clothes, about the boys she dated, about her grades, about where she was going to go to college. It was so constant that, after a while, I stopped hearing it.

"The day before…it happened, they quarreled over me. I was ten, and Brooke did my makeup. Mom was furious with her. With us. She accused Brooke of trying to turn me into a slut, too, and told me to go wash my face. I told her not to be mad at Brooke. We were just having fun. She grabbed my shoulder, and I can still remember the way her fingers dug into my skin."

She reached up to touch her shoulder, as if touching an old bruise. "She looked at me like she hated me. I've never forgotten the look in her eyes." She was silent for a moment, and then sighed and spoke softly. "The next day, Brooke disappeared. For a long time, I thought it was my fault."

Neill stirred abruptly, but Anne shook her head before he could speak. "I know it wasn't. I figured that out a long time ago, but children are so ego-centric, and, at first, when we thought Brooke had run away, I thought it was because she and Mom had fought about me. And when they...found her, all I could think of was that sometimes I'd wished she'd go away so Mom could love me best.''

She turned to look at him, her smile holding a rueful amusement for the child she'd been. "There's nothing like a ten-year-old girl for conjuring up guilt. If we'd been Catholic, I probably would have decided to enter a convent. As it was, I did everything I could to make up for Brooke's death. For a long time I tried to *become* Brooke, only I was going to be the good Brooke, the one my mother had wanted her to be. I got straight A's in school, and I wore clothes I knew my mother would approve of. I guess I'm still wearing them," she murmured, smoothing a hand over the soft peach-colored skirt.

"And I didn't date. I don't know...I still don't know if Brooke was promiscuous." She frowned a little. "I don't think she was. I know she and David dated for most of her senior year. I don't want to think that she was...careless with her favors. But I made sure that I never was. Not that I had to beat the boys off with a stick," she added with a self-deprecating smile. "Since everyone knew what had happened, they all treated me with extra care. I don't think there was a boy in the whole school who would have dared to try and get out of line with me. The couple of dates I did have, they treated me like I might shatter if they breathed too heavily in my direction.'' Her laugh didn't quite conceal the hurt she'd felt. ''It didn't matter, really, because, no matter how hard I tried to fill Brooke's shoes, I didn't have her looks or her personality.'' Anne sighed, remembering. ''She was so beautiful.''

Neill thought of the pictures he'd seen. Brooke had looked like exactly what she had been—a girl teetering on the brink of maturity. She'd been very pretty, with the promise of beauty, but without the character to back it up yet. But he knew Anne wouldn't believe him. In the years since her death, reality had been blurred, and Brooke had become the prettiest, the brightest, the most charming girl ever to have lived. He'd seen it before, the need to almost deify a loved one once they were gone, as if remembering their faults—their humanity— might be somehow disloyal.

''Anne, you can't spend your whole life trying to make up for your sister's death.''

''No. I know that. It took me awhile to figure it out, but I finally did.''

She was suddenly aware of a deep exhaustion.

She'd let herself feel more in the last two weeks than she ever had in her life. Maybe saying that she'd "let" herself feel wasn't quite accurate, either, because, from the moment Neill had come into her life, she hadn't really had any choice. He'd stirred something in her that she hadn't known existed, made her want things she'd never even let herself think about before.

And now, somehow, she'd told him about Brooke, something she'd never talked to anyone about, not even Lisa, who was the only person she knew willing to mention Brooke's name. Now it was out in the open, and she felt drained and almost dizzy, as if the things she'd said had been a weight inside that was suddenly gone.

"I'm...very tired," she said slowly. "Would you mind very much if I went to bed now?"

Neill saw that she was nearly swaying on her feet and crossed to her in two quick strides, catching her up in his arms.

"No." Her voice shook as he carried her toward the bedroom. "I can't tonight. Please, Neill."

"Hush." He nudged open the bedroom door with his shoulder. "I'm not going to try and make love to you." He set her on her feet beside the bed and bent to kiss her forehead—a soft, comforting touch. "Let me take care of you, Anne."

It occurred to her that, in the short time she'd known him, he'd spent more time taking care of her than anyone had ever done, but she was too tired to worry about it. She stood, obedient as a child, and let him undress her. Even when she stood naked before him, his touch remained so gently impersonal that it left no room for embarrassment. He found the rose-colored silk nightgown she'd brought to wear for their first night together and slipped it over her head, letting it fall in soft folds around her body. Then he sat her on the edge of the bed, and she felt his fingers in her hair, pulling out the pins until her hair fell to her shoulders. When he picked up her brush and began to pull it gently through her hair, Anne had to close her eyes against the sting of tears.

In her whole life, she'd never felt so cared for. So loved.

# Chapter Twelve

Anne watched the familiar buildings come into view with some regret. Now that they were almost home, she had to admit that the lovely weekend was really over. Leaning her head back, she closed her eyes. Neill had folded the top down for the drive home and she loved the feel of the wind rushing across her face.

It seemed incredible that she'd only been gone two days. She felt as if it had been a lifetime. She'd left a virgin and was returning a woman well loved. Whatever happened between them in the future—if they had a future—she would always be grateful to him for making her first experience so special, satisfying her not just physically but emotionally.

Last night he'd held her tenderly, asking nothing of her. She had been the one to wake him at dawn, her hands hesitantly exploring his body, testing powers she was only just discovering, until, with a smothered groan, he'd rolled on top of her, taking her with a long, powerful stroke that had brought her nearly to climax in an instant.

Afterwards, they'd slept again, not waking until midmorning. Neill had swept her up off the bed and carried her into the shower, then had made love to her again while the water beat down on them.

They hadn't talked about their conversation the night before. He hadn't mentioned her family, and, oddly enough, she hadn't even thought about them. It was as if she'd been granted this single morning as a slice apart from the rest of her life.

They'd eaten brunch in a restaurant high atop the hotel, then had reluctantly started home. Now they were almost there, and real life was waiting. Still, real life didn't look too bad, either, Anne thought, smiling to herself. There hadn't been any promises between them, but she knew he felt something more than lust for her. He would pretty well have to, since she didn't have the sort of physical beauty that drove a man wild. He hadn't said he loved her, but that didn't mean he didn't. She hadn't said she loved him, either, and her heart was so full of it that it ached. She wasn't counting on anything, but, at least for the moment, life seemed full of possibilities.

Glancing at her, Neill wondered what she was thinking that had put that Mona Lisa smile on her face. They were almost home, and he wondered how much she would protest if he just drove straight through town and kept on going. Or maybe he could turn the car around and drive back to Chicago. They could lock themselves in the hotel and never come out again. Legends would grow up around the eccentric couple who never left their suite. Room service waiters would pass tidbits of information to the press, and Hollywood would eventually buy the rights to the story.

Then again, maybe he should just take Anne home, set her down and tell her that there had been a small misunderstanding about his career. He wasn't a struggling freelance writer at all, he was actually quite successful, and, in an amazing coincidence, he just happened to write books about the sort of thing that had happened to her family.

It really wasn't a big deal, Neill thought, his hands tightening on the steering wheel. He hadn't known about Brooke's death when he met Anne.

He sure as hell didn't plan on writing about it. He was more and more sure that he'd had enough of exploring the dark side of humanity, of trying to explain things that couldn't be explained; of trying to understand acts beyond comprehension.

Anne would certainly understand when he explained it to her—how when he'd let her assume he wrote articles and such, it wasn't really a lie, because he *had* started out doing exactly that. Maybe she would be a little hurt. She certainly had reason to be angry. But it wouldn't be long before they were laughing about the whole thing. He was sure of it. So sure that there was no reason not to put it off until tomorrow, he decided, and then winced at his own cowardice.

When Neill pulled up in front of her gate, Anne thought the cottage looked odd—so small and tidy, hemmed in by picket fences and the neat beds of roses. It took her a moment to realize that it wasn't the cottage that had changed, but her. It looked different because she was seeing it through new eyes.

Wasn't there an old song about what a difference a day made? Well, certainly two days was enough to turn your world around, she decided as she led the way up the walkway.

"Have dinner with me tonight?" Neill asked as they stepped onto the porch. "I'll cook something simple. We can watch the moon come up over the parking lot."

"Sounds romantic." Anne unlocked the door before turning to look up at him. "It's Sunday."

"So?" He arched his brows. "You can't watch the moon rise on Sunday?"

"I always have dinner with my parents on Sunday."

"Always?" He reached out to trail the tip of one finger along the scooped neckline of her T-shirt, making her skin tingle everywhere he touched.

Anne swallowed. "Always. Why don't you come with me?" she asked, and then had to smile at his pained grimace.

"And let your mother chew on my leg as an appetizer? I've got a better idea." He slid his arms around her, bent to nuzzle her ear. "Why don't you invite me in for dinner? We'll take the phone off the hook, and I'll make love to you in front of the fireplace."

She leaned back against his hold, letting him support her. "It's the wrong time of year for a fire, and the floor is oak."

"I'll let you be on top," he said, loving the way color flooded her cheeks.

"It would be hard on my knees," she said primly. She reached out to toy with a button on his shirt. "I'd really like you to come to supper, Neill. I know it seems like a silly tradition, but it means a lot to my mother. I know she can be difficult, but she's lost a lot. I don't want to hurt her if I can avoid it."

Privately, Neill thought Olivia Moore was iron all the way to the core, impervious to hurt. But Anne wasn't, and, if it meant that much to her... "Sure. Just let me slip into my chain mail."

"I'll call and let them know you're coming."

"To give your mother a chance to put crocodiles in the moat?" he asked politely and kissed her before she could protest.

As it happened, Olivia was at her most gracious. No crocodiles, no arsenic in the pasta salad. Though there was little conversation, what there was was civil, impersonal. Neill couldn't help but compare it to his own family gatherings and wonder why Anne's family clung so stubbornly to a ritual that seemed to give them so little pleasure. But perhaps, when there was not much substance, you were willing to cling to at least the pretense of closeness.

"Do you have any idea when your motorcycle might be repaired, Mr. Devlin?" Olivia asked as she served dessert.

"No. Soon, I imagine."

"I'm sure you must be looking forward to getting on your way."

Neill looked at Anne and smiled slowly, unaware of how much the look revealed. "I'm in no hurry," he murmured. Anne flushed and lowered her eyes, afraid of what they might reveal.

To anyone looking—and everyone was—the intimacy in that brief exchange was unmistakable.

Across the table, Lisa felt Jack tense and put her hand on his arm, squeezing in sharp warning. He didn't look at her, but she felt him ease back in his chair. She shot a cautious glance toward the foot of the table and was unsurprised to see the sharp fury in Olivia's eyes. Lisa wondered if she was angered by the idea that Anne might have taken a lover or simply outraged by the possibility that she might be losing her stranglehold over her daughter. Either way, she didn't envy Anne. Or Neill Devlin, though he looked like he could take care of him-

self. She hoped he could also take care of Anne—
and that he wanted to.

"Did you see the way he was looking at her?"
Jack exploded half an hour later, barely waiting for
the car door to shut behind him. "Like he
was...like they were—"

"Lovers?" Lisa supplied dryly.

"Yes, goddammit." He jabbed the key in the
ignition and started the engine. "What the hell
right does he have to look at her like that?"

"They spent Friday and Saturday in Chicago,"
Lisa said calmly. "If he looks at her like they were
lovers, I suspect he has reason."

Under other circumstances, Jack's look of
stunned disbelief might have been funny. As it was,
she could only marvel at his blindness.

"The car goes faster if you take your foot off
the brake and put it in gear," she pointed out after
a moment.

Jack responded automatically. He didn't speak
until they'd reached the bottom of the drive. Neill
and Anne had left shortly before them, and the
sight of Anne's cottage, a single light glowing
cheerfully from the bedroom, seemed to snap him
out of his shock. His foot shifted to the brake,
bringing the car to a shuddering halt.

"I'll kill the miserable bastard," he said furiously, shoving open the door. "If he's with her now, I swear to God—"

"Don't you dare set foot out of this car, Jack." Lisa grabbed hold of his arm, her nails digging into muscles iron-hard with tension. "It's none of your business if he's with her now or any other time."

"None of my business?" He turned to look at her, the overhead light slanting over his features, revealing the glittering anger in his eyes.

"None of your business," she repeated, suddenly every bit as angry as he was. "Anne isn't a little girl. She's twenty-five years old. Now shut that damned door before she hears the car and wonders what's going on." When he hesitated, she hissed between her teeth and tightened her grip on his arm until he winced. "He's not there, you idiot. Unless he parked that stupid car of David's in town and walked back. And there's no reason for him to do that, since there's no reason on earth why Anne shouldn't have a man spending the night with her."

After a long, tense moment, Jack pulled the door shut and put the car back in gear. Lisa released his arm and sat back, wishing she could believe that sanity had prevailed but knowing that, if the Corvette had been there, nothing would have stopped him from storming up to the door to protect his sister's virtue. It would have been sweet if it hadn't been so damned irritating.

Neither of them spoke until Jack pulled the car into the driveway next to the house Lisa rented. He shut the engine off, but neither of them moved to get out.

"Anne's not like most people," he muttered. "I know she's twenty-five, but she's been...sheltered."

"I think the word is smothered."

There was a short silence, and then she saw Jack nod slowly. "Maybe. Maybe we have been too protective of her. But whatever the reason, she's young for her age, and I don't want to see her hurt. I don't like this Devlin. We don't know anything about him."

"We know he makes her happy," Lisa said quietly.

"Happy?" Jack laced the word with contempt. "A quick roll in the hay may put a smile on her face now, but what's going to happen when this bastard walks out on her?"

"I don't know that he will. But I do know that I've seen Anne smile more in the last two weeks than she has in the last two years. Have you ever

really looked at her, Jack? Have you given any
thought to what her life is like?'' There was something about sitting there in the shadowy darkness
that made the truth not only possible but impera-
tive. ''Do you think about her future at all? Or do
you just have this vague idea that things will go
on the way they are, with Anne living in her pretty
little doll's house, all safe and secure, making
everyone feel better because, as long as she's
tucked away in cotton wool, we know it can't happen again. No one is going to take her and hurt her
the way they did Brooke.'' Her voice cracked on
the name, and she saw Jack shift, his hand coming
up as if to touch her face.

''Don't!'' She shook her head fiercely. ''This
isn't about Brooke. Just for once, let's keep Brooke
out of it.''

''What the hell are you talking about?''

''Anne. I'm talking about Anne and the way
your family—the way this whole damned town—
hovers over her like she's made out of spun sugar.
She's a flesh and blood woman, Jack.''

''I know that.'' He sat back in his seat, his lean
body vibrating with frustration. How the hell had
they gotten into this discussion? When had it
veered away from the fact that his sister—his little

sister—had taken a lover? Just thinking about that miserable bastard touching her made his blood boil.

"What the hell is she thinking of?" he burst out, smacking his palm against the steering wheel. "What in bloody hell is she thinking of?"

"Herself, for a change. Did you expect her to die a virgin?"

"No." Jack shifted uncomfortably. He didn't like talking about this, didn't want to think about it. "I figured she'd get married some day."

"To whom?" Lisa's tone was one of polite inquiry. "Frank Miller? Is that what you want for her? A man you once told me was so boring that he could provide the ultimate cure for insomnia."

"There's nothing wrong with Frank," Jack muttered. "He's solid. Decent. He'd keep Anne safe."

"From what?" Lisa spread her hands in question. "From having someone to talk to? To laugh with? From actually having a life? What you really mean is that he'd keep her alive. Is that all that matters? That she's safe? What about being happy? Don't you want her to be happy?"

"Of course I do."

"Then stop trying to shelter her. Life doesn't come with any guarantees. Maybe Neill Devlin will break her heart. Maybe he won't. But being hurt is better than never feeling anything at all. Do you really want her to settle for good old Frank? Is that what you really want for her?''

Jack shifted restlessly, the car keys jangling as he pulled them out of the ignition and then shoved them back in again. ''Maybe I am a little overprotective of Anne,'' he said finally. ''But after...what happened to Brooke, I felt like I had to make up for not being there.''

''That wasn't your fault.'' This time it was Lisa who reached out, her fingers brushing against his cheek, settling on his arm. ''What happened to Brooke wasn't your fault.''

''Wasn't it?'' The muscles under her hand bunched and shifted. The silence stretched between them. Somewhere a dog barked twice. ''I was late,'' Jack said, his voice thinned by the effort of saying the words. ''That day when Brooke...when it happened. I was supposed to pick her up after school, but I was late. Afterward, I said I'd lost track of time, but that wasn't the truth. I was playing basketball with some buddies, and I knew I was going to be late, but I didn't want to quit until we finished the game. I figured she could walk home if she had to. And she did. And someone took her and killed her and cut her to pieces.''

His arm was like iron beneath her touch. The silence was so thick that Lisa could hear the sound of her own pulse beating in her ears. She could feel the pain in him, a pain so huge that it was eating away at him, destroying him from the inside out.

"Brooke—we *all*—walked home as often as not," she said finally. "You couldn't have known that there was any reason why this time should be any different."

"But it *was* different, and she died because I didn't want to interrupt a damned basketball game."

She wanted to put her arms around him and hold him, offer him comfort, but instinct told her that wasn't what he needed. She made her voice cool, faintly impersonal.

"She's been dead for fifteen years, Jack. How many more years are you going to spend feeling sorry for yourself?"

He jerked as if she'd slapped him, and, even in the dim light, she could read the shock in his face.

"I don't feel sorry for myself!"

"Yes, you do. You gave up medical school to become a sheriff. You're drinking too much. Oh, maybe you're not a full-blown alcoholic yet, but you're heading in that direction. I know the signs.

You can't bring yourself to commit to marrying me or having a family." Her voice cracked, but she steadied it and went on, rushing the words, as if afraid she might not get them all out. "Your sister died, and you've spent the last fifteen years turning yourself into some kind of martyr on her behalf." Lisa's voice began to climb, and she let it, not sure she could have stopped it if she'd tried. "You don't even remember Brooke anymore. Your whole family has turned her into some sort of plaster saint so you can spend your lives mourning her perfection. Well, I'm sick of it. I'm sick of this town, and I'm sick of you. I'm leaving as soon as I can pack, and I hope Neill Devlin has the sense to get Anne away from the lot of you before you manage to sacrifice her life, too."

She practically screamed the last words at him, her hand fumbling for the door handle.

"Lisa." Jack reached for her, but she jerked away.

"Leave me alone. Just leave me alone." Shaking with sobs, she nearly fell out of the car in her haste to put some distance between them. Blinded by tears, she stumbled up the walkway and onto the tiny porch. The keys were in the bottom of her purse, of course. Where else would the damned things be when she needed them?

"Lisa." Jack was suddenly behind her, his hand on her shoulder, ignoring her attempts to pull away. "Don't. Don't cry because of me. I'm not worth it."

"You're damned right you're not," she sobbed. "And I'm not crying over you. I'm crying because I can't find my damned keys."

"I'll break a window," he murmured, pulling her into his chest and holding her despite her weak struggles. "I never meant to hurt you. I just...I guess I didn't think I deserved you."

"You're right, you don't deserve me." But she let her cheek rest on his chest.

"I...maybe you're right. Maybe I have gotten in the habit of feeling sorry for myself. I don't know. It's...I've felt guilty for so long. Maybe...maybe it helped to be able to blame someone, even if it was myself. When Brooke was killed, one of the hardest things to deal with was the...randomness of it. It wasn't that someone wanted *her* dead, it was just that she was handy. And the fact that she was handy because I was late—it ate at me."

Lisa closed her eyes and spoke without lifting her head from his chest. "You were twenty years old, Jack. How many twenty-year-old boys do you know who would sacrifice a basketball game to pick up their sister when she was perfectly capable of walking home? Okay, so it was rude of you to let her wait. It was even selfish, but you didn't kill her. She wasn't dragged kicking and screaming into the killer's car. If she had been, someone would have seen or heard something. Whoever he was, he offered her a ride, and she took him up on it. Does that make it Brooke's fault?''

She lifted her head and looked up at him. His face looked gaunt and haunted in the yellowish porch light. ''Do you really remember her at all, Jack? Do you remember the way she liked to play tricks on people, get everyone riled up? If someone—a pleasant-looking stranger—stopped and offered her a ride home, or even to the next town, and she was annoyed with you for not showing up, she'd have taken him up on it.''

''She knew better than to—''

''Take candy from strangers?'' Lisa's mouth twisted in a half smile. ''Sure she did, but there was nothing Brooke liked more than stirring things up a bit. She would have loved to call home from thirty miles away and tell your mother that she'd hitchhiked there. The fact that your mother would tear a strip off you for being late would have been a bonus, but the main benefit would have been to show Olivia that she wasn't the one in control.''

Jack shifted uneasily, and she reached up to cradle his face between her hands. ''*If* that's what happened, if Brooke got in his car thinking that she was just going to stir up a little trouble, if she did something that stupid, that careless—that young— does that make her to blame for her own death?''

''Of course it doesn't.''

''Then why is it different for you?'' When he shook his head but didn't answer, she sighed and let her hands drop to her sides. She took a step back and faced him. ''I love you, Jack, but I'm not going to let myself become a part of this thing your family has going. I'm not going to hang around and watch you move from heavy drinker to full-blown alcoholic. And I'm not going to spend the rest of my life waiting for you to decide that you've been punished long enough and maybe you can grab a little happiness. I want a home, and I want babies, and I want them before I'm too old to enjoy them. I wanted them to be your babies, but, if that's not going to happen, I'll find someone else and I'll be happy. It's your call.''

When he didn't say anything, she scooped up

her purse and found her keys just where they were supposed to be, in an outside pocket. Without looking at him again, she opened the door and went inside, closing it behind her and leaning back against it, waiting to hear the sound of his footsteps moving off the porch.

The silence stretched, and still she waited, her heart beating slow and heavy in her chest. Then she heard the creak of the screen door opening, and he knocked on the door. Her breath hitching in her throat, she opened the door and looked at him without speaking.

"How many?" he said.

"What?" She stared at him blankly. "How many what?"

"Babies." He smiled uncertainly. "We don't have time for more than half a dozen, unless we work some twins in."

"Half a dozen?" It took her a moment to recognize the emotion welling up in her for pure happiness. "I...I was thinking maybe one or two."

"We can start out there and see how we like it." He reached for her then, holding her so tight that her ribs nearly cracked. "I can't make any promises except that I'll do my best, Lisa."

"That's all anybody can do." She combed her

fingers through his pale hair, her heart aching with love. "That's all anyone can ask."

"I want to get married as soon as we can," he said, catching her hand in his and turning his head to press a kiss in the palm. "We can stay here, or we can move. I can find work anywhere. I don't care where we live. Just don't leave me."

"I won't." She tilted her head back and smiled up at him. "I need a father for all those kids you're planning on us having."

He grinned, and for the first time there were no shadows in his eyes. "Maybe we should get started on the first one tonight. I understand it can take some practice to get it right."

# *Chapter Thirteen*

Neill closed the little gate behind him and started up the narrow walkway. The warm twilight air was heavy with the scent of roses, and he could hear the sluggish buzz of bees, gathering a last few bits of nectar before hurrying back to the hive for the night. Looking at the cottage, it struck him that he'd never seen such a feminine-looking house. The neat little walkway, the whimsical colors, the tiny little porch with the roses scrambling across its roof. Just looking at it made him feel large and clumsy.

It had been less than twenty-four hours since he'd seen Anne, and he was caught between an almost painful anticipation and nervous jitters wor-

thy of a teenager approaching his first date. He
could have stayed with her last night, he reminded
himself. If he'd asked, she wouldn't have refused.
But he hadn't asked, on the vague theory that, after
the intensity of the weekend, they both needed
some breathing room. So he'd spent a miserable
night alone in his motel room, and he was just selfish enough to hope that Anne had been every bit
as miserable.

He scowled down at the flowers in his hand.
What was he doing bringing daisies to a woman
who had a yard stuffed with enough roses to decorate a float? But Bill's Grocery didn't exactly
stock an extensive array of floral decorations, and
the yellow and white daisies had made him smile.
Well, if she hated them, she could always throw
them out after he left.

Or after she kicked him out, whichever came
first. He was determined to tell her about his books
tonight. The longer he waited, the more it made it
seem like it was a big deal. And it wasn't. At least,
he hoped it wasn't.

Drawing a deep breath, he rang the doorbell.
Anne opened the door before the sound of the
chimes had faded, and, looking at her, Neill felt
something warm unfold in his chest. She was wear-

ing jeans and a peach-colored shirt, her hair pulled back from her face but left to fall on her shoulders, and all he could think was that she was so damned pretty.

"Hi." Her greeting was breathless, her eyes shining with pleasure at seeing him again.

Without speaking, Neill stepped into the tiny entryway, wrapped one hand around the back of her neck and lowered his mouth to hers. He took his time about it, feeling her hands lift to his chest in a quick little flutter of surprise, then still against him, her fingers curling into the faded cotton of his denim shirt as her mouth opened to him. When he finally lifted his head and looked down at her, he was pleased by the dazed look in her eyes and the warm flush on her cheeks.

"Hi, yourself," he said, his voice husky. "I brought you flowers."

"Oh." Anne stared at the bouquet he was holding out. Her mind seemed to be dipping and swirling, and her knees felt like overcooked noodles. She took the flowers automatically. There was something she was supposed to say. She was nearly sure of it. "Thank you," she managed at last, dragging the appropriate response from her scrambled brain.

Grinning, pleased with himself, he reached around her to close the door. "Water's usually a good idea," he suggested, when she continued to stand there, staring blankly at the flowers. "My mom swears by putting an aspirin in the vase."

Putting his hand on her shoulder, he turned her in the direction of the kitchen. "Something sure smells good."

"Chicken." Anne drew a shaky breath and released it slowly. "I made a chicken casserole. I wasn't sure what you'd like, but chicken's usually pretty safe."

She set the bouquet in the sink and opened a cupboard to take out a tall glass vase.

"I eat most things," Neill said, sniffing appreciatively at the cake that sat cooling on the counter. "I didn't know you cooked."

"I enjoy it." Anne used kitchen shears to snip the ends off the flower stems before slipping them in the vase. "Of course, cooking for yourself can get to be pretty boring, but so can living on frozen food, so I generally make the effort."

"Is that chocolate frosting?" he asked, leaning over her shoulder to eye the bowl on the counter.

"Yes." She was nearly sure it was chocolate

frosting, but with him standing so close, it was hard to remember her own name.

"I love chocolate frosting." There was such naked longing in his voice that her breath gusted out of her on a laugh. Without thinking, she brushed back the plastic wrap and dipped her finger in the bowl. It was only as she turned to offer it to him that she realized what she'd done. Uncertain, she started to pull back, but Neill caught her hand in his and lifted her finger to his mouth.

Anne sagged back against the counter as his tongue swirled around her finger, licking it clean before drawing it into his mouth and sucking gently. He kept his eyes on her face, watching the flicker of emotions. By the time he released her hand, the only thing holding her upright was the counter at her back.

She sighed as he bent to kiss her. He tasted of chocolate, and there was something strangely erotic about the contrast between that sweetly innocent taste and the vibrating hardness of his body against hers.

"Can dinner wait?" he asked as his mouth slid down her throat.

"Yes." She would have said the same if it had been a soufflé in the oven.

"Good," Neill said savagely. "Because I can't."

By the time they got around to dinner, the chicken was dry and the noodles were overcooked. Anne didn't care, and, since he ate two helpings, she didn't think Neill did, either.

"If you're going to keep working me like this, I've got to keep up my strength," he said as she scooped the second serving onto his plate, and he laughed when she flushed pink.

Considering the fact that she was wearing only his shirt, with not a stitch on underneath it, it was ridiculous to feel embarrassed. And she didn't, really. It was just the novelty of having someone want her the way he did. She'd never thought of herself as a sensual person, but obviously she'd been wrong.

After dinner, Neill let her shoo him out of the kitchen while she tidied up and frosted the cake. He almost suggested that he could think of more interesting things to do with the frosting than putting it on a cake but decided she might not be ready for that. She was such a delightful mixture of shyness and sensuality. He'd had other lovers—women he liked, a few he'd simply wanted—but he'd never met anyone who stirred him the way Anne did.

Reluctantly, he went into the living room. There was a cozy domesticity to the scene. All he needed was a pipe and slippers and a shirt, he thought, rubbing his hand over his bare chest. And maybe an apron for Anne. He wondered how she would feel about wearing an apron with nothing on underneath it—maybe something black with ruffles. Aware that he was becoming aroused, Neill turned his attention determinedly in another direction.

There was a set of bookshelves flanking one of the windows, and he wandered over to them, curious to see what her taste in reading was like. There were a few novels—some romances, a handful of mysteries—half a dozen books on growing roses, and the rest were travel guides. Europe, the Pacific Northwest, South America, Australia. Skimming the titles, Neill felt something like anger rise in his chest. She had a bookshelf full of travel guides, but this past weekend had been her first visit to Chicago, which was driving distance away. How long had she been reading about places she was never going to go, dreaming about things she would never see? Choosing a book at random, he flipped it open and saw that she'd used a red pen to mark sights that interested her—the Louvre, the Champs Elysées, a bakery that claimed to have the best croissants in Paris.

Hearing Anne come into the room, Neill turned with the book still in his hand. "Planning a trip?" he asked casually.

She flushed lightly as she set down the coffee cups she'd brought in. "Not particularly. I like to read about different places."

"Why not go yourself?"

"Oh, well, I don't really...I mean, I've never traveled." She fiddled with the collar of his shirt. There was something about the way he was looking at her that made her nervous. She couldn't quite put her finger on it, but he seemed almost angry.

"Nothing stopping you, is there?" he commented, turning to slide the book back onto the shelf.

"I suppose not. I'm just not sure how well I'd do away from here," she admitted.

"You seemed to do just fine this weekend."

"Yes, but you were there." She lowered her eyes to the coffee, reaching down to shift the cups so that the handles were in perfect alignment with each other. "I suppose it seems stupid to you but I...after what happened to Brooke, I've always been a little leery of travel, and, of course, it upsets my mother so much. I almost went away to college, after high school, but she was afraid something would happen to me.'' She shifted the cups a fraction of an inch, keeping her eyes down, so missed seeing the quick flash of anger in Neill's gaze. ''It's understandable. After what happened to Brooke, I mean. You can't blame her for worrying.''

''Brooke was killed right here in Loving,'' Neill said softly. ''If she was going to be afraid for your safety, wouldn't she be afraid for you to stay here?''

Startled, Anne lifted her eyes to his face. ''I'd never thought of it quite like that. I guess that's logical, isn't it?'' She fiddled with the collar some more. ''But emotions aren't always logical, and I'm not afraid here. Not most of the time, anyway.'' She shrugged. ''Anyway, I may surprise myself and suddenly take off on an around the world trip one of these days. So, are you ready for cake?'' she asked, giving him a smile that didn't quite chase the shadows from her eyes.

''Sounds great,'' he said, willing to accept the change of topic. If they talked about it much longer, he might end up saying things about her mother that she wasn't ready to hear.

When she went back into the kitchen, Neill turned to look at the bookshelf again. Paris for their honeymoon, he thought. Or maybe they would spend a month or two and see the whole damned country. But before they could have a honeymoon, there were things that had to be said. Things like I love you and will you marry me, and, by the way, I lied to you about what I do for a living.

"I've never made this recipe before," Anne said as she carried dessert plates in from the kitchen. "The cookbook called it classic dinette cake. I figured any recipe that's been around for forty years or so ought to be pretty good."

She set the plates down and looked at him, her heart stuttering a little at his expression. He looked so serious.

"We need to talk," he said.

"You know, I've noticed that, whenever anyone says that, they're almost always about to say something that you really don't want to hear," she said almost conversationally. "Are you about to tell me that you're married and have ten children?"

His mouth twisted in a half smile. "I'm not married."

"Well, that's a relief. I'd hate to think that I waited all these years to have my first affair, only to start out with a married man." She knew she was chattering to cover the nerves jangling in her stomach.

"Anne—"

"I really don't feel like having a serious discussion tonight." She walked over to him and set her hand on his chest, sliding her fingers through the dark mat of curls as she looked up at him from under her lashes, fear making her bold. She wanted tonight, she thought. If he was about to tell her that he was leaving, she wanted to have just one more night before she had to deal with it. "Couldn't we just pretend that this was a nice, long holiday weekend, lasting all the way through Monday?" she asked. "You can't possibly have a serious discussion on a holiday weekend."

"Is that a rule?" he asked, half amused, half irritated. But the irritation was self-directed. He'd blown this whole confession out of proportion in his own mind, and now he'd made it seem like what he had to tell her must be something dreadful. Besides, it was damned hard to think about anything when he knew she was naked under the thin covering of his shirt. He reached up to toy with the top button.

"It's a city ordinance," Anne said, feeling some of the nervous fear subside. Maybe whatever he had to say wouldn't be so terrible after all. Could he look at her like that—like he wanted to devour her on the spot—if he was about to tell her good-bye?

"Well, I wouldn't want to break any laws," he said, easing the first button loose and starting on the next.

Anne's breath caught in her throat as he slid his hand inside the open shirt to cup her breast.

"How do you think we should spend the rest of the weekend?" he whispered, rubbing his thumb over her nipple.

"I'm sure you'll…think of something," she got out, just before she forgot how to talk.

Anne was measuring coffee into the filter when the doorbell rang the next morning. Startled, she spilled the second scoop of coffee onto the counter. Or was it the third? And what difference did it make, since the only person likely to be ringing her doorbell at this hour of the morning was her mother, who had undoubtedly seen Neill's car parked out front and had probably drawn some fairly accurate conclusions from its presence there at seven o'clock in the morning?

*You're a grown woman,* she reminded herself as she abandoned the coffee and went to answer the door. But her fingers were shaking as she tightened the belt on her robe and she wished she'd taken time to get dressed before coming downstairs. If only she'd gotten up a little earlier or had put a little effort into resisting Neill when he'd shut off the alarm and then rolled her on top of him.

But she hadn't wanted to resist him, and she wasn't sorry he was here, and she had nothing to feel guilty about. With that reminder, she pulled open the door and immediately flushed beneath the accusation in her mother's eyes.

"You're up and about early," she said, with a fair imitation of relaxed welcome. "I was just making coffee. Would you like some?"

"No, thank you." Olivia's cool blue eyes swept over her daughter, from her tousled hair to the bare feet beneath the hem of her pink cotton robe, and missing nothing in between.

Anne was immediately conscious of her rumpled state. She'd planned to run back upstairs and take a shower as soon as she got the coffee going. Even at the best of times, her mother's effortless elegance made her feel like an unmade bed. How on earth did she manage to look so polished at this hour of the morning? Ivory slacks, taupe shirt, her hair perfectly combed, her makeup perfectly applied, tasteful gold accessories. She looked like she'd just stepped out of the pages of a catalog.

"Whose car is that parked outside?" Olivia asked icily. "Or shouldn't I bother to ask?"

Before Anne could say anything, she heard Neill at the head of the stairs. It was obvious he hadn't heard the doorbell, because he was talking as he came down, raising his voice to be sure she could hear him.

"Hey, why don't you call in sick today?" he was saying as he swung around the curve in the stairway. "I'll make us some breakfast and then we can go back to—" He broke off when he saw Olivia, but the word "bed" hung in the air, as if painted in blood-red neon.

Both women had turned at the sound of his voice, and Neill stopped at the bottom of the stairs, feeling pinned by the weight of their separate gazes. Anne looked nervous, apologetic, faintly guilty. Her mother looked furiously angry.

"Mrs. Moore." He inclined his head in polite

greeting and leaned one hip against the wall, the picture of indolent masculine ease. "Anne didn't mention that she was expecting you this morning."

It was a deliberate provocation. If Olivia was going to unleash her anger, he would rather it was aimed at him than at her daughter. For a moment he thought it had worked. Certainly the emotion that flashed in her eyes was blade sharp and just as lethal. But she had it under control almost immediately.

"I wasn't expecting to see you, either, Mr. Devlin but perhaps it's just as well that you're here, since what I have to say concerns you, in a way."

"Mom." Anne moved over to stand in front of Neill. She pushed her hands in her pockets to conceal their trembling, but her voice was steady. "This is really none of your business." She felt Neill's hand drop to her shoulder in silent support. "I know you're concerned about me, but I'm not a child anymore, and I don't need you to—"

"Has he told you why he's here?" Olivia interrupted.

"Here in Loving?" Anne looked surprised by the question. "His bike broke down."

"Convenient, wasn't it, Mr. Devlin?"

"Not particularly." But Neill had already seen

the book in her hand, and he guessed what was coming next. It was his own damned fault, he thought. He should have told Anne, but he'd kept putting it off. And now her mother was going to tell her, and put it in the worst possible light. He drew his hand away from Anne's shoulder, aware of the older woman's look of sharp triumph.

"Did he tell you that he came here to do research?" Olivia asked Anne.

"I did not," Neill said sharply. "My bike broke down. End of story."

"An amazing coincidence," Olivia all but purred.

"What are you talking about?" Anne turned to look between them. She'd never seen her mother look so bitterly triumphant, had never seen Neill look so uncomfortable, almost guilty, and she didn't know which frightened her more.

"Apparently Mr. Devlin is a bit more successful than he led you to believe," Olivia said, holding out the book. Anne took it automatically and stared down at the stark red-and-black cover. *The Killer Next Door* by N. C. Devlin. Turning it over, she saw Neill's face staring up at her from the back cover. He was wearing a black leather jacket and jeans, standing against a background of autumn leaves and clear blue sky. It was a wonderful photo, she thought numbly.

"I thought you wrote articles," she said, lifting her head to give Neill a bewildered look.

"I did. I do." He shoved his hands in his pockets as insurance against the urge to wring her mother's neck—or maybe his own—for putting that hurt look in Anne's eyes. "I started out doing freelance work. I still do an occasional article."

"But this says that you've been on the *New York Times* list. So you're not...I mean, you must be very successful."

He jerked his shoulder in dismissal. "I've done okay."

"You're much too modest," Olivia said. "According to the inside cover, all four of your books have been bestsellers. But what I think is most interesting is the subject matter."

"The subject matter?" Anne felt as if she'd fallen into a play where everyone knew their lines but her. Neill and her mother both knew what was going on, but she was stumbling around in a fog.

"Mr. Devlin writes books about murders," Olivia said brightly. "Nonfiction exposés, I guess you might call them, detailing a heinous crime and exploring its effect on the victim's family. Now do you see why he's here?'' When Anne only stared at her blankly, Olivia's mouth twisted in an ugly smile. ''And why he cultivated a relationship with you?''

''I'm here because my bike broke down, and I've 'cultivated' a relationship with your daughter because I'm falling in love with her.''

The declaration seemed to set the older woman back for a moment, but she recovered quickly. ''Isn't that convenient? Do you make it a point to fall in love with someone in the victim's family on every book you research?''

Neill took a half step toward her, violence in every line of his body. Olivia stiffened, and he took savage pleasure in the quick fear that flickered in her eyes.

''That's enough.'' It was Anne's voice that broke the tension. ''Both of you. That's enough.''

She stared down at the book for a moment, then set it carefully on the end table beside her, before linking her hands together in front of her. When she lifted her head, her expression was perfectly still, her eyes unreadable.

''I'd like you to go now,'' she told her mother.

''Me?'' Olivia couldn't have looked more astonished if Anne had slapped her. "Why should I go? He's the one who—"

"I want to talk to Neill," Anne said levelly. "And I'd like you to go. Please." Though she added the last word, it was clear that she was giving an order, not making a request.

"I...if you're sure. But I don't think you should—" Shock had Olivia stammering.

"But *I* do." Anne's mouth curved in a cool smile. "I *do* think I should talk to him."

"Well, I...of course, if that's what you want." Without knowing quite how it was happening, Olivia found herself moving toward the door. "If you need anything..."

"I won't." Still smiling, implacable, Anne shut the door in her mother's face. She stayed there, listening to the sound of her mother's footsteps moving off the porch, and then, a few seconds later, the protesting squeal of the gate's hinge. Behind her, she could feel Neill watching her, waiting to see how she was going to react.

That made two of them, she thought, swallowing an hysterical little laugh. She didn't know what she thought. Didn't know what she felt. She didn't know which was worse—the idea that Neill might have used her, or the icy venom with which her mother had passed on her news.

Her mother was gone, but Neill was still here, and she had to deal with one before she could face the other. Drawing a deep breath, she turned to look at him.

## Chapter Fourteen

"Do you believe that's what this has all been about?" Neill asked, breaking the silence that had fallen in the wake of Olivia's departure.

"I don't know." Anne pulled the edges of her robe closer together and wished again that she was wearing something more substantial. It seemed like it might be easier to think clearly if she was dressed. And she wished Neill would button his shirt.

"Do you think I somehow planned meeting you at the gas station that first day?" he demanded. "Do you think this was all some elaborate plot to get close to you and pry out secrets about your sister?"

When she only stared at him with those big gray eyes, Neill strode away from her, his gut churning with a mixture of anger and fear—anger that she thought he could use her like that, fear that he might be losing her. Damn her mother for throwing the truth at her like that, making it sound like he'd plotted and planned and used her. And damn him for putting off telling her himself.

"I don't sneak, Anne," he said, speaking more quietly "I don't go undercover and try to weasel information out of a victim's family. I never lie about what I'm doing. I can't. Not if I want to get to the heart of the story."

"The heart of it?" She stared at him without comprehension. "What kind of heart is there when an eighteen-year-old girl is hacked to pieces and then scattered along the highway like she was so much t-trash?" When her voice cracked, Neill felt his heart crack, too. He moved toward her, but she held up her hand, warding him off. "No! Don't. Just…don't." She pressed her fingers to her lips for a moment, breathing deeply as she fought for self-control.

"Dammit, Anne, I—" He broke off, jamming his hands in his pockets and turning away. He didn't know what to say to her, didn't know what to do. Her pain was tearing him apart, and knowing that he was the cause of it only made it worse. Her mother might have been the one to deliver the blow, but he'd given her the ammunition.

"I'm trying to understand," Anne said, her voice almost steady. "I *want* to understand, but I don't. I don't understand why you lied to me about who you are."

"I didn't lie," he said, hating himself for grasping at such a thin straw. "I just...oh hell." He turned to face her, his eyes sharply blue. "I let you believe that I was a struggling writer because it was easier. At first I thought it wouldn't matter, because I'd be gone in a couple of days. What difference did it make if you knew I'd had a couple of best-sellers? Fame is a funny thing. It doesn't just change the person who has it, it changes the people around them. When my first book hit the *Times* list, I had calls from people I'd gone to summer camp with when I was twelve years old, wanting to offer me a chance-of-a-lifetime investment or wanting donations to their favorite charity, which, more often than not, happened to be them. It was like winning the damned lottery."

He jerked one shoulder irritably, as if shrugging off the memory. "I can't say I was disillusioned.

God knows, you can't write the kind of books I write and maintain many illusions. But it was irritating as hell. And it wasn't just the requests for money. If I was at a party and someone asked me what I did and I told them I was a writer, it led to an endless series of questions. *What do you write? Where do you get your ideas? How do you do your research?* I ended up feeling like an exhibit at the zoo. And if they recognized my name, it was worse. Then they wanted to know what Oprah was really like and just how tall was Julia Roberts, like just because I was a successful writer, I knew every damned celebrity on the planet.''

Shoving his fingers through his hair, he spun away from her and stared unseeingly at the delicate china figurines that stood on the mantel. "I'm not complaining. I like being a writer, but I like being a successful writer even more. And I'd be lying if I said I didn't like seeing my name in the paper or knowing that two studios are bidding to option my next book before it's even in print. And I like the money, though I never really felt as if I was doing without before I had it. But I hate the way it makes people look at you differently.''

When he turned, Anne had to look away from the sudden vulnerability in his eyes. "When we met, the only thing I thought of was how pretty you were and how much I wanted to get into your pants." Her eyes shot to his, color flooding her cheeks. Neill gave her a lopsided grin and shrugged lightly. "Sorry. That's the way men think. Then I started to get to know you, and you were so open and sweet, and you didn't want anything from me but my company. It was...nice, and I didn't want to risk seeing it change."

"Okay." Anne folded a pleat into the skirt of her robe, careful to make it perfectly smooth before releasing it. She understood better than he could know. Wasn't it the fear of having him suddenly look at her in a new way that had made her want to keep the truth of Brooke's death from him? "Okay, I can understand that, I think. But what about later? After we...after I..." She couldn't find the right word and finished the question by spreading her hands and looking up at him. "Why didn't you tell me then?"

"By then I knew about Brooke," he said simply. "How could I tell you not just that I was a successful writer, but that I'd written about exactly the kind of thing that happened to your sister?"

"I would have understood."

"Would you have?" He sank down on his heels

in front of her, putting his hands on the arms of her chair, boxing her in without touching her. "Anne, your whole family has spent the last fifteen years caught halfway between pretending Brooke never existed and turning her into some sort of icon of beauty and perfection. You don't talk about her, but she's always there. Your whole life has been...circumscribed by what happened to her. You stay safe in this little town where everyone knows you and watches out for you. You don't take chances or risks."

His tone was gentle, but the words stung like little stones against her skin. Her breath sharp in her throat, she pushed past him, turning in the middle of the room, one hand pressed to the base of her throat, her eyes shimmering with tears she was determined not to shed.

"Can you blame me?" she asked thickly. "Can you blame me for being afraid, for thinking that, if it could happen once, it could happen again?"

"It's not a matter of blame." Neill rose slowly and lifted one hand toward her, letting it drop when she stiffened. She reminded him of a doe at bay, her eyes wide and frightened, her breath coming too quickly. It was like a knife in the heart to know he'd put that look there. But it was time the wound was cauterized, even if she hated him for it. "What happened to Brooke was horrible. You'll never forget it. I'm not saying you should, or even that you could. But there's no reason to let it rule your whole life, either."

"I don't," she protested. "I...I have a life. Friends. You don't have to live in a city to have those things. I'm happy."

"Are you?" He walked over to the bookshelf and pulled down a title at random. *"Travel Guide to Greece."* Another book. *"Europe by Rail."* Yet another. *"Historic Manhattan."*

"So I like travel guides," she cried before he could pull another book off the shelf. "Lots of people do."

"You don't want to just read about these places. You want to see them."

Feeling as if he was stripping away all her protection, one layer at a time, Anne looked away from the demand in his eyes, hunching her shoulders as if against a blow. "There's time. I'll go someday."

"Someday?" Neill dropped the books on an end table. "When, Anne? Is there a magic age? Or a magic year? What are you waiting for? The world to suddenly become a safe place? It's not going to happen.''

"I know that. I'm not a...a child.'' She was mortified when her voice hitched.

No, she wasn't a child, but she'd been kept as sheltered as if she were one. Not loved, Neill thought, remembering the sharp look of triumph on her mother's face as she revealed the truth about his writing. No, Olivia Moore hadn't kept her daughter close out of love but out of a need to control. Maybe there was some fear mixed in with it, he admitted grudgingly. She'd lost one daughter in a particularly horrible way.

He turned abruptly away and found himself nose to nose with the fireplace mantel. Three strides the other way and he knew he would be in danger of walking through the front window. There wasn't a room in this house big enough to pace in. It was like a doll's house, he thought, frustrated. Or a fairy-tale cottage, surrounded by a moat of roses. And within its confines, Anne's family had kept her safely sleeping for more than half her life.

"How can you write about things like that?'' Anne asked, and he turned to look at her. She had his book in her hand, looking at it for a moment before setting it back down on the table. When she lifted her eyes to his, there was confusion under the hurt. "Why would you want to? Isn't it bad enough that it happens? Why do you have to dig it up again?"

"To understand," he said simply.

"To understand what?" Anne asked, bewildered.

"Why it happens." Neill jammed his hands in his pockets, his shoulders hunched with tension. "When I was fifteen, we lived in Saginaw. My dad owned a dry cleaning business, and Mom was working part-time at a library. We lived next door to the Kensingtons." He spoke rapidly, as if the words were pushing to get out. "They had three kids—two boys and a girl. Lacey was just a few months younger than I was, and she was a tomboy. I was thirteen when we moved in, and she could run faster than I could, and hit a ball just as well, and she didn't hesitate to point it out. I hated her on sight, and the feeling was mutual."

He walked over to the window and stared out at the clear sunshine, his eyes looking into the past. "I avoided her like the plague, which wasn't easy to do, since we lived next door. But she didn't like me any more than I liked her, so, between the two of us, we managed to keep our distance. We did such a good job of ignoring each other that I just about managed to forget she existed until our junior year. It was the Harvest Dance, and she wore this dress. It was hot pink, short and tight, but sort of wrinkled or pleated or something.''

Neill waved his hand vaguely up and down his body, at a loss for the right words. "I'd never noticed that she had breasts. I saw her walk into the gym, and that's the first thing I thought, *Jesus, Lacey Kensington has boobs.*" His laugh held a rueful edge. "Fifteen-year-old boys aren't exactly the most poetic thinkers. I asked her to dance, and then I asked her to dance again. I took her home. I never did know what happened to her date, if she had one. But I took her home, and I kissed her goodnight.''

He shoved his hands in his pockets and looked past her, his eyes on something she couldn't see. "I'm not saying I was in love with her or that I ever would have been, but I walked her to school every day that next week. I'd never walked a girl to school before. She wasn't exactly pretty, but she was fun, and she not only had breasts but she liked sports. Talk about your dream come true....''

"What happened to her?" Anne asked when he fell silent.

He shifted his gaze to her face, his eyes bleak. "A week after the dance, her father herded the whole family into the bathroom and killed them all with a machine pistol. Lacey, her brothers, her mother. He even killed the damned dog. Then he walked out to his car and drove away. He already had a suitcase packed and loaded in the trunk."

"Oh God." Anne pressed her fingers to her mouth as her stomach lurched. "Why?"

"When the police caught him a couple of days later, he didn't even try to deny it. Apparently his wife wanted a divorce, and he figured that alimony and child support would take most of his paycheck." Neill's mouth twisted bitterly. "It was a simple matter of economics, I guess. I was home when it happened. I heard the shots but didn't know what they were. Afterwards, I watched them carry out the bodies, all neatly bundled up in body bags. I couldn't understand why he'd done it. Even after they caught him and I found out that he hadn't wanted to pay child support, it didn't seem like reason enough. There had to be something more, something that would drive a forty-year-old welder with no record of violence to kill his wife and children and then walk away like it didn't matter. That was the first book I wrote."

"Did you find out why?"

Neill hunched his shoulders. "I was looking for logic, even for insanity, but I finally decided that the only real explanation is that there is such a thing as evil." He shrugged again, his eyes bleak. "It's an old-fashioned idea, but I don't know how else you explain it sometimes."

Anne thought of her sister, of her own desperate need to know why, to *understand*. That was one of the things that had made it so difficult—the fact that something so terrible had happened for no reason that she could grasp.

"Anne?" Neill waited until her eyes lifted to his. "I meant what I told your mother. I love you."

For the first time since her mother's arrival, Anne felt her throat close with tears. She shook her head helplessly and turned away, pressing her fingers to her mouth.

"Do you believe me?" He didn't touch her, but his voice was relentless. "Anne, do you believe I love you?"

"I don't know," she said finally. "I don't know what to think about anything right now." Sheer willpower forced the tears back, though her eyes were still too bright when she looked at him.

"Please. I'm so confused. I need some time to…just think things out."

Neill hesitated. He wanted to ask her how much time. He wanted to take hold of her and never let her go.

"All right. I'll give you whatever time you need. But I'm not going away, Anne. I'm staying right here until you're ready to admit that we belong together."

Without waiting for a reply, he turned and went back upstairs. When he came down a moment later, with his shoes on and his shirt partially buttoned, Anne was standing just where he'd left her. She looked…bruised, he thought, and felt his anger evenly divided between himself and her mother. If Olivia deserved the larger part of the blame, it was only because she hadn't cared about the hurt she was dealing.

"You know where to find me," he said, stopping next to her. When she nodded without looking at him, he felt something close to real terror. What if, after thinking about it, she decided she was better off without him? Sliding his hand under her chin, he tilted her face up and put his mouth on hers, kissing her with a fierce tenderness. She didn't lift her hands to hold him, but her mouth seemed to cling to his, and he took what comfort he could from that. "Don't think too long."

Anne stood where she was as he let himself out. She listened to his footsteps on the porch, then waited for the familiar whine of the gate and, a moment later, the muted rumble of the Vette's engine. Only when it had faded completely did she move.

Less than an hour, she thought, looking at the clock with mild surprise. Less than an hour ago she had been measuring coffee into the filter and dreaming dreams of a future that was vague but wrapped in rose-colored clouds. There was something Neill wanted to tell her, and that had niggled at the back of her mind, but he couldn't have held her and loved her the way he had if he was going to tell her he was leaving. Some men could, maybe, but not Neill. She didn't have to have experience with other men to know the difference between just sex and...caring, at the very least. So whatever he wanted to tell her, it couldn't be that big a deal.

And it hadn't been, she thought now, fingering the edge of the book on the table. Not really. He hadn't come here to research Brooke's murder, and he hadn't gotten close to her to get the inside story on what her family had gone through. He *had* lied to her—or let her believe something that was less than the truth—but she thought she could understand that. Perhaps she would have looked at him differently if she'd known he was successful and, she assumed, rich. Certainly she wouldn't have felt quite as comfortable with the author of four *New York Times* bestsellers as she had with the freelance writer she'd thought him to be.

So what was the problem? she wondered. Why hadn't she thrown herself into his arms and told him that she loved him? He'd said he loved her, and she believed him. So what was she still afraid of?

Hesitantly, she picked the book up, and, opening it to the first page, she started to read.

Anne knew exactly where she would find her mother. She spent Tuesday afternoons arranging the flowers for the house, which meant she would be in the kitchen. As she let herself in the front door, it struck her that her mother must be a very lonely woman. She'd never made any effort to fit in with the local social life, had never made friends.

Before Brooke's death, Anne could remember her mother's friends visiting from Atlanta, the soft southern drawls and her mother serving mint juleps in the backyard but, for some reason, after the murder, the visits had slowed, and then stopped altogether. Looking back, she wondered if that had been her mother's choice, or if her old friends simply hadn't known how to deal with the enormity of her loss and so had distanced themselves from it.

Olivia looked up as she entered the kitchen, giving her a quick searching glance that revealed nothing of her own thoughts. Flowers were spread on the work island in front of her—roses and baby's breath, lilies, and other blossoms that Anne couldn't immediately identify. They were shipped to her every week, at enormous expense, and arranged in elegant vases throughout the house. Beautiful flowers in a beautiful home that no one but her mother ever spent any time in or cared about.

"I thought you might come up to the house," Olivia said, her slim fingers moving gracefully through the flowers, sorting and arranging.

"I called in sick," Anne said. "Since I haven't taken a vacation in the last couple of years, I figured they owed me one."

"I don't know why you bother working at all, really."

"Because I don't want to spend my days arranging flowers."

Olivia's fingers slowed for a moment, but she didn't look up. "Is he gone?"

"No." Anne set the book she was carrying on the corner of the butcher block table. "I asked him to give me time, and he agreed."

"Time?" Olivia arched one brow in cool surprise. "I can't imagine what you'd need time for. The man lied to you and used you."

Anne decided to ignore the comment. She tapped her fingers on the book. "When you came to the cottage this morning, with this, did you do it to hurt me?"

"Of course not." The tone was impatient, dismissive. Familiar, Anne thought. How many times had she heard that same tone from her mother? "I thought you should know what this man was really after."

"Did you care that I might be hurt?" Anne asked curiously.

"I'm your mother. Of course I cared." Olivia's fingers tightened infinitesimally around the stem of the rose she held, and then she was sliding it into place in the bouquet, stepping back to gauge the effect. Satisfied, she reached for a pair of floral shears.

"Why were you so determined to break Neill and I up? What made you go to the trouble of finding out what he wrote?"

"It was obvious that he was no good. A man like that, riding into town on a broken-down motorcycle. He couldn't possibly have any—" She broke off abruptly, but Anne had no trouble finishing the sentence for her.

"Any money?" Anne arched her brows. "But when you found out that he *did* have money, you still wanted to cut him out of my life. Why?"

"Well, once I found out the sort of books he wrote, it was obvious that he was just using you." Olivia dropped the shears, picked them up again and reached for a long-stemmed rose.

"Why was it obvious?"

Irritated, Olivia set the rose down and looked at her daughter. "Because what could a man like that possibly see in you?" When Anne flinched, she clucked her tongue in exasperation. "I don't mean to be unkind, but you have to admit that you don't have much to offer to a man who's spent as much time traveling as this one seems to have done. You've barely set foot out of this wide spot in the road. And it's got nothing to do with your looks, either, because you're really a very pretty girl. Not beautiful like—well, you're not beautiful, but you're pretty in a wholesome way."

*Not beautiful like Brooke,* Anne thought. *And not pretty enough or interesting enough to tempt a man like Neill.* But she *had* tempted him, she thought on a sudden surge of fierce pride.

"Neill says he loves me," she said quietly.

"Well, of course he does. Men will say anything to get what they want."

"I believe him."

"I suppose you think he's going to marry you and take you away from here." Olivia waved the shears to encompass the town, or maybe the whole state. It was difficult to say just how wide an area her distaste covered.

"I hope so," Anne said calmly. "I think so. If he asks me, I'm going to go. You chose to stay here, Mama." The childish name came easily. "You hated this place, but you chose to stay here and be miserable, and you let everyone else know how miserable you were. I don't hate this place, but I think I could come to, and I don't want to be like you. I don't ever want to be like you."

Picking up the book, she turned and walked away, leaving her mother staring after her, ashen-faced and looking every year of her age.

* * *

"Looking for someone?"

Neill turned away from the garage door and frowned at David, who had just finished changing the oil in a sedan of indistinct vintage and was now rubbing waterless hand cleaner into the grease stains on his palms. The sharp scent of it warred with deeper, heavier scents of motor oil and axle grease.

"What?"

"That's the fifth or sixth time you've gone to the door," David pointed out. "I just wondered if you were looking for someone."

"No," Neill said shortly. It was ridiculous to think that Anne's "time to think" had meant a matter of hours. He'd already decided that he would have to school himself to wait a day or two. Unless he went stark, raving mad before then.

Aware of David's light blue eyes watching him, he moved restlessly over to the workbench and picked up a wrench, studying it for a moment before putting it down again. What was she thinking? Maybe he should have pushed her to talk to him about what she was feeling. Maybe he should have offered more explanations, a more profound apology.

He glanced at the clock on the back wall of the

garage and wondered how it was possible that so little time had passed since the last time he looked at it. It wasn't even four o'clock yet. There were still several hours of daylight, then an endless night, to get through. He'd already tried working, but the words on the screen had looked like gibberish. If he had a muse, she couldn't make herself heard through the chattering fear in his head.

"You figure you can bend that bare-handed?" David asked amiably, making Neill realize that he'd picked up the wrench again and was twisting it between his hands. He dropped it and shoved his hands in his pockets. His eyes fell on the motorcycle, still sitting near the back wall of the garage.

"Do you have any idea when the parts for that damned thing are going to get here?" he asked, seizing on the distraction.

David picked up a rag and began wiping the cleaner from his hands. "Got here ten days or so ago," he said, without looking up. "I put it back together and took it out for a run last week. Seems to be working fine."

"It's fixed?" Neill gaped at him.

"Seems to be," David said calmly.

"I—why didn't you tell me?" Neill looked from David to the bike and back again. "I thought you were still waiting for parts, but you must have gotten them within a couple of days.''

"Friend of mine in California specializes in Indian motorcycles," David admitted. "I called him the day after you brought it in, and he sent everything I needed right out." He finished cleaning his hands and tossed the rag in the general direction of the plastic basket that served as a hamper. Hooking his thumbs in his pockets, he gave Neill a considering look. "I was going to tell you, and then I saw you and Anne having lunch at Luanne's. You remember?''

Bewildered, Neill nodded. "I remember."

"I walked in, and she was laughing." David shook his head. "I've known her all her life, and I've never heard her laugh like that. Never saw her look so...young. And the way you were smiling at her, I figured the attraction was mutual."

"So you told me it was going to take a couple of weeks to fix the bike so I'd stay in town?" Neill arched one brow in question and considered the idea of David playing matchmaker. "You don't look much like a fairy godmother.''

"I don't feel much like one." David rubbed one finger along the side of his nose. "Actually, it was sort of an impulse, and then I felt like an idiot.''

He slanted Neill a questioning look. "I figure you know all about Brooke by now?"

"Yeah. I know what happened to her. And I know what it meant to Anne—some of it at least."

"I dated Brooke. We even talked about getting married," David said, narrowing his eyes reminiscently for a moment. "I don't know if we'd actually have gotten that far." He shrugged the memories aside. "I was pretty shook up after she was killed. It hit the whole town really hard. Things like that don't happen here. They don't happen to people you know."

"I know," Neill murmured, thinking of a young girl with pretty brown hair in her first real grownup dress. "It's tough to deal with."

"Everyone wanted to do something, to help somehow. Mrs. Moore was too cold to be approachable, and Doc Moore just kind of went away somewhere. Jack left town a month after it happened, went back to college. But there was Anne. She was just a kid, all big eyes and skinny legs. I guess there were quite a few who sort of felt like, if they took care of Anne, it would make up for not taking care of Brooke. So everyone looked out for her. By the time she got to high school, I don't think there was a boy within thirty miles who would have even thought to get fresh with her. She didn't date, didn't go away to college. It was like she was—"

"Sleeping Beauty," Neill murmured, remembering his initial impression.

"Yeah." David bounced the toe of his boot off the side of a tire. "Like Sleeping Beauty. It wasn't like she was unhappy. She was just not really awake. And then I saw her laughing with you, and I just thought—hell, I don't know what I thought." Acutely uncomfortable, he jammed his hands in his pockets. "So I didn't tell you the bike was fixed and—"

"Hoped I'd hang around long enough to wake her up?" Neill suggested. Any minute now, he would realize how angry he was. Just as soon as he got over feeling grateful.

He started to say as much when he saw David's eyes shift to something past his shoulder. Neill knew who it was even before he turned and saw her standing there, just inside the garage door. It was almost exactly like the first time he'd seen her—the white glare of the sun behind her, her face in shadow.

David said something about making a phone call and disappeared into the office, leaving them alone. Neill barely noticed his disappearance. She was wearing another of those simple little dresses that drove him crazy. This one was raspberry pink, with a flared skirt that left her long legs bare. She'd left her hair down, and he had to curl his fingers into his palm against the urge to touch it. To touch her.

"I was going to the motel, but then I saw your car—David's car—out front and thought you might be here." She took a shallow step forward and then stopped, linking her hands together in front of her. "I...ah...read part of your book. You really made me see them—your friend Lacey and her family, I mean. I could see what you did for them, how you made them real and maybe kept people from forgetting them. I don't know that I'm entirely...comfortable with the idea of it, of digging all that pain out, but maybe it's a good thing in some ways."

"I don't know that I'm planning on writing any more books like that," Neill said, feeling the knot start to loosen in his chest. It was going to be all right. It struck him as oddly fitting that it should end here, where he'd first seen her. Not end, he corrected himself. It was just beginning. "I seem to have shifted gears since coming here—in a lot of ways."

Anne nodded. There had been so many changes in her life that it had taken her awhile to realize that there had been changes in his, too. She stole a glance at his face and then looked away. She wished he would just grab her and tell her he loved her, but she'd asked him for time, and she knew he wasn't going to rush her. She was going to have to take this step on her own.

"I went to see my mother." She cleared her throat and brought her eyes to his. "I told her I was leaving. With you. Did I lie?"

There was a moment of dead silence, and then Neill gave a shaky laugh, and suddenly he had her in his arms, holding her so tight that she could hardly breathe.

"I just happen to have the modern-day equivalent of a white charger standing ready," he told her. "But it's too hot for a suit of armor."

"Armor?" Anne asked, puzzled.

"Never mind." He laughed again and lifted his hands to bury them in her hair, tilting her face back so that he could look down at her. "No handsome prince ever got this lucky."

*     *     *     *     *

# EVA RUTLAND

**One black woman's life in the turbulence of twentieth-century America.**

Ann Elizabeth Carter is a young, middle-class black woman growing up in the segregated Atlanta of the 1930s. She's charming, confident and has a bright future ahead.

Then she falls in love, and her marriage takes her beyond the world of her childhood. For the first time, she is learning what it really means to be a black woman in twentieth-century America. In the decades that follow, Ann Elizabeth's life—and marriage—will be shaped by the changes that shook the nation. Through it all, she holds on to one truth: *You have to guard the love you find— and overcome the hate that finds you.*

# NO CRYSTAL STAIR

Available the first week of January 2000, wherever paperbacks are sold!

# DALLAS
# SCHULZE

| | | | |
|---|---|---|---|
| 66464 | THE MARRIAGE | ___ $5.99 U.S. | ___ $6.99 CAN. |
| 66290 | HOME TO EDEN | ___ $5.99 U.S. | ___ $6.99 CAN. |
| 66295 | THE VOW | ___ $5.50 U.S. | ___ $6.50 CAN. |

*(limited quantities available)*

| | |
|---|---|
| TOTAL AMOUNT | $_____ |
| POSTAGE & HANDLING | $_____ |
| ($1.00 for one book; 50¢ for each additional) | |
| APPLICABLE TAXES* | $_____ |
| TOTAL PAYABLE | $_____ |

(check or money order—please do not send cash)

---

To order, complete this form and send it, along with a check or money order for the total above, payable to MIRA Books®, to: **In the U.S.:** 3010 Walden Avenue, P.O. Box 9077, Buffalo, NY 14269-9077; **In Canada:** P.O. Box 636, Fort Erie, Ontario, L2A 5X3.

Name:_____

Address:_____ City:_____

State/Prov.:_____ Zip/Postal Code:_____

Account Number (if applicable):_____

075 CSAS

\*New York residents remit applicable sales taxes.
  Canadian residents remit applicable GST and provincial taxes.

MIRA